WAR STORIES
AND
FAIRY TALES

WAR STORIES
AND
FAIRY TALES

SEAN KELLY, WAR CORRESPONDENT

PAUL SINOR

LEVEL
BEST BOOKS

Historia

ESTABLISHED 2019

First published by Levewl Best Books/Historia 2024

This novel is entirely a work of fiction. The names, characters and incidents portrayed in it are the work of the author's imagination. Any resemblance to actual persons, living or dead, events or localities is entirely coincidental.

Paul Sinor asserts the moral right to be identified as the author of this work.

First edition

ISBN: 978-1-68512-597-4

Cover art by Level Best Designs

This book was professionally typeset on Reedsy.
Find out more at reedsy.com

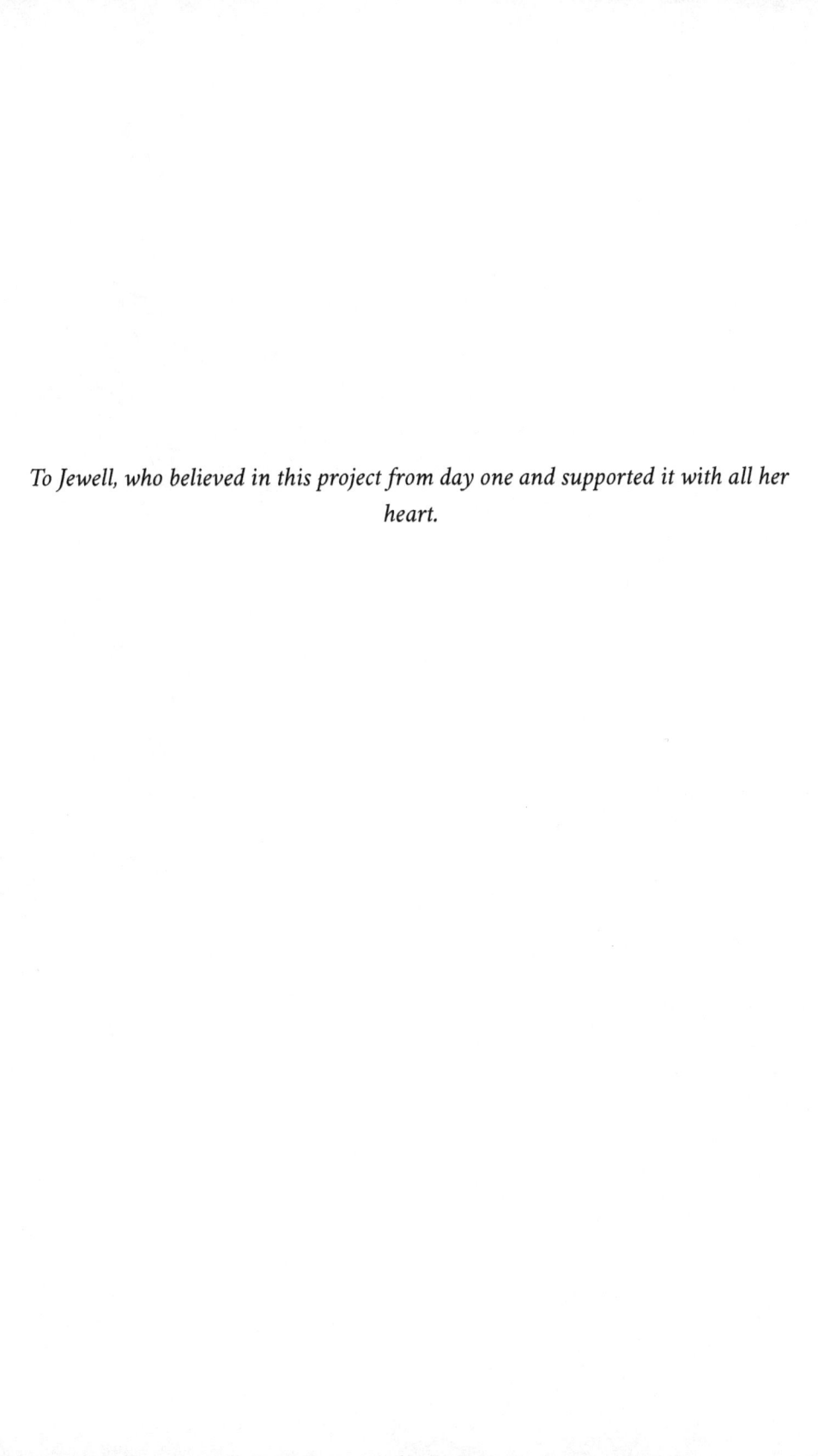

To Jewell, who believed in this project from day one and supported it with all her heart.

Do you know the difference between a fairy tale and a war story?

Fairy Tales always begin with "Once upon a time," and War Stories always begin with "Now, this ain't no shit."

Praise for War Stories and Fairy Tales

"Paul Sinor has the solid background necessary to write about the war in Viet Nam. *War Stories and Fairy Tales*, is a fascinating look at the early days of the American involvement. Sean Kelly, a newly minted war correspondent, is sent to South Viet Nam to write for a conservative outlet, but he ends up witnessing events that are not so easy to categorize. Well-written and thought-provoking!"—James R Benn, author of the Billy Boyle WWII mystery series.

Foreword

From February 1964 until March 1972, I was a war correspondent in Viet Nam. During that time, I worked for two different news agencies and did some freelance work. Although I never gained the notoriety of some of the more famous personalities Americans saw on their television screen as the war was displayed at the dinner table, I did have a by-line in many of the major newspapers and magazines at home.

Because of the attitude back home, many of the incidents I witnessed went unreported. I take my share of the blame for that since much of the style and scope of reporting in Viet Nam was self-induced. Stories from and about Viet Nam were, and have been until the last few years, slanted toward body counts and graphic violence. At times we neglected to mention, or were prevented from mentioning, the bodies were American's and the violence was directed toward these young men, we, as Americans sent to a country most of them, and us, could not even find on a map.

We asked the combatant how he felt about the anti-war demonstrations back home. What we should have asked was how we could either support him or bring him home.

During my years in Viet Nam, I had the pleasure of meeting and working with men and women from all our military services. I went from operations with the Navy SEAL Team in Nam Can in the Mekong Delta to a cross-border operation into North Viet Nam with a Marine Corps Major and a group of C.I.A. sponsored local mercenaries.

I witnessed a light dusting of snow in the mountaintop city of Da Lat and watched helplessly as a young man from Vermont died of a heat stroke in Chi Lang.

Like so many of my colleagues in Viet Nam, when we wrote copy for the agencies for whom we worked, I was unable to tell the human, personal, side of the war. Perhaps what I am doing now is telling those stories that have been lying, sometimes not so quietly, in the back of my consciousness for over a decade.

When I started this project, I was uncertain of the motive. Was it to recognize those men and women whose story I witnessed and, in many cases, shared, or was it to cleanse my conscience of a mistake made in the name of journalistic freedom so many years ago? Perhaps you, the reader, will be benevolent enough to decide for yourself.

For the two and one-half million men and women who passed through Viet Nam and to the fifty-seven thousand who died there, I hope these vignettes from your life are written as you would write them if given the opportunity. Although I have changed the names and some of the locations, the stories and incidents are yours. We shared them in Viet Nam. Let us now share them where we longed to be at that time: HOME.

Sean Kelly

Chapter One

When my boss first mentioned the word Viet Nam, like many Americans, I was hard-pressed to find it on a map. It was in the news, but not a major story. The press had a great time with the stories of an occasional Buddhist Monk setting himself afire to protest the government, and that made the news for a while, but it was not a dinner table conversation. My dad had been in WWII and made the landing at Normandy as a part of the 4th Division. He did such a good job there that later that year, he was sent to a little town in Belgium called Bastogne. Like most men of his age and generation, he didn't talk much about the bad things he witnessed and participated in. He would, on occasion, break into a funny incident like the time he and two of his buddies, after having far too many bottles of wine provided by the recently liberated French, attempted to "relocate," as he called it, a baby grand piano. After carrying it for several blocks through the city, they decided it was too heavy, and besides their unit's mail room would never be able to mail it home, so they just abandoned it. The few times he and I discussed the actions in Viet Nam, he was adamant that it was not a war worth fighting. He saw nothing on the news that convinced him that anyone on this side of the Pacific Ocean was in any danger. Initially, I agreed with him.

I graduated high school in Palm Beach, Florida in 1958. My grades were not good enough for a full-ride scholarship, but I had been editor of our high school newspaper, so I got a partial in the University of Georgia School of Journalism.

After graduating from college with a BA in journalism, I planned to be the stereotypical investigative reporter. My destiny lay before me. Uncover graft, corruption, and crime. Pick up a Pulitzer or two and someday have a syndicated column and radio show.

This had two snags upon which I didn't plan. One was competition from every other liberal arts graduate who knew how to write a complete sentence, and two, a total void of job offers from almost every newspaper and magazine that responded to my resume.

My salvation came in the form of an offer to be assistant editor of the magazine for the Florida Independent Farmers & Ranchers Assn. After six months, I was elevated to editor and asked to produce a weekly half-hour radio show. A year later, I was working for a television station in Tampa, Florida. When the station owner, who also owned a newspaper in Texas, asked me to represent his interest in a small news syndicate, I jumped at the chance.

Viet Nam was getting more play on the evening news and in print, but it was still not something that most people thought about daily. I was at my desk writing the lead for the evening news about a bank robbery when my boss called me into his office. "Sean, I'd like you to think about going on a little trip for us." He accented his words by waving a cigar when he spoke. I think he felt it made him look like Perry White from the old Superman television shows. Sometimes I wanted to call him "Chief" just to see what he would do.

"Where to this time?" I thought he was talking about going to the cattle show in Fort Worth, but I could not have been further off. "Little place in the Far East. Used to be called French Indo-China. They call it Viet Nam, or rather South Viet Nam now. We could use you over there. You'd be sending back dispatches for both the papers and for the two radio stations I've got working up in Kansas and Missouri." He took a healthy pull from the cigar, trapped the smoke in his mouth, since he never inhaled, and then blew a cloud skyward. "I want you to do a weekly column. Kinda like a human-interest thing about what's going on over there." He waited for me to answer.

"I don't know. Tell me more about it."

"I'll tell you more," he said as he filled the air between us with another blast of heavy black smoke from the rope he was smoking. "How 'bout if I tell you if you want to work for me, your next paycheck will be sent to your address in Saigon?"

The conversation got personal after that, and I asked for a day to find out more about this country and the war I was about to cover. I took the afternoon off and went out to the county library and pulled out some *National Geographics* and *Life Magazines* with several stories about the American Army advisors and some of the combat units in Viet Nam. The stories were accompanied by some photos of the country itself. From the photos I saw, it didn't look too bad, but *Geographic* had a reputation for making even the most dismal country look wild and exotic.

It was early on Friday. I asked for the remainder of the day off so I could drive to West Palm Beach. I spent a rather trying evening talking to my father about the offer. As a WWII veteran, any mention of a war or combat zone provided him the needed opportunity to tell me a war story about how he did it in his war. After his fighting and winning the war in Europe, we finally got down to talking about the one in Viet Nam.

I thought I had already made up my mind to go, but I wanted to talk to him and, at least, get his opinion. After about two hours of talking and splitting a six-pack, he leaned forward as if he were about to share a secret with me. "Son, I don't see how anythin' I say is gonna make any difference. You've already made up your mind. I only hope you know what the hell you've got yourself into. God knows, I don't." He reached out and placed his hand on my shoulder and let it lay there for a second as if by doing so, he gave me, through a transfer, the feelings he could not express in words.

The next morning, I went into Mr. Nielsen's office and told him he could send my check to my address, once I got one, in Saigon, like he planned.

"Good, Sean. I know you won't regret it. Let's talk about what I've got planned for you when you get there."

For the next three days, we spoke of little else. I was to be the Southeast Asia Correspondent for the Nielsen News Network or N3 as we called it. He wanted me to send back stories and the weekly column for the two newspapers and for the radio stations in the Midwest. All were to be done with a conservative slant. I was supposed to tell the story of how we were winning the war in Viet Nam and how soon it would be over. The plan was for me to be there not more than eighteen months. That would give me time to cover the war in the field and the victory that was surely upon us. He said I would be working with a couple of other freelancers who did contract work. When we finished, he gave me the name and contact information for a photographer and a soundman who were already there.

I planned to spend the Christmas holidays of 1963 at home and leave just after the first of the year, so my last day in the Tampa office was the 14th of December. After that, I was free to do as I pleased until the day I was to leave for Viet Nam. It was a place I could now find on a map.

My first order of business after I arrived back home was to party. With the holidays rapidly approaching, I began to seek out parties. And did I ever find them!

Buster Williams, my old running buddy since grade school, and I made as many of the parties as we could. Palm Beach was the epicenter of activity for the moneyed crowd from October until April. Across the Inland Waterway, or Lake Worth as it was called, was a different story altogether. West Palm Beach was the town that supported Palm Beach. It was a town of working families and singles. It had several apartment complexes catering to the single crowd, and we made our way through as many of them as we could. By early on Christmas Eve, we had partied out. Buster went to his parent's house, and I stopped off to see Annette Miller.

Annette had been an off-and-on girlfriend in high school and during our first year at the University of Georgia. We continued to keep in touch, and I knew Annette could be counted on to lend a sympathetic ear to a man about to go away to war.

I left her house in just enough darkness not to be seen by the children in the neighborhood as they finally convinced their parents to let them get up and see what Santa had brought them. I don't know about the children, but Santa had been very good to me that Christmas Eve of 1963!

I spent the week between Christmas and New Year's getting ready to leave.

I had tickets for a flight through Atlanta to San Francisco. From there, I had to make stops in Hawaii and Tokyo. Then, it was on to Saigon, the Paris of the Orient. My passport was up to date, so all I needed was what seemed to be, at the time, at least a hundred shots for every disease known to man.

On New Year's Eve, I went to a party hosted by the West Palm Beach Chamber of Commerce. I've never been much for one-night stands, but I made an exception when I met Lillian O'Hara. She and I began the evening making polite conversation and ended making love. In between, we danced, drank, and tried to get to know each other. My attempts to look at her as more than a waystation en route to Viet Nam failed, and we left together for her apartment.

I remember one of the guys at the party talking about getting old. "I'm finding it harder to do some of the things I once did when I was twenty-three or four," he said as we stood by the bar. It had been placed in the corner of the room at the newest hotel, out by the airport.

"How old are you now?" I asked, expecting him to tell me he was much older than he looked.

"Twenty-seven."

I felt good as I stood next to him. I knew I was in better shape than I had been in years and Lillian was going to help me keep the fine edge so important in relationships like we developed that evening.

One advantage, if you can refer to age in that respect, was my age. I was twenty-four in a war where the average age was nineteen. Twenty-four also made me too old to be drafted, a fate which very often was the lead sentence in new conversations I had with the men who would have given almost anything, and in some cases tried, to be in my situation. "You didn't get drafted? You're not in the Army, and you're here anyway. Man, you must be nuts!"

I didn't exactly volunteer for Viet Nam, so I felt I was someplace in between those who volunteered and the ones who were drafted. The difference being I was a non-combatant. Sometimes, the men I was with would argue the point, but technically, as a correspondent, I was not to be involved in combat situations. Easier said than done.

I was free to roam the country almost as if I was a tourist. Most of the free-lance and smaller news organizations worked under a centralized bureau chief in Saigon. He usually knew where he could find me and the others and when to expect us back. The military services had rules about some of the places we went and with whom we spoke, but I, like the other nearly five thousand correspondents who passed through Viet Nam during the war, wrote my own travel itinerary.

Chapter Two

I left on the fifth of January 1964. I spent the first night in San Francisco and caught a flight out the next morning. That first evening in San Francisco, I went down to Fisherman's Wharf and walked around the area. It was my first trip to San Francisco. I fell instantly in love with the city. I went so far as to return to my hotel and cut the pages out of my phone book that contained the radio and television stations. I planned to contact them when I was ready to leave Viet Nam and settle permanently in the city.

The flight to Saigon was the longest day of my life. It seemed the plane was stuck in midair, and we were not moving. Each time I looked at my watch, it had ticked off only a few minutes, leaving uncounted hours to go. Only the stops in Honolulu and Tokyo broke the monotony.

My seatmate was a young Air Force Sergeant who knew less about Viet Nam than I did. He was from Jackson, Mississippi, and the flight from Jackson to San Francisco was his first. Even though this was the second flight in two days for him, he was terrified. I tried to talk about Viet Nam. His home. Anything to get his mind off the flight.

"What made you volunteer for the Air Force?"

"It was volunteer or get drafted. I could spend two years in the Army or four in the Air Force. Seemed like the thing to do at the time. Now, I'm not so sure."

"Did you volunteer for Viet Nam?"

"You got to be kidding me, man. Ain't you heard? There's a war going on over there. People are getting shot at, and some are getting hit."

As though a cruel joke was being played on each man on the plane, we landed in Saigon the day after we left the United States. It was not bad enough we were in Viet Nam; we lost a day in the bargain.

As soon as we landed and cleared through customs at Tan Son Nhut, I was pulled aside by a Vietnamese national who said his name was Nguyen. I was soon to learn almost everyone in the country shared his name, but at the time, he was my only contact with the civilian world. Everyone else began to line up with representatives from their service and waited for transportation to take them to locations throughout the country for further processing and whatever fate was in store for them.

On the seventh of January 1967, I had some very simplistic views of life and the war in Viet Nam. Fortunately for me, they were only fleeting views and not something I had developed that would replace the reality I was about to see first-hand.

"I will help you get to the bureau on Cong Le, and then we will find you a place to live here in Saigon." Nguyen spoke better English than I expected him to.

"If you don't mind my saying so, you speak very good English." I said as we loaded my three bags into an old Mercedes.

"Thank you." He slipped into the driver's seat. "And it is not necessary to speak as slowly as you do. I can usually keep up with conversation."

As we drove across the city, I thought perhaps I should cut out the addresses of the radio and television stations from the Saigon telephone book, if there was such a thing. The city was beautiful. It was dotted with the remnants of French architecture and reminders of the old colonial period. Wide boulevards were choked with traffic. Even motorcycles, riding ten abreast, did not hide the beauty of what had been and what would surely be once again just as soon as the little inconvenience of the war was settled.

Nguyen drove me to the Continental Hotel and told me they were holding a room for me for a week. I could check in and he would be back for me in an hour. "I hope you have not brought a lot of valuables with you. There are those, even in a hotel such as the Continental, who will not hesitate to take from a stranger." He placed the last of my bags on the floor of the lobby and turned to go. "I might add all of them who you may come into contact with are not men." With a half-smile, he left.

The room the bureau had reserved was on the second floor. It had a large set of double doors opening out to what I was used to calling a veranda. I felt certain as I stood there that it had a much more romantic-sounding name in French. The room itself was approximately twenty by twenty feet with eight-foot ceilings. The only furniture was a large bed with a mosquito net, a dresser, and an old brown wooden chest in which I hung my clothes.

The hour passed rapidly, and I heard a knock on my door. I was putting my shaving gear on the shelf over the sink in the corner near the window. As I looked into the mirror, I was happy I had shaved my beard. I fingered my mustache and contemplated cutting it back from a large, bushy one to a nice, thin one or eliminating it completely.

"Come on in. The door's not locked." I yelled over my shoulder.

"That is a very bad habit to have. Do not let anyone in who you do not know. Always look. Do not even trust their voice." Nguyen came in and sat on the one chair in the room.

"Looks like I've got a lot to learn, huh?"

"Some things you will have to learn only once. Others will take time. Be patient. Listen to those who have been here for some time. Do you mind if I smoke?" Before I could answer, he pulled a pack of Salem's from his shirt pocket and fired one up. "Do you smoke?"

"No. Not anymore. I tried it in college and didn't like it too much. My worst habit now is playing poker and having too many gin and tonics when I get the opportunity." I was about to ask about the availability of both when we heard another knock at the door.

"Are you expecting anyone?"

"Are you kidding? Who else knows I'm here?"

"*Ban moi o day*?" He asked in a voice much firmer than I thought possible from such a small man.

"What did you say?" I asked. Before he could respond, we heard a voice answer him in Vietnamese. The voice was female.

"I think one of our working girls saw you in the lobby and wants to get to you before any of the others do tonight. She asked if you were new here."

He walked over to the door and opened it. Standing outside was a very attractive Vietnamese woman of about twenty. She was dressed in red hot pants, a very tight pull-over shirt, and white boots. Her hair was black. It hung straight down almost to her waist. She had a red band around her head.

With very few words, he dispatched her back to wherever she came from and walked over to my side of the room.

"There will be many more of them during your stay if you are interested." There was disgust in his voice as he spoke of his fellow Viets.

We made our way back to the lobby and out to the car he had parked beside the lobby entrance. "Now we will go to where you will work."

The building housing the bureau was like many of the others I saw in the city. It was French design. It was white masonry outside with a stone and wire fence around it. Outside the open gate stood an armed Vietnamese man. As we drove through the gate, my staring at him was obvious to Nguyen.

"Many of the secure places in Saigon have guards. It is one of the things you will have to get used to if you spend much time in Saigon."

I was fascinated by his pronunciation of the word "Saigon." When he said it, it had an "h" in it as if it were pronounced Shygon."

The villa had been converted to a series of offices. Each one had a sign over, or on, the door announcing the bureaus represented inside. I knew I was the only one from Nielsen, so I did not expect to see one with the large "N" used as a logo. "I think this is yours," said Nguyen as he pointed toward a small office in the rear of the villa. There, prominently displayed, was the familiar "N" of the Nielsen News Network.

"You will share an office with several other people," he said as he pushed open the door.

As soon as I entered the room, I was greeted by two men sitting behind desks. Cameras piled high on the desk of the one nearest me indicated he was the photographer. The others' desk was filled with so much junk I could not even guess what he was responsible for.

"You must be Kelly. I'm Wess Price. This is Clayton Stanley." He held out his hand. "We knew you were due in today but over here, today may take a few days to arrive. You could have been diverted up to Da Nang or something. Anyway, glad to have you on board. We'll find you a place to work. Till we do, you can use the table over there."

I sat my briefcase on the table and tried to be as inconspicuous as possible as I looked around. Two gunmetal gray filing cabinets occupied one corner. Next to them was a small wooden table with a hot plate and a metal coffee pot, sending out the aroma of very strong coffee. If cleanliness was next to Godliness, this place was populated by agnostics. As much as I didn't want to admit it, I already felt comfortable with the two of them in the office.

Wess came over and poured himself a cup of the strong black coffee. "Clay and I work for three bureaus. We'll be doing some of the photo and sound work for you, and I suspect you'll be working for a couple of other agencies you have never even heard of in a few weeks." He took a big pull from the cup. "Damn! This stuff is brutal. You drink coffee?"

"I do, but I haven't really given much thought to a cup. Especially in this heat. Is this normal for this time of year?"

"Nothing is ever normal over here for this or any other time of year."

"I see."

"You'll be needing some field clothes. What size fatigues you wear? We'll send Nguyen out to the black market, and he can get you some."

I looked for the first time at what they were wearing and what I had on. My cotton slacks and brown shoes seemed perfectly appropriate until I noticed everyone else was in loose-fitting olive-colored fatigues. "I don't know. Do they come in sizes like regular clothes or what?"

"The Army has one size: too big. You're about how tall? Six even?"

"Five-eleven."

"Boot size? Ten? Eleven?"

"Are you sure you're not a clothes salesman for Robert Hall?"

Clay as he joined us at the coffee pot. "He does it on the side. His real job is to find a place to open a Sears store in Saigon. They promised him the men's department after the war. Should be a fortune in it. Everybody over here wears fatigues or black pajamas," he added.

"I figured I'd shoot a couple of fashion plates for release back home. You know, something about how the well-dressed warrior looks in combat. Should set the standards for years to come."

We decided I needed a set of medium regular fatigues and 11 regular boots. At five eleven and one eighty-five pounds, I seemed to be about average. My hat size was another matter. Both had the Army issue of bush hats, which they wore in the field. I tried them on, and neither fit. I asked Nguyen to get me one that was at least seven and a half.

I was introduced to the rest of the men working in the various offices that afternoon and tried to get a fix on how things ran.

"We work loosely under one man here. Joe Brooks is like a franchise holder for some of the smaller bureaus back in the world. Most of your assignments, if you ever get them, will come through him. The rest of the time, you work on your own. We come and go pretty much as we please. Just keep him informed as to where you are and what you're working on. That way, if the military gets' antsy, he'll know what to tell them, and if you come up dead or missing, he'll know what to tell your folks back home."

"How much time do you spend in Saigon?'

"I've been here almost a year now, and I've probably only been in the citya total of thirty or forty days. There's no stories or action here. It's out in the brush. That's where you'll want to be if you plan to get anything out of this tour."

We walked down the hallway of the first floor, and when we came to the front entrance, he opened the door, and we went out into the courtyard. "How long do you plan to stay, Sean?"

"Stay? I haven't given it much thought yet. Why do you ask?"

"I came over here to spend a year. That time was up last month. I don't know when I'll leave. This place will grow on you. For us, it's like being a general in the military. This is where we get to see if we can do what we are trained for. The generals don't leave. Neither do we."

The remainder of the first day was spent getting settled into the workspace that was to be mine. In a short time, Nguyen came back with a small canvas bag full of clothes and boots.

"For you, Phong Vien. Now you don't look like FNG."

"I'm sorry. FNG?" I asked.

"It's an acronym," said Wess. "Stands for fuckin' new guy. It's kind of a pet name the grunts give the newbies till they've proved themselves."

I was suffering from jet - lag and the time difference when I settled behind the desk they pointed out as mine. I wanted to write my first column on the day of my arrival, so I wound a piece of typing paper into the machine and put my thoughts on paper.

DATELINE: SAIGON, SOUTH VIET NAM

What have I gotten myself into? I had a good job and a realistic future in Tampa, Florida, less than a month ago, and now here I am in what most people now call a war zone. The first indication of that was when the pilot of the plane bringing us here, made his landing instructions. It contained the usual requirement to fasten our seat belts, not get up, and extinguish all cigarettes. What I had never heard on a flight before was a description of "small arms fire round the runway, and a recent mortar attack has left several pits in the runway, which we will attempt to avoid. Once we land and taxi to the terminal, disembark as quickly as possible, as we will be loading with a group of your fellow military members and leaving as soon as possible. We will not shut down the engines on the starboard side of the aircraft, so do not venture away from the exit side. On behalf of the entire flight crew, we wish you the best of luck, and we hope to be able to bring you home as soon as possible." He stopped talking, but we could still hear cockpit sounds. "Oh, and a Happy New Year."

Saigon is, or at least once was, called The Paris of the Orient. As we left the "small arms fire and pitted runway" and ventured into the city, I realized why it had that reputation. The architecture was like that of the French capital. It had the wide boulevards of Paris. The difference was that, as far as I could determine, every citizen of Saigon owned a motor scooter. They moved through the city like ants. I saw one with what looked like the entire family riding on it. The father was driving, the wife was on the seat behind him, one child was standing between his legs, another was perched behind the mother, who also held a baby in one arm, and the other wrapped around the driver. The streets are filled with military vehicles, both American and South Vietnamese. I have already corrected my terminology to refer to the country as South Viet Nam, as there is a distinct difference between this and the country to the north.

Along with the mass of the motorized vehicle traffic, I recognize as cars, trucks, jeeps and motor scooters, there is yet another mode of transport called a pedicab. It consists of either a motor scooter or a bicycle which pulls a small cart or wagon-like passenger compartment. They weave into and out of traffic without paying attention to the larger, more powerful vehicles around them.

I had been here only a few hours when I was introduced to my working location, my new clothing requirements, my travel requirements and restrictions, and my residence, hereafter known as my quarters.

I've learned the military is filled with good guys and bad guys, according to my work associates. The difference between the two is measured in how much they assist you in getting into and out of situations that you should have never gotten into in the first place. I was also given a list of places to go to get food and drinks, send dispatches, attend press briefings, catch flights, exchange money, purchase on the black market, and, as one of the men put it, sample the abundant local nightlife.

The most important thing I got today was a list of acronyms. The first one on the list was underlined with my name on it. It is one used to describe a person who has recently arrived. The initials are FNG. NG stands for "New Guy."

Chapter Three

Back in the United States or "the world" as it was called by those in Viet Nam, I knew where to go to get information when I needed it. If I was working on something that involved the police, I went to the police station. A fire? The fire station. A story about an accident or incident requiring hospitalization sent me to the local hospital. What I did not have to do was go to a central location and speak to a bureaucrat who may or may not give me the information I needed.

Welcome to Viet Nam.

We called them "The Five O'clock Follies."

The follies were held at the Military Assistance Command, Viet Nam, or MACV Headquarters. The first time I attended, it was with two other correspondents who had been in country for almost a year each. As we entered and were required to show our credentials, one of them leaned over and whispered. "Don't believe most of the bullshit they're going to throw at us today. They want us to give their side of the war and not what's really happening."

"Big difference, I suppose," I whispered back.

Before he could respond, a Captain standing in the doorway called out in a loud voice, "Gentlemen, the MACV Public Affairs Officer." I wasn't sure who or what was about to happen when everyone in the room stood, and a man who appeared to be in his late forties or early fifties with a white leaf on the collar of his jungle fatigues went to the front of the room and stood behind a podium. I knew enough about the military to realize this was a Lieutenant Colonel, and he was going to give us the bullshit of the day.

Alone with everyone else, I re-took my seat and gave him my attention.

During the nearly one-hour briefing, which included a question-and-answer session, I learned that we were winning the war, hands down. Much to my dismay, I also found out that the city of Saigon, and probably most of the other larger cities in Viet Nam, were crime-free. He briefed us on two attacks on military personnel that in any city in the world would be listed as robbery and assault. Here, all crime was the result of the Viet Cong.

One man in the reporter pool asked about an explosion at an ammo point north of Da Nang. The briefer explained that even though there had been some reports of enemy activity in the area for the last week, it was determined that the explosion was the result of someone mishandling ammunition.

That was my introduction to the life I was about to lead in Viet Nam. Based on the number of friendly and enemy casualties he provided, I quickly figured at the rate the NVA were reported to be dying at the follies, the military would eliminate the entire male population of North Viet Nam in six years. There was no crime in Viet Nam. All the muggers were terrorists. Even the hookers who rolled GIs were V.C. sympathizers.

Everyone had a different war and a different story. Sometimes, the one we reported was not the one we wanted. We wrote them and turned them in. By the time they got back to the States, the sanitized version bore little relation to what happened.

By the time I got back to the building where we had our offices, I had an idea for my next column. Even though I was only required to write one a week, I thought it best to get a few prepared in case I was out in the field, as Wess indicated. I couldn't imagine being able to type a story and get it to one of the teletype machines all of us shared in Saigon if I was out of the area.

When I sat down at my desk and stared at the typewriter, it washed over me like a tsunami. I was really in a war zone. People were getting killed. Both good guys and bad guys would never live to see another birthday or a family member again. It was a sobering thought that I had an opportunity and a personal responsibility to tell their story.

DATELINE: SAIGON, SOUTH VIET NAM

Is there really such a thing as a free press? If today was any indication, I'm not sure. I was sent to Viet Nam to report what I saw and heard. I was trained as a journalist and I practiced my chosen trade for several years prior to boarding the plane for Viet Nam. I'm sure I was, and still am to some extent, like the many military men and the few women who are here for the first time. We didn't know what to expect, but we had some ideas based on the limited information provided by the news, the military, or those who had cycled through here in the past. I felt like I was playing the childhood game of whispering something in someone's ear and having passed on until the last person was required to repeat it. In every game I played, the last person's version of what was said bore no resemblance to the original statement.

Welcome to the Five O'clock Follies.

A briefing is held every day at a massive complex in downtown Saigon. The Military Assistance Command Viet Nam, or MACV is the largest military force in the country. The force consists mostly of Headquarters personnel, the people making the war happen and not actually fighting it. That job is left to the Army and Marine units with combat personnel and the Air Force who fly from a few bases in Viet Nam, but mostly from Thailand, and the Navy who support by air and gunfire from offshore. The combat personnel that MACV puts in the field are advisors and a few units that no one talks about.

My initial impression is that the war is being controlled by men who think they are living in New York City and all the bad things are happening in New Jersey. From what I have heard from the other correspondents that I have spent time with, that is about a far from the truth as it can be.

I am not here to expose anything or anyone, and I realize that each dispatch is read and censored. If the reader finds something sensitive in it, I won't know how much of what I write makes it to our syndicate until I get a copy myself.

I have only been here a week, so I don't consider myself an expert on anything except managing to get from my quarters to the office without being run over by one of the multitude of drivers of vehicles of all types that crowd the streets and boulevards of the city. My digestive system is slowly getting used to the food and water, and I'm not nearly as sick as I was during the first three days. The medics over here are well-prepared. They have two magical drugs. One is referred to as "no sweat pills." If you happen to catch something you don't want to take home with you, take a round of them, and you're cured. The other is a small white tablet. I have several in a bottle in my desk. My digestive system required a daily dose for the first three days I was here. I think if someone dropped three of them in Lake Mead, it would dry up, and there'd be no electricity on the West Coast for months.

From what I have been able to determine, there are two distinct wars being waged here. One is more of the conventional war, not unlike WWII or Korea, where military units face each other to slug it out until one wins, or the other stops fighting. The other is called un-conventional or a guerrilla war. It's mostly fought by small units of Vietnamese who are protecting their home turf. These small units are assisted by American Advisors, military personnel who are assigned to live in outposts and villages far removed from the normal support provided to soldiers in combat.

This is a new aspect of the war that has not been fully reported. I'm headed out tomorrow to try to change that.

Chapter Four

When I told Wess I wanted to spend some time with a small unit and their American Advisors, his first reaction was that I was crazy. "Most of those guys live like animals. They're on outposts so far from American support that they almost have to raise their own food. Go to one, and you'll be eating shit you never thought possible. No monkey or rat is safe when an American Advisor is out shopping for dinner." He shook his head in disbelief. "You really don't want to do this. Stay here in Saigon. It's the safest place in the country." He walked to the office coffee pot and drained the last of it into a brown mug. "If you're looking for danger, we'll get Nguyen to take us to some of the places he knows about. He took me to one about a month ago. It was a club with live sex shows of all varieties going on for your dining and dancing pleasure. The madam who ran it is paying a military police officer to keep patrols out and the GIs in. There's a story if you want to write it, and you'll probably not get shot in the process. Who knows, you can even participate in the show if you are so inclined."

I took a seat on the edge of my desk. "As tempting as that sounds, I think I'll pass. I'm sure at some point, I'll get around to taking in the floor show, but I want to do a little something toward earning my pay, at least in the beginning."

"If you're dead set, no pun intended, on doing that, you need to get clearance from MACV." He stood up.

"Come on. I'll take you over there and introduce you to the right people."

Wess led us to an old four-door sedan that even he wasn't sure who it belonged to. It was parked in a space behind a building that was used by the US State Department. The lot bordered the State building on one side and a large hotel that served as a Bachelor Officer's Quarters for the Army. He pointed to the building as we pulled out. "That's one of the best places in town to get a good meal and a drink. If you're lucky, some of the women from State and nurses from the hospital down the street come there at night as well. If you can catch it on a night when there is a firefight going on north of the city, you can see it from the rooftop patio. People like to gather up there and watch the light show."

We took Cong Le, one of the main streets from the office, to the main entrance of the MACV compound. Traffic was backed up as military police at the gate inspected everything and everyone going into the compound. We crept forward, and we watched as two large military policemen pulled a Vietnamese man from a motor scooter who tried to slip by them. He was slowed by a turning bus, and one policeman threw a flying tackle on the man, knocking him and his motor scooter to the ground. Another policeman quickly stood over him with the barrel of his rifle stuffed in the man's mouth.

"Holy crap. Is he going to shoot him?"

Wess just nodded. "It's a judgment call. If he thinks the man did it by mistake or didn't hear him, he'll just rough him up and throw him out. But shooting him is also a possibility."

While those two were involved with the man on the ground, traffic continued to stream as if nothing was happening out of the ordinary. Several motor scooters driven by women in the pants and long coat-like covering that most women wore passed the gate. Each one had a cone-shaped straw hat on their head, covering their long black hair.

Wess pointed. "Those are called áo dài. Unless they're hookers or a few who are married to Americans, all the women wear them. Those women are secretaries and other workers who have been checked out and are supposed to be safe."

"But?"

"But a lot of them have different views about the war and who they want to win."

"They're Viet Cong?" I asked.

"Probably, but you won't know until it's too late. They do their work, flirt with the boss, maybe even take him home on the weekend, and then plant a grenade in his desk drawer the day they don't show up for work."

"I guess I've got a lot to learn."

"You ain't said shit, partner," he said as we were cleared by the military and entered the compound.

The MACV Annex or compound was a series of buildings, a great number of which were surplus WWII two-story wooden barracks buildings. There were several permanent structures that may have been built as the Americans moved in or built by the French prior to their leaving the country.

Wess made his way past a theater and a building housing the PX or Post Exchange. "We need to get you a ration card while we're here. You'll need it to buy anything of value at one of the exchanges anyplace in country. You'll get a card good for liquor and cigarettes. If you don't smoke or drink, the cards are worth a fortune on the black market. You buy the things you don't want and sell them for a massive profit." He looked across at me. "Not that you would, but if you did and got caught, you'd be in deep shit."

We found a place to park, and we went into a building with a placard outside indicating this was the Public Affairs Office.

Inside, we were greeted by a Vietnamese woman speaking excellent English who directed us to a desk occupied by a young Army Captain. There was a nameplate on his desk that was hand-carved wood with dragons on one end and elephants on the other. In the middle was the name Sims. On one side of the name was a Captain's bars, and the other had the shield of the adjutant general's corps. The Captain looked up when we got closer.

"Hi, Wess. What's shaking?"

"Just wanted to introduce you to our newest member." He looked at me. "This is Sean Kelly. He's only been here a couple of days." He went on to explain my background and who I worked for. He ended with the reason we were there. "He wants to go out and see what the advisors do. You got any recommendations?"

The Captain pulled a notebook from his desk. "I keep a record of all the teams we have done stories on in the past, so we'll know the good from the bad." He looked up at me. "You want a good team or a bad one? And how deep in the weeds do you want to go?"

I learned that there were forty-four Provinces in Viet Nam, each one operating much like a state in the US. Each Province had a large Province team, usually headed by a Colonel or a high-ranking Department of Defense civilian, or a member of the CIA who was using the job as his cover assignment. Within each Province were districts like our counties, and each had district teams. The lowest level was at the village level, where small, usually five-man teams operated. These were the teams that lived in outposts and went on combat operations daily. After he explained the breakdown, he looked at me. "Your choice."

"How about I start at the district level? That sounds like the mid-way point."

"Good choice. You'll get to see the Ruff Puffs in action."

"Ruff Puffs?"

He looked at Wess. "He is new, isn't he?"

"One week."

"The Vietnamese Army is broken down into three main groups. The Army of Viet Nam covers the entire country. They can fight any place. Then we have the Regional Forces. They're kind of like the National Guard. They can go anyplace in the Province, and finally, you have the Popular Forces. They protect their own home turf. Kinda like a home guard. The last two are referred to as Ruff Puffs." He laughed. "And not to be outdone, some people refer to the Army of Vietnam as Marvin the Arvn." He returned to his notebook. "I've got a good district to send you to."

After getting a map and the necessary paperwork to introduce me to the Province Senior Advisor, we left his office, and Wess took me to a Sergeant who looked like he had been in every war since the Revolution. I guessed his age to be in his sixties, but that may have been because of the large red nose filled with veins indicating a long-standing drinking problem. His rasping cough and voice only stopped when he was dragging on a cigarette. A large brass ashtray made from a cut-down artillery shell overflowed with butts and ashes and spilled them on the corner of his desk. He handed me the ration card and the one for cigarettes and alcohol. "Hang on to these. I got your name and card number on file. You'll get another one next month. Some things you can't buy but one or two of in a year, so don't buy a fan or a refer for the first piece of ass that asks for one," he said without emotion.

I was under the impression that if the United States wanted the Vietnamese to win the war, it must be done at the lowest possible level. That was in the hamlets and villages throughout the country. Each village, whether it consisted of only one or two hamlets or was a metropolitan city like Da Nang or Vung Tao, was hotly contested by both the Government of Viet Nam or GVN and the V.C. The bad guys had a similar government set up with their own Province and district chiefs. The war at these levels was being waged by local military volunteers with the assistance of American Advisors.

Most of the Advisors were volunteers. Many were in Viet Nam for a second or third tour, and the great majority of them believed it when someone, whether it was a Marine or Army briefing officer who had never set foot outside Saigon, told them, "The objective of each advisor is to work himself out of a job. When your counterpart no longer needs you, your job will be accomplished. The war will be over, and the South Vietnamese will live in peace."

That was the opinion I had when I boarded a helicopter for the lift to the Province capital, where I would be introduced to the Advisor team responsible for the Ruff Puffs. That was where I came across one of the most graphic examples of the conflict between the old and the new Army. The old, wanting to fight the enemy all the way to the North Pole if necessary to gain the high ground and win the battle, and the new Army, willing to let the Vietnamese, with U.S. help, fight their own war. If they won, they'd have a free country. If they lost, they'd suffer the consequences.

Each group had their own style, their own methodology and even their own way of talking. They even had a specific group of well-known Army acronyms. The old guys spoke of FEBAs, DMZs and FPFs. The youth spoke in terms like DEROS, ETS, FIGMO, and SHORT.

One acronym both groups recognized was FUMU; fuck up, move up! That sometimes seemed to be the military's way of rewarding incompetence. When a man fucked up sufficiently, he was promoted, at least in position or title, and moved to an easier job. Lose a patrol in Viet Nam, and the patrol leader or NCO was made the permanent report of survey officer or Sergeant back at division base camp and never got to go to the brush again. Do a good job as a Company Commander or First Sergeant, and you find yourself kicking the brush for your entire twelve months.

I thought about that the first time I met Lieutenant Joe York. He was the commander of the Advisor Team on Outpost 21. He was trying to do the best job he could, and his Province Senior Advisor recognized it. He recognized Joe's talents by giving him a series of increasingly difficult Ruff Puff outposts to work with.

I had only been at the Province Headquarters a few hours when the subject of the loyalty of Joe's current counterpart and his trust in him was questioned.

It was during the afternoon's intelligence briefing.

The S-3, Captain Lenton, was handing out an intelligence briefing sheet, "Time to issue the tissue," he said as he passed them around.

"Anybody heard from Lt. York today?" One of the staff asked.

"Nothing last night. Looks like he made it through another one. Jeez. That guy is in a world of shit and can't get out."

One of the many problems confronting Americans assigned as advisors in Viet Nam was the selection process. Once in country, in Saigon, Da Nang, or any large replacement depot, you were simply detailed as an individual replacement to a team or a Vietnamese unit. The fallacy of this system was that, on occasion, an American team was assigned to a unit or an individual counterpart who secretly was a Viet Cong or North Vietnamese regular. Many of these infiltrated the South Vietnamese Army or Ruff Puffs, as the Regional and Popular Forces were called.

The first indication of your counterpart's political feelings usually came out in an intelligence briefing.

"What kind of shit is he in, and how did he get there?" I asked, sensing the beginning of a story.

"He complains all the time about his counterpart. Says he thinks he's secretly a VC."

"So, does no one take him serious?"

"The Province Senior Advisor has been out there several times and thinks that York is seeing ghosts."

"Or maybe he's just getting tired of eating paddy rats and rice," another officer chimed in.

This was getting interesting, and I pulled out my notebook. "Does he offer any proof?"

"All we have in his word. Not much to prove unless he catches his counterpart in a NVA uniform."

"Yeah," the S-3 offered. "Last time we had to listen to him, he said he told his counterpart, Dai Uy Vin, that he had good intelligence from a Navy Seal team that there was a V.C. main force unit operating just northeast of their location. Said he even drew a red circle on the map on the team's second day at Outpost Number 21."

"Was the intel good?" There was a long silence before the officer in charge of intelligence answered.

"Yeah. We got the same report from a second source."

"Did anyone act on it?" Again, there was an uncomfortable silence, and I got the feeling I was asking the right or wrong questions.

"York said when he pointed the location out to his counterpart, he said they should run an operation in the exact opposite part of the Province, well south of where the Navy said the tax collector was operating."

We were seated around a locally made wooden table, waiting for the Province Senior Advisor, or PSA, to come in for the afternoon briefing. We had already been there for fifteen minutes when a Vietnamese man came in with a tray filled with a carafe of coffee, cups, and some type of cake.

"The Dai Ta said to have coffee. He is late." The man placed the tray on the table and left.

"Dai Ta?" I asked.

"The Colonel. That's how to say his rank in Vietnamese. You'll learn the language whether you want to or not if you stay long enough." He reached for a cup, poured it, and placed a slice of cake on a saucer.

I filled a cup and made a note of the spelling of the rank. "What happened after he refused to go where the tax collector was?"

"He decided that he was not going to spend the night on the outpost, so he left."

"That seems to me to be a very bad decision on somebody's part."

"No shit, Sherlock. Living like an animal in one of those places is bad enough, but the idea is to be joined at the hip with your counterpart. You go where he goes. If he ain't there, you don't need to be there either."

A Sergeant who had remained silent spoke up. "I don't know what you're looking for out here, but I'll tell you one thing from my own experience. Living on a Vietnamese outpost is the epitome of hardship for most Americans. There ain't no creature comforts like flush toilets, running water, clean clothes, hot food, or a full night's sleep uninterrupted by rockets and mortars. It means never leaving your mosquito net at night, sleeping with, on, or next to a rifle or some type of weapon. Every meal is mostly what you find in the village, or if you're lucky, you liberate some VC chickens or ducks while you're on an operation. If you don't, it's fish and rice or C-rations and rice until you dream of Big Macs and Milky Way bars. You never trust anyone shorter than you. Living on an outpost was dumb and dangerous. Staying there overnight without your counterpart, the Vietnamese outpost commander is a death wish."

"What did the Advisor do?"

"The only thing any smart-thinking person would do. He got the hell out of Dodge. He called the Province Aviation unit and called for an extraction for his team." The Sergeant seemed to be the most knowledgeable of the group at the table.

"I was working in the Tactical Operations Center (TOC) that night, so I monitored the radio when he called in. His call sign was Speedball two-one. We were Speedball Base. Captain Harry Summers was the officer on duty, so he took the call. When Captain York explained the situation, he authorized the extraction."

"Then what?"

"York got his team out, and both he and Summers got their asses handed to them the next morning when the old man found out what happened."

"He didn't like it?"

The S-3 almost blew his coffee across the table. "Like it? He went batshit crazy. Said York was making accusations against a fellow officer without proof. Threatened to make a note of it on his next efficiency report."

"Did he fix it?"

"The PSA?"

I was getting in over my head in the military chain of command and who was responsible for what, so I knew I had to be careful with my questions. "It seems from what I know about the way this works he's the only one who could make things happen."

"York called for an extraction again about three days ago. It was snuck around the PSA, but eventually, he found out about it. I think when York's tour of duty is over, he needs to look for a job managing a liquor store or something back in the world. His military career will be shot in the ass."

"I heard the old man chewing on his ass the next morning. York was telling him he was sorry, but he wouldn't jeopardize the lives of his men by staying on an outpost without his counterpart being there." The First Lieutenant, who had a name tag indicating his name was Jones, continued. "York was attempting to explain his actions. He said every time we've had an outpost overrun and the commander wasn't there, it was done from the inside. It wasn't an attack. It was from turncoats living inside the place."

"How did the PSA react to that?"

"Colonel Marcus told him that unless he was prepared to back it up, it was not a good idea to go around accusing his counterpart of being a Viet Cong. Even though they were in the Colonel's office, anyone passing by could hear them."

"I don't suppose York had any proof?"

"None, and the old man even told him that we monitored the radio checks from the outpost that night after you and your team was pulled out. Like he said, they came in every hour. On the hour. S.O.P."

Before I could follow up on that, a Lieutenant whom I had seen hanging around the entrance to the room stepped inside and announced that the PSA was here, at which time everyone rose from their chairs until the Colonel went to the head of the table and took a seat.

He went around the table asking each of the staff officers and NCOs to report anything that had happened since the last staff meeting two days prior. When he got to me, he asked what I had found worth reporting.

"Since this is my first trip to a Province Headquarters, I'm still in the learning process. I'm especially interested in how the teams in the field operate."

I saw him bristle at the mention of the teams in the field. "You may be aware that we have one team leader who has expressed some displeasure with his assignment. I am in the process of taking care of that, but other than that, we have a very tightly run operation." He gave me a condescending smile. "I hope you'll report that."

"It's not my job to judge. I only am tasked with reporting what I see and can prove."

This time, his smile bordered on hostility as he stood, indicating the meeting was over.

I knew York's team had been pulled out the night prior, and I wanted to speak to him, but he had already left the area.

Lt. York's' team went back to the outpost. Two days later, they went on a sweep operation with the Vietnamese Captain and seventeen of his men. Not one shot was fired.

Three days of relative inactivity followed, and then a call was received by the Province T.O.C. from Lt. York requesting an immediate extraction for the team. The reason given to the duty officer was the same as before. "My counterpart is spending the night in the village."

Col. Marcus was notified, and he called York.

"This is the third time I've had to pull your team out. I'm not going to let it happen again. As of today, I'm replacing you as team commander with a Captain. You'll be assigned to the T.O.C." Marcus was livid as he spoke.

Even the heated argument which followed the next morning did nothing to alter either the Colonels' decision or the Lieutenants' position.

All the NCOs on the outpost with York requested transfer when the Lieutenant left, so it was a new team that went back to Outpost 21.

It took three days for the new team to mount their first operation. They found an ammo box full of old letters and documents lying almost in front of them on the trail Captain Vin took them on down to the canal.

The patrol returned about dusk, and a victory party was planned for them.

When the team leader called in the find, he said that the Vietnamese outpost commander wanted to have a celebration that evening to welcome the new team because of the items they found on the operation.

That night, the Vietnamese outpost commander raised a glass of ba se da, the potent rice wine as a toast to his new Americans and their accomplishment.

By nine p.m., one of the cardinal rules for surviving as an advisor was violated. Everyone on the outpost, including the Americans, who were not used to drinking the local equivalent of moonshine, got rip-roaring drunk at the same time.

I was in the TOC the next morning after having had a cup of coffee and a small loaf of ban mi, the local bread, when I heard a call being made by the TOC officer on duty.

"Colonel, I think you need to come over to the T.O.C. There may be a problem out on twenty-one." The duty officer spoke into the battery-powered wire phones connecting the T.O.C. with the Colonel's quarters.

"Problems? What kind of problem? What's going on? Do we have a team out there?" There was still a slight sleepy edge to his voice as he spoke.

I quickly removed my notebook from the side pocket in my jungle fatigue jacket and took notes of the conversation. If I needed proof, I felt I was about to get it.

"Yes, sir. It's team six-four. I've got no contact with them either. Looks like the place is on fire. At least that's what the district people are saying."

"All right. I'll be there in ten minutes. Get my chopper ready and get Lt. York."

"Yes, sir. I've already notified the airfield, and both the chopper and York will be waiting for you."

The stone building now serves as the nerve center for American operations in the province, which had once been part of a French villa in the early days. The roof still stood, as did most of the walls, although parts of them had long ago disappeared. The Colonel pushed open the front door to the TOC and entered.

"Tell me what happened. Make it quick. I hear my chopper."

"We had radio checks every hour during the night. The last one was at 0500. I didn't think too much about missing one at 0600, but at 0645, I got a call from the district team. They reported some women coming into the market reported a hell of a fire out there. District wants to go in, but they're waiting on you and a Ruff Puff Platoon." The duty officer handed the evening's duty log to the Colonel.

Lt. York entered the room shortly after the Colonel. The duty officer had already briefed him on the situation at his old outpost.

"Well, what do you think, Lieutenant?" Colonel Marcus asked as the reliever faced the relieved, seeking advice.

"I think we're wasting time here. We can do more, if we can do anything at all, out at twenty-one. Not here." York turned and started toward the chopper sitting on the ground, outside the T.O.C blades churning in anticipation of flight.

Without asking for permission, I fell in behind York and boarded the chopper. I don't think Marcus even noticed I was on board until we lifted off. He looked at me and had to yell to be heard. "You stay beside me at all times when he hits the ground."

The black smoke and flames were visible more than seven miles away. The north side of the outpost and several small huts inside it were engulfed. The southeast corner, where the American team lived, was relatively unscarred by the fire.

The chopper made one rapid low-level pass over the outpost. On both sides of the ship, gunners stood ready with their M-60's. Even through the smoke and flame, bodies were visible on the ground.

The men of the district team popped a canister of green smoke and marked a landing area for the chopper. As soon as the ship settled to the ground, the

Ruff Puff platoon was visible around the perimeter of the landing zone.

"Get these men together, and let's get out of here. Lieutenant, get up with the point element." Marcus motioned as he took charge.

It took less than fifteen minutes to cross the paddies between the district town and the outpost.

The Vietnamese officer in charge of the Ruff Puff platoon spread his men out on the approach and surrounded the area as the small group of Americans entered the still-smoking ruins.

"He did it, Colonel! The bastard finally did it! Your allied officer took over his own outpost." As he spoke, Lt. York stared down at the body of a frail young Vietnamese teenage girl he remembered from the days he and his team spent there. She looked a little different this time. She and the child next to her on the ground both had their throats slashed.

He spoke to no one as he walked alone to the team hut that he had occupied less than a week before. Without looking inside, he knew what he would find.

Two men lay in mosquito-net-covered bunks. Long, American-made hunting knives had been forced into their hearts. Their mouths were open. It was as if they had been killed in the middle of a gasp or a snore. Their eyes were open and stained dark from the smoke.

Two other Americans and the team interpreter lay dead on the dirt floor. The new team leader, the Captain who replaced York, had been stabbed repeatedly.

Altogether, twenty-four men, women, and children had been systematically murdered by a Vietnamese, who, for reasons known only to him, made good his plan to defect or return to the Viet Cong. He took at least thirty-eight people, all the weapons, radios, ammo, and food on the outpost with him.

Once the word of the massacre reached MACV Headquarters, the area around the Province Team's Headquarters was filled with helicopters. Several gunships and loach or light observation helicopters worked the area around the outpost, looking for any signs of a large troop movement. They searched all day and into the night but found nothing. It was a well-planned operation from the side of the Viet Cong, and it worked exactly as they wanted it to.

I caught one of the last helicopters carrying a Captain from the intelligence office in Saigon. He spent the entire flight making notes in a book and never said a word to anyone on the chopper with us. Even though the temperature was almost one hundred degrees on the ground, I felt a chill as the wind blew through the open doors of the helicopter on the way back to the helipad at MACV Headquarters.

When we landed, I saw Wess standing by the building that served as operations for all rotary wing flights coming or going from the Headquarters. He waited until the blades had stopped turning before coming toward the helicopter where I was pulling out my gear.

"Holy shit, man. I heard what happened. Did it really go down like they're saying?"

When Nguyen got my initial issue of clothes and boots, the also got me a ruck sack. I shouldered the olive-green rucksack, which I used to carry my gear. "If the rumor is that the outpost was overtaken by a Vietnamese Captain who murdered everyone in it and had been previously identified as Viet Cong, but the warning was ignored…then, yes, the story is true."

The next day, we heard the Colonel was on his way back to the US on a compassionate reassignment. Lieutenant York was sent to Pleiku to work on a staff job most men called the SLJO, which stood for the Shitty Little Jobs Officer. It guaranteed that if he had wanted to make the Army a career, his plans were as dead as the men his old counterpart left behind on the outpost.

The Captain and his entire team were murdered in Viet Nam.

Later intelligence indicated that Dai Uy Vin was considered a hero by the local Viet Cong and N.V.A.

There was no mention of turncoat Vietnamese Officers the next week during "The Five O'clock Follies."

DATELINE: SAIGON, SOUTH VIET NAM

Who do you trust?

How does that person earn your trust?

Is trust given or earned?

Is trust situational?

I had to answer all these questions to my own satisfaction recently. I have discovered that there are two wars in Viet Nam. One is being fought in the traditional way our fathers and grandfathers fought in The Great War and in WWII. The other is unlike any in which we have ever been engaged, with the possible exception of what I know of some of the jungle fighting in the Pacific in WWII.

It's a war where you can see tanks against tanks. High-performance jets engage in dogfights over clear blue skies with an endless landscape of rice paddies below. It's also one where you never see your enemy, let alone even know who he is.

The beauty of the countryside of Viet Nam is something that I wish everyone who reads this could witness. It's a country with endless possibilities being torn and twisted by a war it does not deserve. It has split not only the country (that happened long ago and is not something for discussion in a weekly column) but communities and families as well. Viet Nam is populated by thousands of small villages populated by people who, for the most part, want to be left alone to live their lives in peace. The country has a unique system to protect these small villages. They have two military forces made up of local men from these villages and larger towns. They are charged with the protection of their fellow citizens, and many do it by having everyone move into a system of outposts at night.

An outpost is a group of small hootches or bunkers surrounded by a dirt berm. Gun emplacements are placed all around the perimeter to protect the inhabitants. There, everyone can live in peace and safety and be protected by those who would do them harm.

Recently, I spent several days at a Province Headquarters. A

Province is a political entity, much like what we call a state. There are forty-four in Viet Nam. The protection of the Province is relegated to Regional Forces, the equivalent of our National Guard. Each Province has an American advisor team assigned to it to assist with security, logistics, administration, and the other things we promised the government in their fight against Communist aggression. The teams work and live with the locals on the outpost. Most teams have an American Captain who is of equal rank to that of the Regional Forces commander on the outpost, called his counterpart.

If there is a need for the Regional Forces to engage in combat actions, the Americans are there to assist by calling in air support, artillery, or other assets that may not be available through Vietnamese channels.

In Viet Nam, all the bad guys do not wear uniforms or carry a sign that tells everyone they are not what you think. That was the case when I went to spend some time with a team on an outpost in a Province north of Saigon.

The American advisor was convinced his counterpart was a Viet Cong sympathizer, if not an actual member of a V C unit. He made every effort to convince his superior officer of his suspicions, only to be chastised about not trusting a "fellow allied officer."

That trust was viciously stripped away one morning when villagers going to market noticed heavy black smoke coming from the outpost. When radio contact with the team on the outpost failed, a helicopter from the provincial capital was sent to investigate, and I was onboard.

What we found can only be described as being the first troops into Dachau in 1945. The Captain was right. His counterpart was Viet Cong. He and who knows how many others under his command in the confines of the outpost murdered most of the men, women, and even the children of those who did not share his political leanings. Probably the first to die were the Americans,

34

so no assistance was ever requested.

The Captain did not trust his counterpart.

The Colonel did not trust the opinion of the Captain.

I do not trust my mind to ever forget what I saw.

Chapter Five

I f I thought about it, I'm sure there are many things I would change about the years I spent in Viet Nam. Perhaps going at all would be first. Maybe not. Until recently, it's never been something I gave a lot of thought to. Back then, it was a job. Now, who knows?

There is one thing that stands out in my mind, in particular, about Viet Nam. I never got accustomed to seeing an American get hit. It didn't matter whether I knew him or not. They were Americans. U.S. GIs'. Just being in jungle boots and fatigues made us brothers when one of the family got hit. I'm sure this feeling was not unique to me. Most of the men I knew here felt that way.

The military services, all of them, have great medics in Vietnam, and they went well beyond the call of duty when they picked up and patched the wounded. Once they did what they could in the field, a medevac chopper slid into the L.Z., picked up the wounded, and flew them to an aid station or hospital. The wounded in Viet Nam stood a better chance of survival than in any war.

It's that small number that didn't survive and the even smaller percentage I saw and talked with that bothers me.

It was the winter of 1964. I had been with several Army units since my arrival, but I wanted to see how the Marines operated. To do that I had to go up north, closer to the border between North and South Viet Nam and Laos to the west. I caught a ride from Saigon to Da Nang on a C-130, and after hanging around for a day, I grabbed a seat on a C-46 and did a resupply run to a firebase near the border. Since I didn't have a specific place in mind, a firebase was a firebase as far as I was concerned.

When I got to the firebase, I jumped from the plane and asked a lance corporal to take me to the base commander.

He was pulling boxes of ammo from the tailgate of the plane and didn't look at me as he spoke. "I don't do guided tours. I unload ammo." He jerked his head backward. "Keep walking in that direction. When you see the biggest bunker on the base, duck your head and go inside. He's probably there." He continued to unload as I walked in the direction he indicated.

I found the bunker, and as he advised, I ducked my head and went inside. It was dug into the hillside, so half of it was beneath ground level. It was the size of a large bedroom, but instead of bedroom furniture, it bristled with radios, map boards, and weapon racks. A string of low-wattage, bare light bulbs hung overhead. All along the walls were Coleman lanterns, some providing a dull glow. Old C-ration cans with the lids removed and filled with cigarette ashes and a stack of Playboy magazines sat near one of the radio consoles. The centerfold of the Playmate of the Month was pinned to the wall. I saw a Captain talking on the radio while standing. He looked like a recruiting poster for the corps. He was at least six feet three inches tall, and his arm and chest muscles filled the olive-green tee shirt he wore. The only reason I knew he was a Captain was the rank on the boonie hat he wore. I noticed a sign above the radio he was using. It was a warning to pilots in the area: *Notice to all aviation assets. Be warned, there is no gravity surrounding the firebase because THIS PLACE SUCKS!*

When he finished his radio transmission, he noticed me. "Who let this civilian on the firebase?" The question was directed to anyone in the room who cared to answer. No one did, so I responded.

"I'm Sean Kelly." I extended my hand. "I'm doing a story on various units in the country, and you're the first Marine unit I have visited." I waited for him to take my hand, and he finally did.

"Who authorized your coming here? We have enough trouble with the NVA. I don't need to be looking out for a non-combatant."

I pulled a paper from my pocket. It was my authorization from MACV to travel by any means available to points of my choosing. I handed it to him and watched as he read it.

"I don't know if you've noticed or not, but we're Marines, not Army. We don't exactly play by the same rules." He handed it back.

He acted like he wanted to be a hard-ass. "Not a problem. If you'll patch me through to your division Headquarters I'm sure I can get someone who will authorize my being here." I held out my hand and pointed to the radio handset.

He shrugged his shoulders. "Okay, what the hell. We can use some hometown news releases. Just stay out of the way, and when the shit hits the fan, come in here and sit in the corner out of the way." He turned to one of the privates. "Take him to my bunker. The XO is on R&R this week, so he can use his rack."

I spent the first day talking to the men who kept the firebase running. I found a gunner from Iowa, a cook from New Hampshire, and a radio operator from California. I promised to do a hometown news release for each of them and several other men I spoke to.

Several times a day, a chopper landed at the artillery firebase. Each time, it was an intermediate stop for their medics to patch up an American or two who got hit in the field. Most of the time, they had a small morphine syrette dangling from their shirt. The only thing, in many cases, the people in the field could do was hit them with a quarter grain of morphine.

Most of the time, the Marines on the firebase fired support for an operation and then secured the tubes, which they called their artillery pieces. After that, everyone waited for the First Sergeant to come on the compound loudspeaker.

"Attention on the compound! Attention on the compound! Wounded coming in on the short strip. All you canker mechanics, get ready. It's time to earn your pay."

The guys on the firebase said two things never changed: his announcement and the sound of the choppers. The Vietnamese called them "my by wop wop." "My by" was their word for airplane and they added the rest because of the sound the blades made as they chopped their way through the air.

I had been on the firebase for three days and I felt I had gathered all the information I needed to do a story on the men and what they were doing.

That was the day we heard a lot of "wop wops" as the choppers began to fly into our short strip landing area.

When a dust-off lands, everyone gathers around like it's an accident on the highway. No one expected to know the people, but it didn't matter. They were us, and we were wounded and dying.

The first choppers usually held the one wounded the worst or the ones dying. The guys who weren't wounded too badly, or those who were already dead, landed last, if at all.

In the movies, a guy seems to know he is dying and is really calm. He coughs a few times, asks for a cigarette, and then closes his eyes. Those never made it to the firebase.

When the choppers came in, I went over to the pad with Corporal Crosby, a man I had just finished talking to. We went with the medics from the firebase. Crosby wasn't trained as a medic, but after a while, they began to count on him to help. There wasn't much he or anyone other than a formally trained medic could do, but he always did what they told him.

I always carried a camera with me in the field, so I was shooting stills with my trusty, though beat-up Nikon. I felt I was getting better, but Wess always found room for improvement in my pictures. He made his comments, and I tried to respond.

Crosby and I were standing in the dust of the landing choppers. I knew he wanted to talk, but I didn't think this was the time.

"What I really want to do is climb on board the chopper and fly to the hospital with those who we knew couldn't make it," he said as we stood at the landing zone. "I want to ask them if I could tell anyone something for them. Not like a priest, but a last messenger. I would like them to say, "Tell my wife and kids I love them," or "Tell dad to remember when we..."

He stopped as if he was embarrassed. "These wouldn't be great revelations, just letting someone know a son or husband was thinking of them when he died."

Four choppers came in at almost the same time. They were all that was left of a flight of seven. They had taken five Marine advisors and a Ruff Puff company on a combat assault. The L.Z. was super-hot, and even with the firebase providing prep and support, fire three choppers, and most of the men never made it off the L.Z.

Each chopper was filled with both American and Vietnamese wounded. The second ship held a Vietnamese Sergeant with both legs missing. He had two M-16 slings tied on the stumps as tourniquets. The senior medic knew a little Vietnamese from his girlfriend, so he spoke to him in his own language. "Don't be afraid. You will see a real bac si in a little while." The Sergeant was in shock by then, so it's doubtful he even heard anything.

Three of the medics assigned to the firebase rode in the first two ships back to the hospital with groups of the wounded. When the last ship was ready to leave, the senior medic threw an aid bag inside the chopper and told Crosby to go with them and do what he could. Along with the bag, he handed him a bottle of saline and told him to start it on the man who lay quietly in the middle of the floor. As the chopper began to lift, I jumped inside and slid in behind the pilot with my back braced against his seat. I wanted to get some shots of Crosby in action.

Crosby was working on a crew chief from the second ship to land on the assault. As usual, the V.C. let two ships get on the ground without opening fire. When the second chopper got hit, it caught fire and rolled over on the right side, trapping him inside and almost under it. His pilot and co-pilot pulled him out, even though both were also severely wounded.

The two pilots worked as quickly as they could under the hostile fire conditions. Even so, he was covered with large patches of burned, black, hard skin. His clothing, what little was left, had melted into his skin. It was impossible to tell if, an hour earlier, he had been black or white.

As soon as Crosby climbed on board, he hung the bottle of saline overhead and prepared to insert the needle into a vein and replace some of the liquid the fire had so quickly and cruelly taken from the man's body.

Insertion was impossible. Crosby could not find a vein on either arm. Each time he tried, the skin simply fell away or collapsed. Even trying his legs was useless. I continued to shoot photos of the action in front of me.

One of the other wounded men, the pilot from the downed chopper, turned slightly in his seat and watched the futile efforts. "He was my crew chief. Do what you can for him. He deserves a better end than this."

He spoke softly, not even looking at Crosby. His eyes were fixed on the man between us on the floor.

If this crew was like most of the others I knew about, they shared closeness unlike most men in Viet Nam had with friends in country.

As Crosby continued to try to find a place to start the I.V., he looked helplessly at the nameless pilot again. The third man from the downed chopper sat immobilized by his own injuries but tried mentally and emotionally to help the chief.

Crosby pulled out a small knife and clipped the end of the tube. He placed it against the chief's lips. The steady drip of moisture was slowly lost on his blackened lips as, even in his obvious last minutes of life, his body tried to take the liquid.

At one time, he tried unsuccessfully to lick the solution with his tongue.

Doors were open on both sides of the chopper, and wind blew through the ship as we flew. In all the time I had been in country, I spent time in almost every city and climate Viet Nam had to offer. For the first time, I felt extremely cold in Viet Nam.

The chief's eyes stared at the young man trying to help him as Crosby held his head in his lap. He tried to comfort him as best he could, but even for someone with more medical training than Crosby, it would have been useless. The chief's only hope was the early arrival of the chopper at the field hospital. That was still a fifteen-minute flight away.

The stench from his burned flesh now filled the chopper. Even with the wind blowing through it, the ship was consumed with the smell. His eyes once quickly shifted and stared at me as my own head reeled with the odor and I fought my stomach's urge to reject the knot now building in it.

The co-pilot flying us in turned slightly in his seat, tapped me on the shoulder, and held up his gray-green gloved hand with five fingers extended, indicating only five minutes more to touch down.

We had lifted off from the firebase less than thirty minutes ago. Crosby tried his best to help the Chief. He wasn't a medic. He was an artilleryman. A cannon cocker. "What the hell are we doing here?" I thought. Maybe if he had a real medic, he would stand a better chance. I knew that wasn't right either. He didn't need a chance. He needed to be home. Like me, like all of us. Home where we belonged. Not flying in a chopper with a dying man lying in the lap of a man trained to fire artillery.

One night, a couple of days prior at the E.M. club, Crosby confided in me that before coming to Viet Nam, he had only been to three funerals in his whole life. Three dead people in nineteen years! He broke that record his second week in country.

I don't remember when I stopped taking photographs with the camera. When I placed the camera beside me, I began to take them with my eyes. My mind.

Since coming to Viet Nam, I began to accept death as inevitable. That attitude held up while I watched the enemy bodies carted off after a foiled attack. It even worked several times when I shot photos for a story about the rows of American body bags at Da Nang. It worked until I climbed aboard that chopper. For the first time, I had to watch another human being die. He was dying because he was in the wrong place. The wrong uniform. The wrong everything.

I didn't realize until I turned back to the man who lay dying in front of me that tears were now rolling down my cheeks.

With the hospital compound in sight, the chopper began to descend toward the large Red Cross marked on the ground. The sound of the blades began to pop as we descended. "That's why the Viets call choppers wop wops," I said to no one.

For the first time, one of the other men in the chopper called the man by his name. "Come on, Mike! You've got to make it. Stay with us. We're a team." Words of encouragement fell on deaf ears. Mike did not hear his friend.

Mike's eyes began to cloud. He coughed once and died.

Silently.

Quietly.

Just like in the movies.

DATELINE: SAIGON, SOUTH VIET NAM

Saturday morning television shows at Bubba Hart's house. That was where was where we all met. His parents ran a restaurant, so they slept all day, and the house was empty for us in the morning. They had the biggest television in the neighborhood. If either of his parents came into the room, they would have seen four or five rowdy young boys reacting to what we saw on television. If someone got shot on one of the westerns, we would grab our chests and roll on the floor as we died with them. That was how death looked to us and how we responded to it.

That was when I was a kid.

It's different now.

It's real.

I was up north in what is designated as First or I Corps near the border between South and North Viet Nam. My purpose in going was two-fold. First, I wanted to see how the Marines operated, and second, by being that close to the border, I could see and experience a B-52 bombing strike.

My second objective was fulfilled the second night I was on Firebase Savannah with a Marine artillery unit. Word came to us that a strike was imminent. It was going in west of us, close to the Laotian border and the Ho Chi Min trail. The air war conducted by most of the jet and fixed-wing aircraft was directed against the trail where supplies and men came down from North Viet Nam or to dog fights between Navy and Air Force jets over the ports, rail lines, and cities of the north.

I was standing next to a gunnery Sergeant who was on his second tour of duty in the country. "You ain't gonna see nothing if the strike is that far away. All you're gonna do is hear it and feel the rumble."

"You can feel it this far away?"

"Bet your ass, you can. Damn things'll knock you out of your rack if it happens when you're trying to get some sleep. Just wait, you'll see." He fired a blast of tobacco juice on the ground and walked away.

Just as he predicted, less than an hour later, I felt the ground shake like I was in the middle of a mild earthquake and then came the soft roar of the bombs as they exploded. I don't know how far away we were from the strike, but I could feel the difference in pressure in my ears created by the shock waves. If anyone lived through the strike, they were going to be deaf for the remainder of their lives.

Navy and Air Force pilots drop bombs and shoot down other planes. They never look the enemy in the eyes. They never see the results of the bombs or the crippled airplanes spiraling to the ground and exploding. Finish the mission, return to the carrier or the airbase, relax, have a drink, maybe a steak, and sleep in a real bed.

It's not like that for the men on the ground in the field, no matter if it is in the highlands, the mountains, or the Mekong Delta.

Death is all around them.

There are all kinds of death. The kind they see and the kind they cause.

Unlike many past wars, the soldier and Marine in Viet Nam normally did not look his enemy in the eye. He shot at movement in the jungle, shadows at night. Things heard but not seen.

What he did see was his buddy when he got hit. That's when it became real. A bullet can cause a lot of damage, which results in massive loss of blood, and that blood must go someplace. It may splatter on the man next to him, or it may pool beneath him so that when he is picked up...

Death is real.

It's a part of war.

It's permanent.

It's not like the movies or Saturday mornings at Bubba's house.

Chapter Six

I caught a pedicab from my quarters to the Continental Hotel one night while I was back in Saigon. I had been to several units throughout the country since I arrived, so I had a feel for who was doing what. There were several places I wanted to go and units I especially wanted to see, but I was taking things as they came. My quarters were taking on the look of a college dorm. I had several new pieces of furniture I'd bought. Each piece was hand-made using mostly discarded military ammo boxes. My dresser still bore the markings inside one of the drawers, indicating it was made using 3.5 rocket boxes. I used my ration card to buy a small refrigerator and a fan. I followed the advice I was given and did not waste it on some Vietnamese hooker who wanted to be my girlfriend.

Like most of the men, I had partaken of the local "steam and cream" parlors. These were the massage parlors that filled every available space around the city. For the equivalent of a few dollars in military payment certificates, converted to piasters, you could sit in a steam room, get a shower and a massage with any kind of ending you were willing to pay for.

That night, I was drinking and playing a ten-cent slot machine when a Marine Sergeant sat down on the stool next to mine and put the first of a roll of dimes he held into the machine. It only took a few pulls of the handle until we were talking like we had known each other for years.

He was on at least his third scotch and second cigar since we started feeding the machines and talking. I found out he had just returned from an R&R trip to Bangkok. One of the perks of being in Viet Nam was a mid-tour five days of leave to go to any number of R&R or Rest and Recreation Centers.

Most of the single men looked at the R&R as meaning Rape and Rampage. It was a time for them to get as much sex and booze as they could afford prior to coming back to the reality of the war.

"A reporter, huh? You want to live like an animal for a while? Come spend some time with one of our CAP Teams," he managed to slur, and the bad booze and good smoke began to lift him out of his field environment into the more civilized decadence of Saigon. "You'll be surrounded by the Viets, we live with them, eat with them, do everything with them." He stopped momentarily. "You ever eat a rat?"

I hit a small jackpot on the dime machine for twenty-five dollars. I bought him another scotch and left after getting more information on just what a CAP Team was. I found out it was called a Combined Action Program team which was a small group of Marines who lived in a village with the locals. It sounded like something I needed to find out more about.

The next day while nursing a slight hangover, I left my quarters and checked in with the office. When I was finished with all the backlog of paperwork I had missed or ignored since returning to Saigon, I left and caught a ride to the large helicopter pad in Saigon known as Hotel One.

The choppers came and left Hotel One at respectable intervals. Destinations were announced as soon as the crew knew, or in some cases decided, where they were going next. It was difficult to pinpoint a destination. One didn't ask to go to Da Nang or Pleiku. North was sufficient. It could be narrowed down later. My ride made two stops, and then I was dumped at an Army aviation unit, where I spent the night.

I caught a Caribou the next morning and flew all the way to Bien Bap. It was a fair-sized city everyone called Be Bop. My ride to the senior Marine team Headquarters was provided by a Navy Seabee. Like most of the men I met in Viet Nam, the ride cost me the promise to mention him by name in a story his mother back home in Phoenix would read.

"You just go on over there to the team house. They'll help you find the CAP guys you want."

As we pulled up to the compound, the ear-busting whump of an outgoing 155 howitzers round welcome us. Six more followed in short order as the unit fired prep for one of its patrols. Although the natural instinct was to quickly duck, crouch, or find a rock to crawl under, if the rounds were outgoing, the impulse was controllable. With incoming, it was immediate and uncontrollable. No one had to explain the difference. We knew. As we responded accordingly.

I found someone at the team Headquarters, introduced myself, and showed him my press credentials. He wasn't wearing a shirt with his rank on it, so I had no idea if he was an officer or enlisted. He seemed to be in charge, so I watched as he looked over my papers. The Marines were usually the only ones who wanted to see them. One night at the Continental, we decided it was because the Marines didn't like the competition of professional reporters screwing with their efforts. Candid comments like that were reserved for the bar in the Continental. Not for places like Be Bop!

"You really want to go out with them? Cap 27 is not in one of our best areas. If you go, you can count on some activity." The man was busy packing a well-stained black briar pipe. Its stem was cracked and broken at the tip. He pulled the smoke through a stem, which, from the gurgle it made, was filled with salvia. "Of course, we're in a defensive mode with our teams. We don't go on offensive operations unless the Viets ask us along as advisors."

"I understand the role," I assured him.

"Fine! I think we can get you out to 27 this afternoon."

I was told by the Sergeant I met back in Saigon that when the men in Viet Nam were assigned to the CAP teams, it seemed the Marine Corps forgot them. A team was put together by finding a Lieutenant or Captain for the skipper, getting a strong gunny to take care of the skipper, and filling in with a couple of grunts. The team was pointed in the direction of a village filled with Vietnamese who couldn't care less about the war, the Americans, the Viet Cong, or anyone else. The team was then told to go forth and pacify.

The initial move-in was usually clean. A chopper set them down. The team made a grand entrance. They handed out scotch and cigarettes to the officers and the local politicians, gave a little candy to the kids, and moved into the nearest empty hootch.

By dusk on the first night, they knew what the local leaders drank and smoked, who could supply them with genuine Viet Cong flags and 'yard crossbows, and what time the rats started coming out from wherever-the-hell rats go in the daytime.

It took only a few days to learn what was expected of them, who they could trust, and what they had to do to prove themselves and not embarrass the Vietnamese Commander.

I spent a week with Cap 27. During that time, they introduced me to all the local Viet leaders. Most of them were like the hundreds of other local officials I met in Viet Nam. They had just enough money or power to get a job with the G.V.N. Depending on how they worked it, they could become very effective, comfortable, or rich. Some, to their credit, tried only to do the job for which they were responsible. Such was the case with Mr. Vinh. Mr. Vinh was the village deputy chief and the man responsible for local security. The men on the CAP team called him Crazy Vinnie.

I quickly learned Vinh was a gutsy mother. He went on search missions at night with the CAP team. I saw him go out with a steel pot on his head, a .45 pistol in one hand, and a big stick in the other. He looked like a cross between Moses and John Wayne when he went up to a villager's front door, knocked once with his stick, then kicked the door open. The guys on the team had a bet on when Vinh would break in on some ARVN soldier home on leave playing humpty-bumpty with his wife. That's when they expected to get to see Marvin the Arvin blow Mr. Vinh to hell.

That's how he got the name Crazy Vinnie.

Anytime the CAP team was with him on his midnight raids, they stood aside when he headed for a door. Gunny told them to do that. He said there was a certain amount of honor if you were killed in combat. Getting blown away with Crazy Vinnie was the shits!

After a while in the village, most teams began to see results from their programs. They gave classes on patrolling, ambushes, first aid, planting a garden, raising chickens, or anything else to convince the Viets the war was about over and the good guys were winning. One of the men on CAP 27, Corporal Gaither even started music lessons when he found an old Silvertone guitar on the ville black market.

After a while, the Marines began to develop a certain amount of dedication to their mission. Because they were so far from other U.S. forces, they had to depend entirely on themselves and the other men to share the outpost for everything they needed. That dedication manifested itself in what Sergeant Morris told me my first night in Be Bop. "We'll do whatever we have to do as long as we can keep our head and our ass down and get home." He popped the top on a barely cool bottle of O.B. beer. "We know we can do it for twelve months. Then we get the hell outta Dodge."

Crazy Vinnie was just the opposite. He really believed he and the Americans could make a difference. By applying them and their talents, he said, the enemy will be defeated, and his country will be free. Knowing his father bought the farm in the early '50s at the hands of the Viet Minh made it a little difficult to believe we, or anyone else, could stop the war.

He didn't let the team's sometimes ambivalent attitude rub off on him. He continued to believe he could plan raids, ambushes, and his favorite, house-to-house searches, and rid his village of the V.C.

I had dinner with him and his wife one evening, and through the team's interpreter, he went to great lengths to tell me about what he considered to be both his job and his destiny. "We are not so far from Hanoi that they cannot send people to our area," he said. "We must cut off their support in our village. If we do not feed them, either their body or their mind, they will not come back. Those who do, I will kill."

His comments were made without emotion. It was as if they said, "Pass the salt."

One day, Vinh called Gunny and the skipper over to the little hootch that served as the office, community kitchen, and tavern, which he owned. I went with them.

"I have word of three Bac Viet officers. They will soon come to our village. We must find them. Then we kill them!" He told us.

Gunny was right when he told me about Vinh. He said the little guy never minced words when talking about Bac Viet or the North Vietnamese. He never wanted to capture one. It was always his purpose to snuff them. Take no prisoners!

Two nights later, I went with the team on a search mission. Vinh's' plan was to set up an ambush about two klicks outside the village, then double back and check out a few of the houses. It was an old trick, but it usually worked. Few of the villagers expected the raiders to return before daylight. When they did, it was to a specific house or section of the village. Being paid a visit in the middle of the night by Crazy Vinnie was enough to transfer the allegiance of many of the villagers.

As soon as the evening light began to fade, we left the village going east.

It was Tuesday night. It doesn't really matter, but I know it was a Tuesday.

The sun was just beginning to set over the mountains. If there was anything you could call a simple, beautiful sight in Viet Nam, it was sunset. Some of my friends say it's prettier down in the Delta, but dusk in the highlands gets my vote. We began to check out and load our equipment as the sun threw its last shadow for the day.

I was going out with the team, so Gunny checked me for anything that I might have that gave a reflection, rattled, or made any other noises. All of which are deadly in an ambush position. "You want a weapon?" he asked as we taped the snaps on my harness with black tape. "I know you're a non-combatant, but Chuck don't give a rat's ass. We get into some shit tonight, a weapon may come in real handy. That is, if you know how to use it!" I thought his last remark was sarcastic until I saw him pat himself on the small of the back and smile.

Somehow, the old Marine had seen the small snub-nosed .38 revolver I had strapped on. I won it in a poker game one night in Can Tho, and I kept it in my bag unless I went out with the troops. Then I quickly, or so I thought, slipped it on a belt in the small of my back.

Before I could answer, he made his way down the line to check his men.

Sergeant Vickers, the man who invited me to the team, was carrying the M-79 grenade launcher with buckshot rounds. It was a great weapon for close-in action like ambushes or for a point man to carry. It was worthless at ranges over 25 or 30 meters with buckshot. After that, it was like having a grenade that you could throw a hundred yards. When Chuck got close enough for the gunner to need to use the buckshot, the man was usually so

51

scared he just pulled the trigger, reloaded, and pumped out as many rounds as possible.

Crazy Vinnie had all his men stand over to one side so he could personally check them out. He made them hop up and down so he could listen and hear if anything clanked or rattled. I couldn't help but laugh as a fully armed ambush patrol of U.S. Marines, and Viets jumped up and down to see who rattled. I knew Gunny failed to see the humor in all of this.

We covered our necks, hands, and faces with bug spray to keep the mosquitoes off. The vile liquid in the little brown squeeze bottle worked well unless you accidentally got some in your mouth. Do that, and your lips go numb. That's probably why it worked. It must be a bitch to be a mosquito trying for blood and have your drill go numb.

By dark, we were ready to go. Gunny, me, Vickers, Gaither, and Crazy Vinnie, with nine of his people, began to move slowly and cautiously through the western edge of the hamlet. There were four hamlets making up the village. This one was next to the largest, with about twenty houses.

We skirted the hamlet and moved along a natural draw about a thousand klicks out to a canal. It was here we placed our ambush. The Viet Cong used this canal as one of their main lines of support, so the team came here about once a month. Most of the time they came away empty. Vickers said an empty ambush never seemed to bother anyone except Crazy Vinnie and perhaps Gunny, although I'm not certain about him.

One thing about the Viet Cong, they usually kept a good schedule. If they were in your area, you made contact about nine thirty when they went to work or about two a.m. when they returned home. For them, being a guerrilla was a part-time job. They did it on the midnight shift.

We sat in the ambush site for three hours with no action, so we split.

I was amazed at how quietly we slipped back into the main village area. This time, the return was through the middle of the smallest of the four hamlets. The men spread out in a column about fifty meters long. I had just passed the first hootch when the Viet in front of me quickly threw himself to the ground beside the trail. I immediately did the same.

The Viets and CAP teams played around a lot, but they were well-trained.

In situations like this the training takes over, and actions become automatic. Even mine. Without a word, Crazy Vinnie moved up to where his point man lay, covering the hootch by the end of the trail. Gunny and Vickers slid in place silently next to him. I quickly moved up beside Sgt. Vickers.

Vinnie whispered to the second man in line and pointed to the hootch. By now, I could make out a faint glow of light, either hidden or burning very low, in the rear of the house. I heard voices from the hootch, but I couldn't understand them. I made a mental note to work on the Vietnamese language program I picked up in Zion. The team interpreter told Gunny what Crazy Vinny was planning.

Before I realized he had the place surrounded, Crazy Vinnie stood up, pulled his .45 from his belt, and motioned for Gunny and Vickers to follow him. I didn't want to be left alone with the action going on in front of me, so I fell in and followed Gaither and Vickers' lead and moved about three meters to the left of them and Crazy Vinnie while Gunny did the same on the right. Vickers M-79 was loaded with buckshot, and I watched as he quietly pressed his thumb along the safety and backed it off. Six more rounds were secured in his green webbed vest.

Vinnie moved quicker than I ever saw him. I don't think he even knocked. All I remember is seeing him kick the door down, yell something in Vietnamese, and start shooting. As soon as he started shooting, so did his men. For about thirty seconds, it sounded like the D-Day invasion of Europe.

Everyone except Gunny and Vickers was shooting into the hootch. Most of the Viets had their weapons on full-automatic. I was in a half crouch behind Vickers who was covering the left side of the hootch when I saw the man scramble through the window and hit the ground.

Vickers instinctively pulled the grenade launcher to his shoulder in a quick kill stance and yelled at him. Later he said he wanted to tell him to stop in Vietnamese. I knew enough Vietnamese to know how to say it or recognized it when someone else yelled it, but even now, I'm not sure what Vickers said. All I know is he yelled something in Vietnamese and fired.

By that time, Crazy Vinnie was yelling for everyone to hold their fire.

He pulled a woman from the hootch and even though she was crying and bleeding from small wounds all over her body, he was slapping her around. He wanted her to explain what was going on and why the men in the hootch were sitting around an American radio like the team carried when it went on patrol. The Prick 25 radio the men had been listening to was in the hootch with its guts shot out.

Gunny came up to Vickers side. He held his M-16 hip-high on the guy Vickers had just splattered with buckshot. "You o.k." He asked as he crouched beside Vickers. I was also alongside the young Sergeant.

"He was running, Gunny. I tried to tell him to stop, but he wouldn't. I just gave him a snapshot. He wouldn't stop Gunny. I tried, but…" The older man placed his hand on Vickers shoulder as he continued to try to explain what had just happened in a small hamlet in a village everyone called Be Bop.

I know Gunny understood, even better than I, what Vickers was trying to say. I had seen it before. Usually, war is a very impersonal endeavor. The men called in artillery or air strikes and moved through the area afterward, counting bodies. Occasionally, when they made contact on patrol or an ambush, they fired at forms or movement, never at people. This was different. Enemy or not, Vickers had quickly and instinctively killed a man.

Vickers spent his last thirty days in country at Division Headquarters. He didn't really have a job. It was a pay-off for staying in the brush for eleven months. On the 27th, he loaded on the freedom bird and felt it lift off for home. His war, at least in the in-country part, was over.

Gunny extended for six months and wrote me a couple of weeks after I left the team and returned to Saigon. He said a V.C. hit team came to the ville and got Crazy Vinnie one night in his own hootch. It's hard to believe a man like Crazy Vinnie died in his sleep. I don't think even he would have liked that.

DATELINE: SAIGON, SOUTH VIET NAM

Is there a good time to die?

A good place to die?"

Unless a person takes his or her own life, that decision is not left up to us. Call it fate, a higher power, karma, or whatever you believe in, but most people will never know the time, place, or circumstances of their demise.

There have been several instances where a soldier or Marine dove on a nearby grenade to save the lives of those around him. Each one who did it was awarded the Medal of Honor, posthumously. If ever a decoration for bravery was deserved it's in those instances and noted on the headstone of those individuals who are interred in military cemeteries.

Was it a conscious act? Obviously, we will never know and perhaps the person who did it did not know at the time. Muscle memory? Training? A love of his fellow man? From the time the pin is pulled from a grenade, it has approximately five seconds before it explodes. Take away the two or three seconds it travels through the air from the person who threw it until it hits the ground, and that leaves about a second to decide. Most people can't decide how much cream or sugar to put in their coffee in a second, and they've been doing it for years.

Some people, for whatever reason, think it is an honorable death to give their life for their country. I cannot argue that point as it is a personal decision and not open for discussion.

Such a person was a Vietnamese man I had the pleasure of meeting recently. He was the village deputy chief for security, and he took his job very seriously. Nights would find him, along with a small group of Marines, conducting missions to find and eliminate any threat to his village from the enemy. I watched him in action, and he showed a complete disregard for his own life. When I asked him about it, his response was like Nathan Hale's: "I regret that I have but one life to give for my country."

Everyone who knew him expected him to go out in a gun battle. That was not to be.

Mister Vin, the person everyone called Crazy Vinnie, is dead. Not in a gun battle as befitting him, but in his sleep.

Killed in his sleep by assassins who crept into his house in the dark.

He was killed by the Viet Cong, who were afraid to face him on the field of battle.

Chapter Seven

I think Charles Dickens had Viet Nam in mind when he said, "It was the best of times. It was the worst of times." That was an accurate description of Viet Nam, especially the larger cities in the latter part of 1964 and early 1965. For me, Saigon was the epitome of both the best and the worst times I had ever had or ever expected to have in my life.

While in Saigon, I lived at the Continental Hotel. The grand old lady of Saigon had been playing host to diplomats, correspondents, and an assortment of civilians who had participated in the wars in the area since the French first locked horns with the Viet Minh under Uncle Ho. Even now, you could see the upper crust of the limited Western social elite sitting around the veranda bar and being served in the massive dining room. Steaks were abundant and cheap. Drinks were equally abundant and scattered among the guests,. One could usually find a round-eyed woman.

After a while, those of us who lived at the Continental began to search out some of the other clubs and bars for our evening's entertainment. We tried the clubs on Tudo and Plantation Road. We went to most of the Officers and NCO Clubs at the various compounds throughout the city.

Anyone who ever thought officers didn't get as drunk and disorderly as their enlisted troops never visited the bar at the Vietnamese Air Force Officers Club at Tan Son Nhut. One trip to the bar called the Snake Pit and that mystique was destroyed forever.

We made the rounds and finally decided to live at the Continental, drink and have dinner at the Massachusetts or Mass BOQ, and then throw our fate to the Gods.

I had promised to meet Wess at the Mass that evening.

"Hey. Sean. Come on over. Join us. There's plenty of room." Wess was motioning me to join him and two other men at his table. "Where the hell you been?" Without waiting for an answer, he motioned for the waiter, an older Vietnamese man in black trousers, white shirt, and black bow tie, to bring the three of them another round of drinks and bring me a gin and tonic.

"Down in the Delta. How about you? Last time I was in town, you were going to Lai Ke. You were trying to get the Marines to take you on a patrol with them. Did you ever get out?"

"Holy shit! Did I get out? Those grunts nearly got me, and my cameraman killed. You know Ben, don't you? He works out of Da Nang." He stopped long enough to reintroduce me to Ben McCoy and the other man at the table.

"Yeah, I know Ben. We were together a couple of times at the briefings General Westmoreland had up in Long Binh."

"Anyway, I was shooting stills for Nielsen, and Ben was filming for ABC. These Marines wanted to show me how they really operated, so when we set up in an ambush, they picked a spot where there was sure to be a kill that night." He stopped long enough to take a drink. "About midnight, all hell breaks loose. We got main force VC and hardcore NVA regulars both on our ass. I think they used everything except air strikes against the squad I was with. Out of an eleven-man team, two bought the farm. Four were wounded, and I almost got religion. I kid you not. Man, it was hairy."

Wess was still telling me about his near-religious experience when she walked by the table. She crossed in front of me and behind him. As she approached, I saw she was alone. The lady quickly scanned the dining area as if she were looking for someone. I held my drink midway to my mouth as I watched her. When she did not find the person for whom she looked, the maître' d escorted her to a table, and she sat alone.

"You still with us, Sean?" Wess saw my actions as I stared openly at the woman.

"Physically, yes, I'm right here. Mentally. That's another question. Right now, I'm across the room with the lady with the black hair and the dark eyes."

"Damn. It didn't take you long to zero in on her." Ben said as he fished for a cigarette.

"You guys know her? What's her name?" I wanted to know all I could about her as soon as possible.

"I think she works for the State Department. Some kind of low-level spook. Friend of mine said she comes in here every two or three nights. Usually, she has a couple of the locals sniffing around her by now. Maybe this is your lucky night, Sean. Everyone else seems to be tied up somewhere. If you're gonna make a play for her, it better be tonight." Wess hesitated for a second, then raised his glass in a mock salute,turned toward her, and added, "For tomorrow, we may die!"

We continued to talk about a multitude of things that evening. Most of them revolved around the three main topics of conversation in Vietnam at that time. How the media was getting fed a ration of shit by the brass and their briefing teams about the war and its effect on the country, how we were laying our lives on the line for no real reason that we could agree upon except the fact we got a by-line in a stateside publication or our families saw us on the evening news, and most importantly, where to get laid without the risk of taking something home that wouldn't show up for the next three generations in your family.

All during the conversation especially the part about getting laid, my attention was riveted to the woman sitting alone two tables over from us. She finished her meal, had another glass of wine, and left. Except for the few words she exchanged with the people who obviously knew her, she spent the time alone. I made myself a promise not to let that happen again if I saw her during the next six days I planned to spend in Saigon.

I awoke the next morning and spent several minutes trying to remember where I was. I vaguely remember it being Saigon, but my fuzz-covered brain refused to narrow it down any from there.

I looked around the room and spotted a green fatigue jacket with the name Dunning over the right breast pocket. I was in my friend Captain

Chuck Dunning's room at the Massachusetts BOQ on Cong Le. At least it was convenient. I could make my way over to my place or to the MACV Headquarters or the annex by military vehicle or by pedicab if necessary. The air base was close by, so when I got ready to leave, it, too, would be a short ride.

Chuck was assigned to the Provost Marshall's office and lived in the BOQ. His room was like so many of the others occupied by the permanent party military in Saigon. He tried to make it as comfortable as possible within the restrictions of the hotel. He had a small refrigerator, a fan, and a wall full of his stereo and its various components. The walls had been painted white so many times the paint stood like thick chalk in the corners of the room. Overhead, suspended from the ten-foot ceiling, a great fan tried to keep the heavy, moist air moving. Its flat wooden blades cut through the air with each revolution. It was little help but seemed so much a part of the room and its environs that it was never shut down. It made endless revolutions for all who cared to watch.

I slowly made my way out of bed, pulling the mosquito net back to gain access to the cool blue and white tiled floor. I remembered once having slept, or perhaps passed out is a better term, on these tiles, and even now, I could recall how cool they had felt against my bare skin.

It was after his birthday several months back. Chuck was an excellent source of information from the military police, so when he mentioned his upcoming birthday, we decided to have him party. It lasted a day and a half. Unlike last night when I didn't even remember seeing Chuck, much less coming to his room, I remembered finishing the party on the cool tiles of his floor.

After a quick shower down the hall in the communal latrine, I was ready to meet the rest of the day in Saigon.

I spent most of the day at the Press Corps Headquarters in the villa next to the American Embassy. The old villa had served us well. Most of us used it as a mail drop when we departed for unknown areas around the country. As I entered the building, I recalled the four-day drunk we pitched here between Christmas and New Year's Eve one year when the locals had agreed to a cease-fire. The fact that neither the Viet Cong nor the Americans honored the cease-fire was irrelevant. We spent the time in as close to a drunken stupor as we could.

"Morning, Sean. Where you going this week?"

"Morning, Dennis," I said to Dennis McDonald, the reporter for the Atlanta newspaper in Saigon. "I'm taking a little R&R. I'll be in town for the next week or so. I haven't decided where I'll go next. Possibly up in II Corps. I heard about a recon team I want to check out. How about you?"

"I'm in Saigon for a while. You coming over to the Mass tonight for dinner? I'll probably see you there."

I watched as Dennis went to the teletype machine and did an input of a news article he had just completed. This was the communal teletype machine used by all who needed one. Most of the time, we dropped our dispatches off, and they were entered and sent by one of the Vietnamese women who worked in the office.

As soon as he mentioned Massachusetts and being there tonight, I immediately thought about her again. "If she's there tonight, I'm going to find out more about her," I said aloud to anyone who cared to listen.

There was no such thing as happy hour in Viet Nam. Drink prices were so cheap, if the prices were cut any more, the military would be giving them away. I arrived at the Mass at about five. The beginning of the cocktail hour was what Wess called it as we took a table near the window overlooking the western portion of the city.

By six-thirty, we already had several drinks and were well into a series of war stories neither of us believed. Wess was telling me about his trip out to a Navy ship whose choppers were flying pilot rescue and pick-up into North Viet Nam, when he completely lost me. I found my eyes riveted to the entrance to the club.

She came in alone again tonight. Like before, she quickly glanced around the room. Then, she walked over to the table next to ours. As she approached, I stood and pulled the chair out for her.

"Whoa! Look at this. Chivalry is not dead. It is alive and well and living in Viet Nam." Wess stood and bowed toward her as he spoke.

I was delighted to see the smile break across her face. "Thank you very much," she said as she took her seat.

Since coming to Viet Nam, I have had my share of the local women. There was nothing that could not be purchased in the better houses of Saigon. On two occasions, a couple of friends and I rented a villa for several days and kept it stocked with a variety of women. Each had her own specialty. In the States, I had one lengthy involvement with a coed while in college. I knew none of these would even be worth a second thought after getting to know the lovely lady sitting behind me at that very minute.

After about thirty minutes, when no one came to her table, I turned to face her and asked if she would let me buy her a drink.

"A glass of wine, please," she said after a moment's hesitation.

I picked up a slight accent, but it was so soft I could not determine its origin. It could have been Spanish or Italian. For all I cared, it could have been that of a Russian Cossack.

I introduced Wess and me and told her who we worked for. "I have to ask," I said, as I slowly turned my seat to face her, "Where do you work? I'm assuming you're not military."

"No. I work for the State Department." Her eyes burned across the distance, separating us.

"Holy shit! The lady's a spy!" Wess immediately began to pull his notepad from his pocket and leaned forward. He began to whisper. "Give us a good story. We're cleared for rumors as high as ridiculous. We won't mention your name. We'll just say you're a beautiful lady spy."

"I'm afraid Wess is a little more discrete than I. If I mention a source in a story, I like to have a name. You know ours. What's yours?"

"Carmen"

"What a great name for a spy. Carmen. Besides being beautiful, she's got a most appropriate name." Wess was losing his threshold for pain and reality as the drinks began to take effect.

The club was starting to fill as the military officers assigned to the Capital Military Region left their air-conditioned offices and had their drivers drop them off at the club for dinner. I wanted to see if I could sit with her or have her move to our table before someone she knew arrived and took over.

Before I could ask, Wess stood and excused himself, saying he had to go find a Vietnamese man he had been trying to locate for a story. "I really hate to do this, but I'm going to leave my partner, Sean, in charge. You take good care of him. I promised his mama I'd look out for him. He's your responsibility tonight." He paid our tab and made his way to the door.

"There's no reason to take up two tables. May I sit at yours, or would you join me?" Behind her, the sun's last rays set the sky afire with a blaze of reds and oranges visible nowhere else on Earth.

"Sit with me if you like. I like to see the sunset and then watch the moon as it rises. This is a great time of year for that. There's so little time between the two. Have you noticed the moon here?" She asked as she turned to face the open country visible behind the flat expanses of the one-story houses and slightly taller villas of Saigon.

She was wearing a red jumpsuit. It had large metal buttons down the front. All but the one at the top was secured. It was belted with a multi-colored canvas web-belt. She had a circular pin on the left lapel. The pin, an "O," reminded me of the virgin pins girls wore when I was in high school.

Her hair was as black as the night into which she starred. It lay just at the collar of her suit.

A Korean band began to lay out their music for the night's show. Five men and two women who were the strippers for the band putzed around tuning guitars and testing mikes.

"I heard these people last week. They're pretty good," she said.

"What kind of music do they play?" I spoke just to listen to her respond.

"Top 40. Some rock. Things like that. What's your favorite?"

"I'm afraid I'm a little out of step over here. I'm a die-hard Elvis fan. Plus," I said almost apologetically, "I love good blues and some of the old big band stuff."

"Guys like BB King, Muddy Waters, and Blind Boy Davies?"

"You're kidding? I thought I was the only one in Viet Nam who even knew who those guys were."

The sun had completely disappeared, and the three-quarter moon rose to watch over the landscape of this country at war with itself.

By nine-thirty, she had switched from wine to gin and tonic. We talked openly of the things that mattered to us. How long we had been in country, why we were here, and what we did back in the world. She told me of her youth in Monterey, California, where her Spanish mother met her father, a bank executive. After living throughout the Southwest, she went to school in San Diego, then got a job with the State Department. All she would tell me about her position was that she was a foreign area specialist. I knew enough not to press her.

"And now, about you. Tell me something. Why do you go on the patrols with the men? You could just write from the intelligence reports and from interviews. Why do you do it?"

For the first time I had to answer a question I and many of my friends had asked ourselves. I knew I didn't have an answer suitable for her, and it was no use lying. "I don't know. Perhaps it's a holdover from some past life where I was a warrior with unfinished business."

Her eyes took on a far-away look as she contemplated what I said. "Do you really think so? I mean, do you think you were a warrior or lived in a past life?" She picked up her drink and walked to the large windows overlooking the city. I followed her.

"I sometimes think I lived before. I feel at home near the sea. Like it's a part of my past, I can't explain." She turned to face me. "Have you ever walked on the beach at Coronado in San Diego? It's one of the most peaceful places in the world, late at night or early when there are no others on the beach. I sometimes went there and just sat and watched the water."

I remembered my own mother's fascination with the beach when I was a child. She seemed to get a years-worth of energy out of a weeks-vacation in the summer.

I stood behind Carmen and hesitated. I wanted to place my hands on her as we watched the lights of the city. It was a crazy sensation. We were in an active combat zone in Viet Nam. In the distance, I could see the planes from the American air base in Saigon as they took off for a bombing or support run for some other Americans not as lucky as the two of us. I felt as if we were cheating the elements by being here in the relative security of the city. As we stood silently, the moon began to cast its light on the peaks of the highest buildings in the city.

"It really is pretty," I said as I watched it rise to its silvery radiance. In the past, I thought of the moon only when I was with a unit in the field. It was a light to both sides. One used it to move their men into ambush positions, or move through the jungle, The other side used it as a beacon to guide them as they tried to avoid the ambushes. Only by birthright was the decision made as to who was who.

I held my drink in my left hand and slowly placed my right on her shoulder. She did not flinch or move as I let it lay casually on the red material of the jumpsuit she wore. She stood motionlessly for a minute and then turned to face me. "Please don't. Not tonight. Let's just share the moonlight."

In my life I had been turned on and off by any number of women, but never so quickly as by this lady in the moonlight. I knew I would have to stand in line to see her if I ever got close enough again, however I fully intended to try each time I came back to Saigon.

"I really must go," she said as she stood in front of me. "It's going to be a long night. I have some things I need to do."

"Will I…I mean, can I see you again? Tomorrow?"

"I'm afraid not tomorrow. I'm going up north. I'll be there for three days. Perhaps when I get back. I come here almost every evening for dinner. You'll see me the next time you're in town. Better yet," she said as she withdrew a small notepad and pen from her purse, "drop me a line at my office and let me know when you'll be back. I'll try to make it on those days." As she spoke, she placed her hand lightly on my right forearm and let the tips of her nails slide gently down my bare flesh. She gave me a quick kiss on the cheek, and I watched her walk slowly away.

I passed the days, waiting for the nights. I wrote her office address and called early on the day she was to return.

"Good morning. My name is Sean Kelly. I'm with the Nielsen News Network and I'd like to speak to Ms. Cinfuegos." I tried to sound as official as possible.

"I'm sorry, sir. She is not here now. She will be in the office in the afternoon," said a Vietnamese female.

I left my name and said I would be at the Mass at 1800 as we planned. If she got the message. If she remembered me. If she came. If. If.

All my "ifs" were cast aside at half past six when she walked through the door, looked around quickly, and walked directly to my table when she saw me stand.

"I got your message. All of them." She laughed. "I'll say one thing. You're persistent."

She waited for me to pull the chair out for her.

"Unlike opportunity, I'll knock more than once. Especially for you." I added.

"I brought you something," she said as she placed a cassette on the table. "It's a copy of a tape I brought with me. It's Mississippi Blues. I think you'll like it. It's even got one by Lightening Hopkins on it."

We spent the evening with dinner, and then when the band began to play, I suggested we go to the Continental.

"Isn't that where you live?" she asked.

It took a second for her comment to register. "Just to the bar. It's quiet. Unless you want to stay here."

"No, that's all right. I'll go. To the bar."

At eleven, she asked me to get a taxi for her. I offered to go with her, but she refused.

"Do you like French cooking?" She asked as she waited for the cab.

"Love it."

"Good. Let me take you to dinner tomorrow. Have you ever eaten at the Mayflower? They have the best food and the most horrid wine in the city."

"It's a date. I'll meet you...where?"

"The Mass at seven."

I opened the taxi door for her. "Are you certain you don't...."

"I'll be all right. I promise." Another quick kiss, and she was gone.

The Mayflower was the most heavily guarded restaurant in Viet Nam. Maybe even the world, though the executive dining room at the Kremlin

66

may have it beat. Outside, on the street, armed guards stood behind sandbag bunkers just inside several strands of concertina wire. Diners were required to show an I.D. to enter.

The reason was two-fold. Its location, across the street from the Presidential Place, made it a favorite of both President Tu and Vice President Ky, and almost every foreign politician, celebrity, or dignitary who visited the city ate there. The walls were covered with photos of these people dining at the Mayflower.

We were taken to our table at exactly the time specified on our reservation. "I'm impressed," I said, noting the Vietnamese usual disregard for time.

"If you are that easily impressed, you'll be amazed by the food. Do you like French Onion soup?" Carmen radiated charm, class, and beauty. I felt like I was a schoolboy on a prom date.

The meal was excellent. Crocks of onion soup with chunks of dark bread and cheese, thick and strong, sealing the top. Shish kabobs served on flaming skewers made up the main course.

"How many females work for State over here?" I asked as we sipped coffee long after we finished our dinner.

"Is that the reporter after a story or the young man wishing to expand his little black book?" She asked.

"I think the answer is none of the above. I've got enough stories projected for a while. And as for a black book, I think I've torn out all the pages except one."

"Only one? Is that enough?"

"I think it's more than enough. What do you think?"

"I think if we do not leave on our own, we will be asked to give up this table very soon. Do you dance?"

"Not very well. But I give 'em hell at intermission!"

"I'll just bet you do." She reached into her bag and extracted a roll of piasters.

I reached across the table to stop her. I placed my hand on hers. It was to keep her from paying, but just touching her sent a charge throughout my body.

"You can't do that."

"Do what?"

"Pay for dinner."

"I invited you, remember?" She was looking at me with the deepest, most piercing eyes I ever saw.

"I know, but...."

"No buts. My treat. Don't worry, you'll get a chance to repay."

She paid, and we left. We caught a cab and told him to take us back to the Mass, where we planned to try to dance to the Korean band.

She slid into the back seat, and as I got in beside her, I realized she had not gone all the way over. Once in, I lay my arm across the back of the seat and across her shoulders. My right hand lay on her arm.

Halfway to the Mass, we heard the unmistakable sounds of small arms, automatic rifles, and grenades exploding near us. "I think we should get off the streets. Let me take you home." Without waiting for her reply, I tapped the driver on the shoulder and told him we weren't going to the Mass. "Tell him where to go," I said.

"I almost let myself forget where I was tonight. I guess it took a firefight to bring me back to the reality of Viet Nam." She had leaned back, gently resting her head on my arm.

"Why are you here?" I asked.

"Good question. Sometimes, I'm not certain myself. My family had a fit when I told them. They were all for my being a Foreign Service Officer, but they wanted me to work my way to the embassy in Spain or Mexico. Do you speak Spanish, Nito?"

"Nito?"

"Sean translates to John, which becomes Juan which becomes Juanito. Nito is what you would call a special friend. A pet name of sorts. You don't mind, do you?" She sat up, a puzzled look on her face.

"No, my dear. Call me what you will. Just keep calling."

For the first time, I kissed her. She offered no resistance, yet I knew she held back.

"Carmen...."

"No. Please," She placed a finger against my mouth. "Now is not the time."

The cab pulled in front of the address she gave him. "I'm all right here. Thank you for this evening. For everything, Nito." This time, she kissed me.

I watched her as she stepped from the cab and then disappeared behind a metal gate. The moon seemed to illuminate her every step.

From that second, I knew I would spend as much time as I could in Saigon with the lady in the moonlight.

DATELINE: SAIGON, SOUTH VIET NAM

Puppy love.

Love at first sight.

Lust disguised as love.

I came to Viet Nam to write about the war and the men fighting it. I have met many of them and have written their stories. Several of the stories have gotten national attention, for which I am both personally and professionally grateful. I have kept in touch with a few of the men I met and have discovered by reading casualty reports that far too many of them have lost their lives over here.

I have seen the beauty of sunsets over the mountains, the beaches of Vung Tao, the endless green of rice paddies in the Mekong Delta, and the magnificent French influence in the Saigon of years past. I never expected the country to produce anything so memorable in the midst of a war, but I was wrong.

There is something more I found here in the city than I had expected. I make my living using words to describe people, places, and things but for the first time, perhaps since I was a small child, I find myself at a loss for words.

I saw her for a fleeting moment the first time. It was like being struck by lightning. It was a sensation I had never felt, and I still don't know how to describe it.

I was with friends at dinner in one of the better places in Saigon, were people gather to have a drink, a good meal and forget for a while that if they look out the windows on the top floor of the building, they can see tracer bullets cutting through the night as men not so lucky are fighting for their lives a few miles away.

I was told she was off-limits. Not because she was married or had a steady boyfriend, but because she could choose from almost any man in the room as each approached her at some time and was turned away. It was if she had a 'wet paint' sign on her. It was almost human nature when we saw a sign like that to touch it to see if it was real.

She came in two nights later, and through a set of circumstances, we managed to sit at the same table. As we talked, the building could have collapsed around me, and I would not have noticed. By the end of the evening, her 'wet paint' sign had disappeared, and we made plans to meet again several days later. She worked for the State Department in a classified position, but she gave me her office address and phone number, which I used to arrange dinner meetings.

Dinner.

Two days later, we sat on the terrace at the top of one of the hotels, and I watched as the moonlight played across her features. It was a sight I will never forget.

Another dinner. Then drinks.

A taxi ride to her quarters and a kiss good night.

Love at first sight?

In a war zone with my moonlight lady?

Chapter Eight

There were numerous large, division-size military commands in Viet Nam. Army divisions like the 1st, 4th, 9th, 1st Cavalry, 173rd Airborne, Marine Expeditionary Units, Air Wings, and Navy commands dotted the landscape with parts of some out to sea and some in neighboring countries. Each one of them had someone down to the Battalion level who was responsible for public affairs. That meant keeping their units in front of the folks back home, answering news queries, escorting anyone from the media who happened to stumble across the unit, and writing hometown news releases about the men in the unit. Some had actual public affairs training, others got the position by screwing up in another job and then getting placed where they could do little damage to themselves or someone else. They had everything they needed to do their jobs. The one thing they didn't need was me. For that reason, I tried to stay away from the major units and spend my time with the people in the field who would be the ones who would make a difference if a difference could be made in Viet Nam.

Every time I attended the Five O'clock Follies at MCV Headquarters, I paid special attention to anything said about a small unit anyplace in the country and what they were doing, no matter if it was good or bad. I figured if they made the Five O'clock Follies, there would be something of interest about them, and I wanted to know what it was.

One day, the public affairs officer doing the briefing mentioned a small unit that had recently captured a senior Viet Cong leader who was in their area. Their Vietnamese counterpart had provided the intelligence, and it

71

came so quickly that they had to act on it without running it up the chain of command and getting permission. The briefing officer said the team leader was counseled on the proper manner of sending intelligence up the chain and getting permission, even when it was a short-fuse issue. It was almost tongue in cheek as he knew if they had done it the prescribed way, the man would still be running loose.

This was the kind of unit I wanted to find out more about. I did some background work on them and found out that for more than ten months they had all been together: Captain Ron Taylor, the commander, Bob Evans, the executive officer, Frank Scott team medic, and the Dutchman, the weapons expert. They worked hard to maintain a close friendship not only with each other, but also with the Vietnamese to whom they were assigned as advisors.

I didn't need permission or clearance to go to where they were, but I like to keep some of the others in the office informed as to my plans…just in case. After stopping and briefing Wess, I caught a pedicab to the entrance to TSN. I got out and waited until a military vehicle stopped at the gate and offered me a ride to the terminal.

I checked the board with the scheduled flights on it and found one headed in the right direction. I signed up, and thirty minutes later, I was seated on a C-119. After landing at an almost abandoned airstrip, I caught a ride on a Huey to the outpost where I was going.

My first morning at the outpost was spent getting introduced to the Vietnamese and attending an early morning intelligence briefing.

"Trung Uy, we will find many Viet Cong tonight. I have a new ambush location where there are many local V.C." The Vietnamese Lieutenant Colonel in charge of the battalion-sized outpost gave Lieutenant Evans the orders of the day.

"That's good, Trung Ta. We can use the money we will get from the war trophies we capture and sell in Saigon." Bob kidded with the short, stocky man who shared a dedication to his cause with Bob.

"I'll get the team together. Have you told Dai Uy Taylor yet? He will want to go out on this one." As he spoke, Bob turned, and we began to walk back toward the side of the compound reserved for the Americans.

The compound on which the team lived was part of a larger outpost system comprised of four crudely constructed outposts along a canal junction. The team part of the compound was the smallest of the group and was on the northeast corner. This was the most easily defended by the internal weapons they had with them and with the little artillery support they could count on when the going got rough.

A wall of mud and logs, reinforced with sandbags, made up the perimeter, circling all the compounds. Our wall was only about four feet in height, so just walking around the compound was like being a duck in a shooting gallery at the county fair.

The small log-and-mud hut in which they lived was set into a corner, thus giving the benefit of two walls instead of a single thickness of mud. Overhead, they were lucky enough to have several pieces of perforated steel planking or PSP, easily worth its weight in gold during a mortar attack. The team obtained it by trading VC flags and other war trophies to the Navy Seabees. A thickness of only one sheet covered with a layer of sandbags would usually stop a direct hit from a small mortar. Even with the PSP, a direct hit on the roof of the hootch would make the ears of anyone unlucky enough to be in it at the time buzz and whistle for a few days.

Since the roof did not allow enough height in which to stand, time inside was usually spent sitting at the small table and chairs placed near the door. Captain Taylor scrounged another table and single chair for me. He placed this near the one they used and nailed a neatly hand-lettered sign over it, which read, "War correspondent. Not cleared for rumors higher than ridiculous!" My table was quickly named the War Room.

Scotty and Taylor were playing hearts when Bob ducked down to enter. "Go ahead and stiff him with the queen, Scotty. You've probably got an extra one in your hat anyway." He looked around. "Has the Dutchman got dinner ready yet? It looks like we got ourselves a little mission tonight." Bob slid the third chair back across the hard-packed dirt floor and sat at the table with them. He motioned for me to take the remaining one. At six-foot-one, even sitting, his light blond hair almost touched the roof.

Each member of the team took turns cooking over the grill fashioned out of an old oil drum. Most team members had their own specialties. The Dutchman was the exception. When Scotty cooked, it was Scotty's Soul Shack, and they had fried chicken, greens, and sweet potatoes, if they could be found in the village. Bob ran Bob's Bar-B-Que with an iron hand. His beans and chili were known throughout the Area of Operation or A.O. However, it was the sauce he concocted for the large slabs of ribs he scrounged from the Navy that made him famous, or infamous, depending upon one's digestive system.

He even made a mild version that he put on the meals he gave to the children on the compound. "I can't eat this and see them all so hungry" was his usual excuse to share most of his food with the kids.

Like the rest of Team 75, he wrote home for clothing for the kids. When his two daughters outgrew an item, it was not passed on; it was mailed to Viet Nam.

"See that dress? I remember buying it for Jamie. She was so cute in it." He told me one night as we walked the perimeters at dusk. He seemed to have total recall for clothing.

Taylor was on his second tour in Viet Nam. It was the same for Scotty and the Dutchman. Only Bob was a virgin. After his Special Forces training at Ft. Bragg, he spent seven months with a team at Ft. Devens, Mass., and made first Lieutenant. He was then assigned to Viet Nam as an executive officer on the team.

The three of them, Scotty, the Dutchman, and Taylor, knew they were closer than they wanted to be. I was tolerated and accepted because they knew I would leave in a week. Unlike in past wars that we all read about or grew up on from fathers and uncles, people in Viet Nam did not get to be life-long friends. Unfortunately, Bob changed that for Team 74 when he arrived.

Bob had an almost little-brother-like personality. The NCOs felt like his father, and Taylor took on the role of an older brother. He fit into the little family from his first day at the outpost.

Scotty liked to tell the story of Bob's arrival. He was on radio watch when the chopper first brought Bob to the outpost. "Slicks coming in. They got some groceries from the country store, another box of claymores, and a newbie to replace Lt. Lewis." He handed Taylor the handset for the radio as he left to mark the LZ with a smoke grenade. "See if they got a fresh copy of Stars and Stripes. I think I need to check my horoscope and see if it's going to be a good day," he added as he left the radio shack.

Taylor heard Scotty telling me the story and began to give his version. "Great," I said as I spoke to the pilot, "Another green replacement. What's the guy look like? How much junk is he bringing with him?"

I could picture them as they spoke to the pilot. The vibrations from the incoming chopper always reminded me of a kid trying to talk from behind an electric fan. The voice was slightly broken from the steady rhythm of the vibrations.

"Doesn't look too bad. Maybe a little overweight. He's only got a rucksack and a duffel bag. I don't see any TVs or air conditioners," the pilot responded.

"I knew we were stuck with the newbie," Taylor laughed as he continued with the story. "I wanted to know about the important stuff."

"At least he doesn't expect us to have electricity. What kind of beer and soda you carrying? If it's Fresca and Olympia, I swear I'll have the tigers blow up the chopper when you set down."

The pilot's lack of response to Taylor confirmed that, once again, the field soldiers were at the ass-end of the supply chain, and the Cokes and Coors were in the NCO and Officers clubs in Saigon and Da Nang.

"Say again your last..."

"Don't even unload it. My Viets won't drink it, and they're worthless on the black market. I'll see you on the ground. Out here." Taylor cut him off.

A large column of green smoke drifted slowly skyward in the heavy, humid Delta air as Scotty waited for the chopper to land.

Even before the skids touched the hard, cracked mud of An Xuyen Province, boxes and bags were being tossed out. Just as the chopper settled for a two-bounce stop, the crew chief was firmly dislodging the new replacement and all his worldly possessions.

Wind from the rapidly spinning blades blew debris including Lt. Bob Evans's bush hat, across the L.Z. As it tumbled by, Taylor snatched it and held it for him.

"Welcome to the Song Bay Resort, Golf, and Tennis Club. If you will remember a few simple rules, your stay will be most enjoyable. Never swim in the canal north of the outpost. That's where all the native plumbing facilities are located. That's also where we catch the biggest fish. Never leave after dark unless you're wearing formal attire. Basic black will do, black pajamas, black cap, and black face. We don't want to distinguish ourselves from the fun-loving native nightlife. And last, but certainly not least, you will be required to cook once a week. What can you do with paddy rats and rice?" Taylor was trying to jokingly give him the rules of survival.

Scotty came over to help him carry some of the new man's equipment. Taylor picked up Bob's rucksack, and Scotty took the duffel bag.

"They told me at Bragg, the locals would always be anxious to help me, and I could pay them with cigarettes. What brand do you two smoke?" The newbie was fitting in already.

During their first operation, four days later, the team learned two interesting things about Bob. First, he had an uncanny sense of direction, and second, he had a total lack of a sense of balance. He could cross the unbroken expanse of rice paddies and know exactly where he was at all times, but when he tried to navigate the native monkey bridges crossing the smaller canals, he immediately slipped and fell into the water. By the afternoon of his second day out, as soon as they came to a bridge, two of the tiger squad, the bodyguards assigned to the team, slid into the water and waited for Bob to come crashing in behind them.

"Shit! This time, I'm going to do it." Bob was looking at a two-log bridge made of coconut tree trunks approximately twenty-five feet long. Taylor had already crossed. Scotty was behind Bob.

From the waist-deep canal, one of the tigers chided Bob in Vietnamese to hurry up and fall and get it over with.

Since Taylor and Bob usually were at opposite ends of the column when they went out, each of them had a Viet who carried their radio. Bob's RTO stood by patiently, smoking one of the Salem's with which he was paid. In less than a week, Bob had taught him two words in English, his favorite expressions, "heavy" and "shit." Both were interchangeable as everything new or unusual was rated "heavy," and virtually everything was prefaced or ended with "shit." Even the other Viets picked up on this and began to call Bob's RTO "Heavyshit."

Slowly, Bob inched out on the logs. "Wait, I'll meet you halfway," Taylor said as he returned across the bridge. "Just keep your head up. Don't look down at the logs." The team leader talked to him as he came back.

Suddenly, Taylor found himself in the middle of the bridge, facing Bob, and had to walk backwards to return.

As they began to inch back to Taylor's' side, one more tiger eased himself into the water.

No one will admit to being the first to slip. Both Taylor and Bob blame each other.

Fortunately, Taylor fell to one side of the logs, Bob to the other. When they surfaced, Scotty and Heavyshit stood on the logs and looked down at the two of them. "Playtime's over, boys," Scotty said. "It's time to come out and dry off. You don't want to catch a nasty old cold, now do you?"

From Bob's bridge side companion came only one heavily accented word, "Heavyshit!"

Mail was the only link the teams in the brush had with civilization and reality. No matter how infrequently it came or what it said, it meant someone still cared. Even a box of crushed cookies or a cake, green and inedible with mold, was treasured.

Bob had a wife, Jane, and two daughters in Florida. Both Scotty and Taylor were single. The Dutchman was divorced but occasionally received a letter from his grown son in Utah.

Bob's wife numbered each letter and wrote daily for about ten days, and then she stopped. It always ran in cycles, and when it stopped, they said Bob went slightly crazy. I was there when he experienced such a cycle break.

"Hurry up, Scotty. Shit! Open the bag. See if I got a letter today." Bob stood by as the team's senior NCO went through the small pile of boxes and bags the chopper left for them.

Scotty's lack of response was enough to tell Bob this was the first day of another dry spell. They knew what came next.

I was about to find out.

"I've been thinking, Rabbit, maybe we should go back to V.C. Lake tonight. We haven't had an operation down there in three weeks." When the mail stopped, Bob got bloodthirsty!

When Bob began to mentally prepare himself for an operation, he called each man using the radio call sign we used. Taylor's was "Rabbit," a name he picked up during his first tour in Viet Nam, when he scrambled through a seemingly impenetrably growth along a canal while under fire. His men told him he looked like a rabbit running from a fox as he burrowed through the undergrowth.

Bob was "Summerwine". He gave no explanation; however, I'm certain it had a somewhat mystical, perhaps even romantic, connotation from days spent beachside in his native Florida.

I had been given permission to go along on any operation so long as the local American commander approved, and I went as a noncombatant. I had long ago picked up the nickname Deadline, which would be my call sign.

Our target, a large inland body of water they called V.C. Lake, was a bust. A night spent silently lying in ambush positions resulted only in each of us being covered with fresh mosquito punctures. Insect repellent, netting, and gloves didn't dissuade these little bloodsuckers from their midnight raids.

We returned at daylight and prepared for another relatively inactive day at the outpost. Bob and I sat in the shade of the berm as we talked. "Where do you want to go when you leave here?" I asked. "You're pressing your luck personally and professionally if you stay in Special Forces too long." I tried to get a little personal information on each of the men. Bob sometimes talked about what the others said they planned to do after leaving Viet Nam. He was the only one who did not plan to remain in the Army.

Later, we moved to the little shade offered by a piece of green Plexiglas the Dutchman had traded for in Vin Long when the rest of the team joined us. He placed it between two hootches during the day and sometimes hung a jungle hammock under it.

"I don't know," Taylor spoke first. "Maybe the Advanced School at Benning, then a nice cushy job pushing recruits at some basic training post. Who knows, maybe I'll be your kid brother's C.O., and I can continue to take out my hostilities on a member of your family," he said to Bob.

"Shit! He's playing football for Florida State now. He'll show you hostilities if he gets drafted by anything other than the NFL."

We talked for over two hours. We went through two six-packs of beer, which we had left in the canal to cool. It didn't work too well, but cool beer is better than no beer at all.

"Why are you still here? Talk about pressing your luck; even as a war correspondent, you've been here a long time." Bob spoke as he handed me another barely cool beer.

Night noises inherent to an outpost full of Vietnamese Regional Forces began to fill the air. From the area containing the families, a baby began to cry and was quickly silenced by its mother, who immediately drew the infant to her breast. Children up to the age of three or four were often quieted in this manner.

The high-pitched squeaks of rats were heard as they, too, began night operations. Around the perimeter, gun positions were readied as claymores were set, and weapons clicked when magazines were inserted.

Lights were dimmed and placed inside the small hootches the Viets called home. Frogs, who would quickly become meals if detected in daylight, began to call to each other across the paddies.

"Eighty-seven and a wake-up," said Bob the next morning as he left his position at radio watch. He bent to enter the covered area we called home. As he settled in for what little amount of sleep he could get, he had eighty-eight more days left in country.

Taylor and I were sitting outside when Scotty found us. "The Lieutenant's looking for you," said Scotty as he and the Dutchman came around the corner from the operations center. "The swing ship just landed and threw off all our stuff. You got a small box and two letters. Here's that film you wanted." He handed me a small package from the pilot. "This is four days in a row for him without mail. That's about as long as he can stand it without looking for a village to plunder." Scotty handed us the box and letters, and then he and the Dutchman went across the canal to work with the gun crew to place up new aiming stakes for our mortars.

"Hey, Rabbit! I got some heavy information on a couple of NVA officers snooping around up in Chi Lang. Our guys say they crossed the border from Cambodia two days ago. They're working with a local VC tax collector. Let's go have a look-see." Bob placed his map of the area on the communal table.

The Viet Cong had a unique system of tax collecting. Once they went into an area, they would levy a tax on crops, livestock, and even possessions. Payment was in cash, livestock ,or rice. A few, like the guys they were after, were reported to have a nasty habit of taking some of the village children until the parents paid their taxes. In other places, other times, that was kidnapping.

"Slow down, Bob! Man, you're too short to be thinking of looking for an NVA cadre with a tax collector."

It was as if Taylor had been speaking to the green nylon sand-filled bags stacked outside the walls of our hootch.

"Even Navy Intelligence has a report on them. We could slip in by chopper, do a quick cordon, search the village where they're hiding, and un-ass the area. Shit! It'll be a piece of cake." Bob was now drawing a broken line around a small village complex west of the outpost.

"Bob, you can leave here anytime you want to now. You've got less than ninety days left in country. Forget it! The war is over for you. I can call back to Ben Thuy and have you out of here in one day!" That was the first time I heard Taylor come close to pulling rank on anyone on the team.

"It's a hell of a system," said Bob as we sat in the green-tinted shade of the team hut. "The Americans and the South Viets come by in the daytime and police up the men. At night, the VC take the ones that hide from us. At least we're not stealing their kids and taking what little money they have and calling it taxes."

I finished the warm beer I was drinking as he talked.

"One more, Rabbit! One more! Let's do one more, and I can go back to

Florida. You can go wherever lifers go after the war is over."

It was like arguing with a kid. "Last time?" Taylor said as we looked at the map Bob unfolded between us.

"Heavy! Rabbit, Heavy!" Bob smiled like a child who just got his way.

It took two days to get all the clearance and logistical support necessary to mount the operation. We would go in on Wednesday morning. The choppers would drop us off about three klicks away from the village, and a reinforced company of Regional Forces would meet us there. Bob, Scotty, Taylor, and I would take the troops in, and with the R.F.'s acting as a blocking force. Taylor expected the Vietnamese with us to make quick work of the North Viet Cadre and the tax collector in the village.

One chopper lifted off in the predawn darkness as Taylor yelled to Bob. "It's not too late to stay. You don't have to go." I knew Bob heard him; however, we received only silence as he gave us the thumbs-up signal and slid aboard the helicopter that would soon place us close to a Viet Cong village.

Wind blew across the chopper as we began to climb and prepare for the assault team to hit the ground. This was usually the quietest time. Landing into an unknown area usually played hell with nerves, stomachs, and memories. I made notes as I sat on the floor next to Captain Taylor.

Almost unconsciously, I waited for Bob to slowly and silently remove his bush hat and say a prayer. Taylor confided in me that each time Bob went on an operation, he said a quick prayer, first for his wife and daughters, then for his men and their safety. Equal thanks were given when he returned.

As we approached the village where the tax collector was operating, we dropped down to fly at treetop level. The choppers skimmed along, barely missing the tall coconut and mangrove swamps. At times we were so close bits of twigs and leaves from the trees were sucked into the open choppers and swirled about as we flew.

The gunner on the left side of the ship in which we rode to war broke the silence. The echoing of his machine gun reverberated through the inside of the chopper. Sun glistened as it picked up the light from the rapidly tumbling brass cartridges expelled from the gun and swept the wood line nearest to where we were landing.

We jumped off before either chopper settled to the ground. A quick thumbs-up signal was flashed to the pilot by Summerwine as he ran in a crouch to a rendezvous with the men from the first chopper.

To maintain control over the little people, as the Americans call the Vietnamese, the team split up. Bob and Scotty took the right flank of the village. Taylor, the Dutchman, and I went to the left. At exactly five a.m., we went our separate ways. Bob smiled and waved as he left. "I'll see you on the other side. If you see the NVA before I do, try not to put too many holes in their uniforms. I'd like to have one for a souvenir. If you see me do something stupid like fall off a bridge, don't write it up," he said to me. "Come on, Heavyshit. Let's go." Bob, Scotty, and Heavyshit moved slowly to the right.

I was almost in a daydream as I watched a few of the old people emerge from their wood and thatch huts and dip the morning cooking water from the large round crock jugs standing by the front door openings.

One of the huts was less than a stone's throw away. I saw the inhabitants moving about in the semi-darkness of the hut. An old lady came out of the hut where she probably had spent every day of her life. The old mama-san was dressed in a loose pair of black pants ending well above her ankles and bare feet. She wore a blue scarf tied turban style about her head. Even from my position, I could tell the nearly toothless old lady was chewing bedel nut with her few remaining teeth. As she dipped water into a brass pot, occasionally, a short blast of blood-red juice from the nut was splashed to the ground. Bedel nut was chewed as a sign of age and respect by the village elders.

Taylor gave the signal to move out. As I stood and moved, I wanted to remember this village with its unique sounds and early morning smells.

Taylor and each of the men with us, picked out a nearby hut as they passed, shoved open the small door, and entered prepared to do whatever was necessary to emerge alive. In the hootch Taylor and I entered, a woman and two small naked babies huddled in a darkened corner under an old wooden table, which they used for cover and protection. They knew the rules. It was the same for the Americans in the daytime as it was for the VC at night. Be cool, don't move. Don't come outside when the shooting starts, and you might live to do it again the next day.

Each hut was the same. Young women and grandparents. No men, no husbands, no sons, no brothers. It was always the same. Those the team found were put into the South Vietnamese Army. The Viet Cong took those who escaped. There were no draft dodgers in Viet Nam.

"Rabbit, this is Summerwine. It looks like we got ourselves a little heavy action over here. Scotty's dropped back a little way to see if he can determine what it is. You got anything over there yet?" Bob's calm voice came over the radio as we exited the hut.

"All quiet here, Summerwine. I'll shift and work my people in your direction. The RFs are still blocking, and I haven't heard any fire from their area. I'll try to get a couple of gun-ships on station for us."

Before Taylor could change to the other radio to request the helicopter gun cover, I heard two rapid explosions. They were both made by B-40 rockets. We now had a more heavily armed force than we originally thought.

"Rabbit, Summerwine. I'm taking B-40's over here. Looks like some of my little people are down. We're moving up to see what's so important."

We cleared the hootches as quickly as we safely could. *"Bac Viet o day?"* We asked the occupants in our best paddy dialect. "Where are the North Vietnamese?" After three villagers told us there were no NVA in the area, the little people torched a house as a punishment for their lying. I could picture myself either on trial or a witness at a court martial after Viet Nam for war crimes.

I saw the rapid movement of the men as they ran between the small patches of coconut trees lining the edge of the clearing, where even heavier fire was being directed against Bob and his men.

"Summerwine. I see you. We're coming in. We'll close in on your left flank in zero-three." Taylor spoke as he moved. His R.T.O. had the radio handset on a long line to stay as far away from him as possible. Americans, especially those with radios, drew an inordinate amount of fire in the field.

We were now less than fifty meters from Bob. We were too close for the radios to function, so we used hand and arm signals to communicate. With a few deft movements, Bob indicated the direction from which he had been taking the most fire. It was a small series of bunkers approximately fifty meters to his front and just out of our line of fire because of his position.

"Cover us, we're coming over!" Taylor yelled as a burst of automatic rifle fire dug up the ground in front of our position. "De! De!" I told the three Vietnamese with me. They didn't need to be reminded of the need to hurry as they ran to the tree line now occupied by Bob, Scotty, and six Viets.

"I just talked to the advisors with the Ruff Puff blocking force. They're moving up on the back side of the bunkers. Looks like we found the tax collectors." Bob spoke slowly and calmly as he showed us the position of the four bunkers to our front on his map.

"We're getting the heavy stuff from the second one from the left. Some guy keeps popping up, fires a B-40, then drops back inside the door before we can get a shot at him. That must be their C.P. I've got a LAW on the way up. As soon as it gets here, we can…" He stopped, frozen in mid-sentence.

"Shit! Look what that son of a bitch has done!"

I turned to face the bunker causing the look of total shock on Bob's face.

Half crawling, having obviously just been thrown from the bunker, was a tiny frail Vietnamese girl about four years old. She was crying uncontrollably from the horrors of the situation in which she now found herself. Her only clothing was a ragged blood-stained piece of a dress nearly in shreds on her small body. Her right arm hung at a wicked angle, obviously with a shattered bone. Her weak, spindly legs would not respond to her attempts to raise herself and escape the nightmare around her. Even a primeval attempt to crawl to safety was fruitless.

She appeared to be about the same age as Jamie, the youngest of Bob's two daughters.

I was shooting pictures with my camera when Bob stood, slid his rucksack off, and, with only an M-16 in his right hand, left the relative security of his position. Scotty and Taylor both reached for him, but they were too late.

"Don't move, sweetheart, I'm coming. It'll be okay. Daddy's coming." He spoke to the child as if it was a Sunday back in the world and they were on a picnic.

Bob and the little girl were in between the bunker and us. "Keep the North Viets pinned down," Taylor yelled in a combination of English and Vietnamese as he tried to get his troops to fire on the bunker from positions which didn't endanger Bob or the girl.

"Cover us as best you can, Scotty," Taylor said as he left the Sergeant and went after Bob. Although Bob was running in a crouch at top speed he was only halfway to the child who now sat in shock, in front of the bunker. Bob still had over twenty yards to go to reach her.

Just as this child, born into a war in which there no winners saw this strange man running toward her, a figure emerged from the half-opened doorway of the bunker behind her.

Bob was less than ten meters from the child when he slowed his pace to a near walk, stood erect, and held out his hands to her. He was smiling at the blank-faced girl as the North Vietnamese soldier emerged, rifle in hand from the bunker.

Now, only a few steps away from the child, Bob did not see the rifle pointing at his midsection as it prepared to spew forth a load of lead. Each piece was plainly marked with Bob's name. No "To whom it may concern," no "occupant," just Bob, Summerwine, friend, brother.

"Don't cry. I'll take care of you. Please don't cry." I could hear him speak to her. All other sounds now ceased for me.

The bunker door stood open. Small bits of wood flew off as silently, lead and steel from the weapons of warriors tried to end the panorama before me.

I saw Bob reach down to pick up the child. Her left hand was extended toward this wild yet gentle man who was taking his little girl away from dangers only a father could understand.

One evening, Bob and I talked about how impersonal war seemed to be. It was always artillery and air strikes or ambushes shooting at movement or forms. Never real people.

I saw Bob buckle under the force of the rounds entering his body. An old feeling began to build in me. I had seen Americans of all ages, all ranks, and colors die in Viet Nam. I never got used to it. I could feel it creeping in like a San Francisco fog as my eyes were riveted to the horror I was helpless to stop.

In confirmation classes years earlier, as a young man, my family priest, Father Douglas, tried to explain to me the difference between "Thou shalt not kill and Thou shalt not murder." I wondered if Buddha taught the difference.

The last few meters between Bob and Taylor slid slowly by as the Captain made a dive to catch Bob before he fell to the hard-packed earth in front of the bunkers. I saw Bob jerk involuntary as the unmistakable sound of an AK-47 rifle spit death towards the man and the child in front of us.

A slight half roll to the left allowed Taylor to catch the man called Summerwine as his legs lost the strength to support him.

"Don't…cry…don't cry, Jamie," Bob whispered to the little girl as Taylor tried to keep the life in him.

I could hear a helicopter approach. It didn't matter now if they were gunships or medevacs.

The warm, slick, dark red blood from Bob now covered Taylor's hands and arms. I knew the feeling. In my mind, I could taste the salty liquid through my own skin.

"Easy, Bob. Hang on. Don't go! Bob, don't go! Stay for Jane and Jamie and Victoria." He pleaded. Foam, red and slick, began to form at the corners of Bob's mouth. Bob's main purpose in living was his wife and two daughters. He often talked of them as we watched the Delta sun disappear. At last light, he would show me a well-worn photo, always kept wrapped in plastic in his left top shirt pocket.

"If I ever get captured, at least I'll have a picture of them," he said.

Clear plastic stuck out in jagged bits from the pocket where bullet fragments had torn through his photo and his chest. His pleas to the child now were nothing more than guttural sounds.

"They're coming in for you, Bob. It's a medevac! Stay with us! Do it for the girls." I heard myself plead.

The bleeding stopped. The foam did not reappear. Eyes, clear, open slightly, stared up at Taylor as he sat with Bob lying prone in his lap.

Beside him, a tiny girl lay silent and still as she, too, left with Summerwine.

DATELINE: SAIGON, SOUTH VIET NAM

We all have heroes at some time in our lives.

Babe Ruth at age 10.

Elvis Presley at 15.

The Beatles at 20.

Summerwine forever.

Since I've been in Viet Nam, I've preferred to spend time with small units, mostly made up of what the military calls Advisors. For these men, life about as far removed from the normal military and its bureaucracy as possible. They were, for the most part, free to wage war as they saw fit or was necessary. When a senior officer decided to visit one of the many outposts that dotted the country, he had to announce his arrival in advance. This was to make certain the Americans were on the outpost. It became a game played between the two elements. If they didn't want to have him land, for whatever reason, the team member who was on radio watch simply told him the rest of the team was on a mission. They would wait a few hours or sometimes days, then contact the officer and report on what they had done, even if it was not true.

Each team was given a budget called the AIK, or Assistance in Kind, fund. Since they were usually far removed from normal military support in the form of food and other comforts of life, they used the funds to purchase what they needed from the local villages. The funds probably were destined for the black market, but they had no other choices.

I found out about Team 75 in a briefing at the Five O'clock Follies, and it sounded like a place I needed to go. After catching a hop on the "swing ship," the name given to the weekly helicopter trip that resupplied the teams with ammo, mail, and any other thing they could get, I arrived at the outpost in the middle of a day with no real activity. I settled in and immediately formed a bond with the entire team, especially the Executive Officer, 1LT Bob Evans. Both of us were from Florida, so that gave us a basis for many conversations.

I accompanied the team on an ambush one night to a place everyone called VC Lake. It was a bust, and the next day, when the swing ship came and didn't leave any mail for Bob, I found out it set the beginning of a pattern. His wife numbered each letter so he could read them in order. She sent him news from home, pictures of his two young daughters, and the occasional box of cookies. No mail for a week, and Bob went slightly nuts.

He was down to what they called a two-digit midget, which meant he had less than one hundred days left in country, when the fifth day passed without mail. That afternoon, he went to the Vietnamese outpost commander and found out a VC tax collector was in their area. Tax collectors in Viet Nam had a reputation for taking money, children, and even lives when they went through a village.

Against the team leader's better judgment, he agreed to mount a mission to stop the tax collector. I went with them and it's a day that's burned forever in my memory. The tax collector was with a larger force than we had anticipated, and a huge firefight erupted. We were pinned down by fire from a series of bunkers where one man would rise up, fire a B-40 rocket, and then disappear back inside. Everyone was pouring fire on that bunker when he suddenly opened the door and tossed something out.

That something was a little girl, about four years old. She was dressed in rags. Her right arm hung loose and helpless, and even from where we were, the bone was visible. She was bloody and in tears. This was not good for a man who had two little girls of about the same age.

Without hesitation, Bob stood and half-walked, half-ran to the bunker. The other team members tried to stop him, but he was a man on a mission. Ignoring the bullets digging into the ground around him from the bunker, he slowed, extended his hand to the little girl, and spoke in a soothing voice, telling her everything was going to be okay and that he was going to take care of her. When he reached her and cradled her in his arms, his body was cut down with AK-47 rounds from the bunker. The shooter was killed, and Bob's team leader came to his aide. A helicopter was circling and had been called in for a medical evacuation, but it was too late.

A little girl whose name we never knew and a man who used Summerwine as his radio call-sign died on the hard-packed dirt in front of a bunker in a place few will ever be able to locate on a map.

A little girl died in the arms of a hero she never knew.

The hero left behind a wife and two daughters who will never know what kind of hero he was.

If a postage stamp is ever made for heroes, it will have the face of Summerwine on it.

Chapter Nine

I've often heard from the guys in the brush that you never hear the round that hits you. I can now attest to the fact that a statement like that is pure, unadulterated bullshit! Not only did I hear it. I felt it! And it hurt really bad. Not like the wounds I grew up with on Saturday morning westerns at the movies. "It's just a flesh wound, ma'am. It didn't hurt. He just winged me." All wounds are flesh wounds. That's where the bullet or shrapnel or whatever enters. In this case, the flesh was mine.

My editor sent me a short message that said he wanted to know more about the real combat troops, as he called them. He went on to explain that I had written news releases, and my weekly column had a slant toward the advisory effort and not the men who were fighting the enemy. The enemy, as he called it, was being fought in pitched battles between American military personnel in combat uniforms, driving tanks, firing big artillery pieces, and flying helicopter gunships with machine guns blazing as they came to the rescue of the men fighting the enemy. He said the evening news was filled with these images, and that's what the American public wanted to read about.

I disagreed, but since he was paying my salary, I fell back on the adage that "the boss ain't always right, but he's always the boss."

I spent two days in Saigon, getting a great steak dinner one night and a great hangover the next morning. I managed to find time to even make a trip over to the MACV Annex and lay around the swimming pool they had. It was now an 'every man for himself" situation since they no longer had a lifeguard. When the pool was first opened, they had a tall chair with an umbrella over it where a lifeguard sat and watched over the military and their girlfriends who came to swim. Next to the swimming pool was a large tennis court enclosed by a fence or net that was about twenty feet high. Beyond the enclosure was a minefield that the Americans had put in after taking over the compound. The minefield separated the compound from a seedy side of Saigon where there was a lot of crime and some VC activity.

One day, the lifeguard was sitting on his chair doing what lifeguards do when they are not blowing their whistles at people running or breaking other rules. He was, so the story goes, occupied watching two young Vietnamese women in bikinis frolic when a sniper's round tore through his umbrella. A second one hit the back of his seat just as he left the seat and hit the water. It was soon decided that a lone man sitting ten feet in the air was a far too tempting target, so lifeguard services were eliminated.

After drying out in the sun, I made my way to one of the many liaison offices at the Headquarters and found one who was receptive to the idea of my accompanying a unit on a road-clearing operation on Highway 1. This was the only main thoroughfare from the DMZ to the Delta. It was always clogged with military convoys, busses filled with locals going or coming from the market, and refugees trying in vain to escape the war. Due to its importance, it was also an almost daily target for the bad guys to mine and place ambushes. Daily road-clearing missions ran north and south to keep it open.

I caught a flight the next morning up to Pleiku, the base camp for the 4th Infantry Division. I checked in with the division Headquarters and was shown to the public affairs office, where I met a young black second Lieutenant. Officers who were not Caucasian were still a rarity, but as soon as we began to talk, I noticed the US Military Academy ring on his hand. He fell into the classic group of men referred to as 'ring knockers' since they seemed to go out of their way to let you know they were wearing a ring indicating they were a service academy graduate. In addition to the ring and butter bar on his collar, he wore the shield of the Adjutant General's Corps. I had spoken to enough graduates to know that an assignment to a non-combat or combat support branch was the kiss of death for a military career.

He introduced himself as Lieutenant Beckton and offered me a cup of coffee. If the Army ever runs out of coffee, I think it will cease to function. I accepted, and we went to his desk. Not his office but a desk set along the side of a room occupied by several other men, most of whom were senior NCOs.

After explaining what I wanted, he said he'd like to accompany me, but his duties at the Headquarters dictated he remain there. He offered to introduce me to an officer from the first Battalion of the thirty-fifth infantry who was going on an operation the next day from Pleiku to the Duc Lap special forces base near the Cambodian border.

He had one of the Sergeants drive me to the unit, where I was introduced to First Lieutenant Lamar Howard, who was the officer in charge of the road-clearing operation the next morning. Howard found me an empty bunk in a transient billet and left me alone for the remainder of the day.

I was awakened the next morning at zero four hundred and told the convoy's ETD, or departure time, was in thirty minutes. Coffee and some donuts made in the Battalion mess hall were outside if I wanted some.

We left and took KL-19 that ran from the base camp to the west toward Duc Lap. There were several two-and-a-half-ton trucks carrying ammo and other essentials for the base in the middle of the convoy. Leading it was an engineer mine clearing team. Behind them, bracketing the trucks were armored personnel carriers, and interspersed intersperced in the convoy were several jeeps with Howard, medics, and communications personnel. When Howard suggested I ride in one of the personnel carriers, I quickly accepted.

The carriers offer much more protection than the canvas covering the trucks and the open jeeps in case there happened to be any action on the way. I found out it was a good choice, but it did have its drawbacks.

I was in the armored personnel carrier when the first explosion hit the vehicle in front of us. The deafening sound of a command-detonated mine echoed through the carrier in which I was riding. I was standing up in the troop compartment at the time.

"Get down, man! We're in a kill zone." The black Private standing next to me pushed me roughly to the floor of the carrier. As he did so, I felt the brass from his M16 as it tumbled into the open area. The second explosion tore open the road between the first two carriers. We were now cut off from the lead vehicle, which was on fire.

"Hang on to your ass, guys, we're going cross country!" Someone yelled. The driver quickly pivoted the large, tracked vehicle and moved to the right side of the road.

Our maneuver took us into the secondary kill zone of the ambush!

I could hear fifty-one caliber rounds hitting the side of the carrier. Two of the men above me were slumped down. One was wounded, the other, the Private who pushed me down earlier was missing most of the top of his head. The driver was attempting to drop the rear cargo door for those of us who had not made it over the side. The door would not open. The hydraulic lines were hit. "When I pull this lever, push that mother open, or we're dead meat." The driver pulled the red handle beside his seat, and three of us pushed it as the door began to drop under its own weight.

As the door hit the ground, a second automatic weapon opened up on us. This time, it was zeroed in on the rear as we tried to get the one wounded man out of us. No longer was it the dull "Thump! Thump! Thump!" of the heavy fifty-one caliber machine gun. This was a light machine gun or someone with an AK-47 and it was pointed in my direction.

Behind us, the other carriers were returning the fire as best they could; however, my immediate concern was the sight and sound of the rounds quickly finding our location. I heard the sharp "ping" as they bounced off the thick skin of the carrier and watched as they dug into the ground in front of us. I knew it was only a matter of seconds before one found its mark.

With a machine gun spitting out more than 200 rounds per minute, it's not too hard for me to believe I was struck twice before I hit the ground from the impact of the first round.

The first thing I felt was in the recess of my mind. I recall a fight I got into once in high school. It was to be a simple after-school fight between two boys who were fighting over a point of honor that the years had erased from my mind. I remember circling, fist up, like my favorite fighter, Jake

Lamotta. Unlike the opponents whom the champion faced, mine had a flat, leather-covered slap jack concealed in his rear pocket that he removed and pasted me with. The blow to the side of my head knocked me from my feet and ended my participation for the afternoon. It required six stitches to close and cost me a suspension, and him an expulsion, from school.

As I fell to the ground, I had the same sensation of the quick shock and dull pain of the blow. This time, it was to the lower left leg and thigh. As I tumbled to the ground, I rolled off the tailgate and tried to get as close to the limited overhead protection the heavy ramp provided as I could. By the time I slid into place, the firing was beginning to subside, and pain was taking its place.

"Medic! Medic! Over here! I've got three wounded." I heard the driver yell to the men in the carrier behind us. "One of 'em is that civilian I had with me. Better get someone over here quick. We're gonna be in a world of shit if he dies."

The driver came over and knelt beside me. "You all right? It looks like it's just your leg. The medics will be here in a minute; then we'll get you on a chopper." As he spoke, he took the first aid packet from the harness I wore, tore it open, and placed it on the gaping hole in my thigh.

"I'll take care of him," the medic said to the driver when he looked at my wound. He placed his bag on the ground beside me and opened it. He extracted a larger bandage and a brown can. He looked at the driver. "You go check out the others in your crew."

"What's in the can?" I asked as he placed it beside me.

"Simple answer is canned blood. If I can't get a medivac here in the next few minutes, I may have to start a transfusion. You're losing blood, but they didn't hit a major artery."

The medic was bent over me and applied bandages to the other two places in my leg. "Looks clean to me. We'll get a doctor to look at you in about an hour. We've got some that need a dust off before you."

Around me, I could hear sounds of the choppers in the air. Cobras fanned out, looking for targets. Gunships flew protection for the relief and clean-up of the mess on the road. The debris scattered when a chopper set down to extract the wounded. I waited for the time when I would be on the chopper to the aide station in the division rear area.

"You're next. Can you roll over onto this stretcher?" Two men stood beside me and placed a green canvas stretcher on the ground next to me.

"I'd like to say I can make it on my own, but I'm afraid you guys will have to give me a hand."

"No sweat. As long as you can try to make it by yourself, you're not hurt too bad." The three of us placed me on the stretcher.

As they carried me to the LZ, the man at the foot end of the stretcher said, "You're that reporter, ain't you? How you gonna write this up? If you get the chance, mention one of your chauffeurs was from Colorado Springs."

I was placed aboard the chopper for the trip to the first of three aid stations I was to visit that day. The first two were simply to clean and evaluate the severity of the wounds. At the second, when it was discovered I was a civilian noncombatant, the decision was made to fly me to the Field Hospital in Saigon.

When I got to Saigon, I went to an operating room where they gave me something for pain and then knocked me out so they could dig around in the wounds and see if there was anything left behind as a souvenir. Many men in Viet Nam wore a bullet on their dog tag chains. It was usually the actual bulled or one like it that was removed from a wound after their getting shot. It didn't take long after I came out of surgery with a mouth that tasted like forty acres of cotton and maybe the mule as well, to be assigned a bed. The first thing I wanted to do was contact two people and let them know I was there and in the hospital. I needed to get word to my bureau chief and Carmen.

I don't know how long I had been in the bed, but a very large man dressed in all white came to my bed and asked if I needed anything. He introduced himself as the ward master but did not give any name or rank, just his title.

I asked if there was a phone on the ward that I could use and was informed that this was a military hospital and patients did not generally ask for the use of a phone, so he'd have to check. "But first," he said as he pulled the sheet from me. "You need to pee. Let's see if you can make it to the latrine.

I'll be here to help or catch you if you can't."

With those comforting words, I eased out of my bed and made an unsuccessful attempt to stand on my own. I could tell he did not want to carry me or empty a bedpan, so we compromised with a wheelchair. Thirty minutes later, I was back in bed, and he came back and informed me that I could not make it to the phone, but he'd make the calls for me. I gave him the number for our office and told him to inform Wess and for Wess to tell Joe Brooks and Carmen what happened and where I was. He agreed and gave me a pill that put me to sleep almost before I could place the water glass back on the nightstand beside my bed.

Wess and Joe Brooks, our bureau chief, came in to see me that afternoon. "Does this mean you won't be finishing that story on the troops in the mech unit and the road-clearing operation?" Joe joked as he pulled a chair over to sit beside the bed. "I've got to check this out to see if you have any sick leave left. We may have to dock your pay for laying up here on your ass while we have to follow the war."

His comment made me wonder. I knew my contract called for vacation or time away from Viet Nam, but I hadn't given any thought to sick leave. I made a mental note to check my contract.

"Speaking of ass, do you know if you had been facing the other way, that's just where you would have gotten it?" Wess said.

"Great thought, Wess. What if I was seven inches shorter?"

"Then you'd be short another three inches!"

We were continuing to banter back and forth when the nurse on duty came up to my bed. "It's time for lights out. You guys can come back tomorrow. I'm certain Mr. Kelly will still be here and will be more than glad to see you." She was a blonde, about twenty-five, and wore Captain bars on her white uniform. She brushed them away with a motion of her hand. When they stood, she put the chairs back in place and began to tidy up the area as a subtle but firm signal she meant what she said.

"Would you like us to bring anything tomorrow?" Joe asked as he turned to leave.

"No, they're taking pretty good care of me here. If I need anything, I can get it at the little PX here in the hospital."

"Can you walk there, or have they given you a wheelchair?"

The Captain answered for me. "If Mister Kelly needs anything, someone will get it for him if he is unable to do it himself. We try to discourage the use of wheelchairs unless they are absolutely necessary."

Wess nodded in understanding. "Is there anyone you would like me to bring tomorrow?" Wess asked, knowing the answer.

"Uh, yeah, if you can get in touch with her. See if she wants to..."

"I went by to see her today, but she wasn't in. I left a note for her to meet me at the club tonight if she gets back in the city. I'll bring her as soon as I can. Take care."

"Thanks, Wess."

Carmen came the next day. When she walked into the ward, she couldn't hide the look of concern on her face. The pain was worth it just to see that, for whatever reason, she cared for me.

"I didn't get Wess' note until today. I came as soon as I could." She walked over to my bed and placed her hand on mine. "Are you all right? God, why did I say that? If you were all right, you wouldn't be here in this bed."

"It's okay, really. I'm not in much pain. I'm uncomfortable, but I think I should be able to get out of bed in a day or two."

"Do you want to talk about it? I'll listen if you do." She sat on the edge of the bed, squeezing my hand tighter.

"Not much to tell. I helped some Viet Cong qualify for a VC sharpshooter badge, and I get the zag zig badge. I was zagging when I should have been zigging."

For the first time since coming in, she seemed to relax, and a smile quickly flashed across her face. "Do that again, Carmen. I love it when you smile like that."

"Ay Nito there's something about you..." She laughed into my eyes.

"Someday, you'll have to tell me what you mean by that."

"Oh, I think you know very well what I mean, mi, Nito." She leaned down and quickly gave me a kiss.

After a long silence she stood up and walked over to the other side of the room and looked out the window facing the large grassy area where some of the patients were playing volleyball. "You know I really am concerned about you. Don't you?" She spoke with her back to me.

"Yes, I know. Come back over here, please."

We talked about a multitude of things for the next two hours until she had to leave. Each topic seemed to take us back to talking about us and the situation in which we found ourselves. I knew we grew closer with each passing day. So did Carmen. I also knew there was a limit over which we could not pass and expect our relationship to remain static.

She came to see me for the next three days, and then she had to leave Saigon.

I had my final check-up, and the doctor said I could leave the hospital if I had a place to go and take it easy for a week. I got a message to Wess and he agreed to come and pick me up and take me to my quarters. I didn't know it at the time, but that was also the day she returned to Saigon.

Wess managed to get an old French Citroen to drive when he came to take me back to my hotel. When he and I made it out to the entrance to the hospital, I was surprised to see Carmen sitting in the front seat of the low squatty automobile.

"Do you think it takes two of you to get me in and out of the car?"

"No, but it may take both of us to get you up the steps to my place." Carmen turned and spoke to me as I spread out in the back seat of the car.

"Your place?" Now I was really surprised. "But I thought I was going back to the hotel... For good Ol' Wess to take care of me."

"Don't worry, I think I can take as good care of you. Perhaps even better than Wess. If not, you're free to leave," she laughed.

"No. No. It's just that... never mind." I settled down and watched Wess as he pulled the almost antique French car out into the mass of Saigon traffic. In less than fifteen minutes, we pulled up in front of an old, whitewashed stone villa left over from the French colonial days.

Huge black wrought iron gates covered the front entrance. An old Vietnamese man stood guard with a shotgun resting in the crook of his right arm. As we approached, he brought the weapon up to where it could be swung into position and fired in a millisecond if necessary. Once he recognized Carmen, he relaxed. With a jerky walk, he moved over to the gate and unbolted the lock, and slowly the entranceway was cleared, and we entered.

"I didn't realize you were taking us to the embassy," I joked as we pulled into her compound.

"This is one of the very few advantages to being a woman working for the State Department in Viet Nam. They send me to the field, and I'm on my own. Here in Saigon, they give me full protection. I think you'll be safe here."

Two Vietnamese women stood by the front door to the villa. One was an older woman. The other looked to be in her late teens. Carmen greeted them in what sounded to me like flawless Vietnamese. They both responded and returned to the inside of the house. "That's Mai. My housekeeper. The young one is Kim. She cooks and does the shopping. Unfortunately, neither of them speaks very much English. I'm sure if you want something, you will be able to communicate with them."

With help from Wess and Carmen, I managed to hobble inside and then up to the second floor, where Carmen opened a door and led me into a bedroom. One look around the room, and it was obvious. This was not just any bedroom. This was hers.

"I'll set your bag over here in the corner." Wess placed the bag I had asked him to bring to the hospital on a wooden chair near the window. "I've really got to be getting back on the road. I promised to get the car back in time for the owner to go visit his lady friend tonight. I'll stop by tomorrow with some extra things from my place that you left there, last time you spent the night. Do you need anything else?"

"No, I think I'm in good shape now."

Wess winked at me as he caught the double meaning of what I said.

"See you later. Take care of him, Carmen. He's still got a lot of miles left to cover here in country."

As Wess left the room, Carmen turned to me and firmly but tenderly told me to get into bed. "You can stay here until your leg has healed completely.

If you need anything, Mai or Kim can get it for you. If they can't, perhaps I can. Her dark eyes burned into my soul as she spoke.

"This is your room, isn't it? Where did you plan on staying for the next few days?"

"Don't worry. I'm sure I can find a place. After all, this is a very big house. Now, you get comfortable. I'll be back up later." Carmen came to me and put her arms around me, and, for the first time since meeting her, gave me a kiss worthy of being called passionate. She stepped back and placed her fingertip on my lips. "See you later."

Before I could say anything, she disappeared down the steps to the main floor.

I found myself in a room probably built many years ago to the specifications of a French diplomat or businessman. Like so many others of the style in Saigon, the house was two-story white stucco with stonework inside the main entrance. Outside, a cinder block fence approximately six feet in height surrounded the grounds. Atop the fence, pieces of jagged glass sparkled in the sun. This extra deterrent was placed in the wet cement on the top row of blocks and became an additional barrier to entry. I saw the guard as he, too, made his presence known.

The room had a large wooden cabinet instead of closets like those found in Western-style houses. In addition, there were two small wooden chests in the room. One sat at the end of the bed, and one near the window. A cushion was placed on the window side chest, and I knew without her telling me, Carmen spent many hours here watching the lights of the city, and the moon from which she seemed to get strength.

She had a Western-style bed. It was covered with a lightweight comforter that kept off the occasional early morning chill, especially during the monsoon season. The main item in the room was not on the bed but was over it.

Hanging from the ceiling and draped over the bed, tent fashion, was a mosquito net straight out of the Arabian Nights. The silky white mesh material hung loosely down and surrounded the bed. It was pulled back in the daytime to allow the maid to clean the room and make the bed. At night, it became a gossamer cocoon for the occupant of the bed.

I spent the remainder of the afternoon in bed. Nothing I did eliminated the sharp pain I felt when I happened to roll the wrong way and put pressure on the still-healing wound in my thigh. Twice during that time, Mai entered the room, and I was able to speak to her in my limited Vietnamese. "How long do you know Car Men?" She asked.

"Perhaps six months." The Vietnamese use the word "Perhaps" as a catchall when nothing else will describe what they want. In that context, I could have known her for six hours, six years, or, as I sometimes felt, six lifetimes.

I took a chance and tried to ask Mai how many men Carmen was dating. My understanding of her answer was that Carmen never dated men or that I was the only one she had ever brought back to her home. Either way, I was pleased with the answer.

Mai brought me a lemonade drink and was placing it on a table near the bed when Carmen returned home. It was about five in the evening. "Looks like I made it in time for happy hour." Carmen's smile lit up the room.

"If I had some gin to put in this lemonade, it would really be a happy hour. I've been trying to con Mai out of a drink all day." I sat upright in the bed and pulled a pillow up behind my back.

In less time than it took me to explain it, Carmen spoke to Mai, and the young Vietnamese woman quickly left the room. In a minute, I heard the unmistakable sounds of drinks being prepared. "Just how many languages do you speak?"

"Oh, just enough in two or three to get along. As much time as you spend in the brush, you should speak pretty good Vietnamese. Do you?" As she spoke, she walked over and sat on the edge of the bed.

"I know enough to know not to try to speak to adults. I'm okay with kids. We're at the same level, but…" Mai brought a tray with two large gin and tonics on it and set it on the trunk at the end of the bed.

"Why don't you thank Mai for the drinks? In Vietnamese."

"You know my drinking the rest of the evening may well rest on how much I screw this up?"

"I'm certain she'll understand."

"*Com on,*" I stammered.

"You are welcome, sir." Her response, in English, caught me by surprise.

"I suppose she speaks just enough in two or three languages to get by?"

Carmen dismissed Mai and handed me one of the tall, cool glasses. "When I first arrived here, I was told to put the drink in the ice and not to put the ice in the drink. You need have no fear of this ice," she said as she touched her glass to mine. "The water has been boiled prior to making ice. To what do we toast?"

Once again, I was confronted with the eyes that I had so often thought about while away from her. As she looked across her glass to me, I could imagine a thousand toasts I would like to make and hope that they all came true that evening. "How about one that's actually a line from a movie? I'm sure you'll recognize it, but it seems rather appropriate tonight?"

"And what might that be?"

"This could be the start of a beautiful friendship."

With a gentle clink, she once again touched my glass. " I think it may be the beginning of more than a friendship, but I'll drink to Bogie."

I tried to get off the bed, but the leg was still sore enough to cause me some noticeable pain. "I've been here all day. I think I'll try to make it down to the main floor since you're here." I tried to hide the fact I really was in pain.

"I have a better idea. You stay here and don't make your leg hurt like that. Mai will have dinner ready in about an hour. I'll freshen up and we can have dinner up here. You relax. I'll have her bring up another drink."

Without waiting for an answer or a protest, she disappeared into the hallway, and in a minute, I could hear water running in the first-floor bathroom. I couldn't help but imagine her in the shower. I felt like a teenager as I lay on her bed and let the picture run through my mind. I was in that state when Mai returned.

This time without speaking, she placed another tray of drinks at the end of the bed, and walked over to the large chest containing Carmen's clothes, and began to pick through them. She carefully selected several pieces, but from the way she stood with her back to me and between the cabinet and the bed, I was unable to see what was taken. After she was satisfied, she took the clothes, pushed the door shut, and silently exited the room.

I was watching the sun set over the city when Mai brought the tray with dinner into the room. "*Saigon dep lam*," I ventured, trying to tell her that Saigon was very pretty.

"*Yeah, xin vui long.*"

"Very good! You two have had your second conversation for the day."

Mai excused herself when she saw Carmen standing in the doorway.

The first time I saw Carmen, she immediately got my attention. This time, I was speechless. She stood framed in the waning light of the evening in a war zone in Viet Nam as if she was in her home a million miles away. She wore a deep wine-colored silk gown with white trim around the neck and sleeves. It had to have been custom-made for her from the finest silk available on the black market. It clung to her as if she was wrapped in a wine-colored cloud. I could tell from the gentle movement of her breasts as she breathed that she wore nothing else.

"Aren't you going to invite me to have dinner?" she asked.

"I'm not sure. I may let you stand there so I can look at you all night."

Carmen laughed. "First things first, my friend. I think I'll let you buy me a drink! Then I'll think about where I want to be all night!"

"I've got a couple of gin and tonics from room service. Would you like to help me out with them?"

She slowly approached the bed where I had propped myself into a sitting position. She picked up both drinks and handed me one. As she touched glasses, she said, "Here's to classic movies."

She placed our dinner on a small table and sat beside me on the bed while we had the dinner that was prepared for us. All during dinner, she kept getting up to walk to the window and look at the city as darkness fell. In the far reaches of the horizon, we were treated to a firefight as flares drifted toward the earth after having been fired from an artillery unit.

We talked of past times in the States and future plans, wherever they may take us.

Mai returned with another drink and a bottle of wine. She set the tray by the window and picked up our dishes. After a short conversation, Carmen informed me that Mai and Kim were gone for the evening. We were alone with only a new guard in the courtyard by the front entrance.

As Carmen stood by the window, I pulled myself out of bed and slowly eased over to stand behind her. Without acknowledging my presence, she placed her hands behind her head and slid her fingers through the ends of her hair. As she did so, I leaned forward and gently kissed her at the base of her neck.

As my lips touched her, I felt a slight shiver as she responded to me. I placed my hands on her shoulders and pulled her back slightly so that she rested her head on my right shoulder. The rich feel of silk was all that was between me and the woman whom I had taken so many times in my dreams.

I turned her around to face me. As gently as I could, I touched her cheek and ran my hands across her face, touching each feature of this woman who stood, eyes closed, in front of me.

With a hand on each cheek, I finally kissed her like I had wanted to do for so long. With lips slightly parted, her mouth gave way to me as I probed.

"Hold me. Hold me tight," she whispered.

As I held her, she began to whisper in Spanish. *"Ay, corazon! Amame... acariciame tiernamente."*

Although I spoke no more than a few words of high school Spanish, it didn't take an interpreter to tell me what she was saying. I understood only the word "tenderly," but that was enough for me. The rest could wait. I began to move as tenderly as possible.

As I slipped the gown from her shoulders, I savored each inch of her body I exposed until she stood before me, naked in the light of the city.

"My precious. If I could, I would carry you," I said as I took her hand and made our way to the bed.

I stepped out of the cut-off jeans I wore and slipped into the bed where she now lay. The last thing I did before I pulled her to me was drop the mosquito net over us.

I wanted to hold her and feel her warmth as she lay beside me. She was cradled in my right arm. I turned on my side and savored each inch of her. Overhead, the large blades of the fan kept the air moving as we gave ourselves to the night.

She lay with her eyes closed. I ran my hands over every inch of exposed skin. The smooth feel of the silk gown earlier in the evening was replaced by the even silkier feel of her skin as we prepared to make love.

I had several women prior to coming to Viet Nam and a couple of others since arriving in country. As soon as Carmen opened her arms and gave herself to me, I knew every other woman I had ever been with was simply practice for this one main event. I was in the big leagues now. This was the Super Bowl, the Masters, the Pulitzer. Nothing I ever had counted as she gave herself to me. She held nothing back. I possessed her completely.

I spoke to her as we made love. My words were reassurance. We were the only two people in the world at that time, and the earth belonged to us. As we lay there, she gently kissed my neck. Her breath was warm against my skin as she whispered, *"Otros hombres han pasado por mi vida, pero ellos no mas han poseido mi cuerpo. Solo tu mi Nito, tienes mi corazon...ni alma...mi vida..."*

I stroked her hair as she softly continued, *"Has tocado mi corazon...mi alma... mi vida! Y te quiero tanto, mi Nito. Pero se que es posible que no mas nos queda esta noche, y por eso, mi amor, te doy todo que soy, todo que tengo..."*

The last sounds I remember from that first night with Carmen was the gentle rhythm of her breathing as she slipped into the waiting arms of sleep.

The sounds of Saigon as it awoke and began to move about after the nightly curfew brought us back to the reality of where we were and what we had done. Like a slow, svelte animal, Carmen stretched as she lay beside me. "If this was the real world, we would make love again this morning, have a nice leisurely brunch sent up from room service, make love again, then talk about yesterday, today, and perhaps..."

She placed her finger to my lip. "We can only talk about today. We can remember yesterday, but we must not let ourselves even contemplate more than we can hold in our hands. We can have forever in our hearts, but..." She raised up and kissed me.

For the first time, I was able to see her naked in the full light of day. Her skin had the light olive tint befitting her Hispanic ancestry. Her smooth, flat stomach was unbroken by the slightest hint of excess as it lay bare before me.

"This may not be the real world, and we may not be able to have brunch sent up, but I think I can do something about the rest of our early morning fantasy," I said.

A moan in agreement was the only response she gave.

I stayed with her for a week as I gave my leg time to heal. During that time, we continued to sleep together, and I could tell the bonds between us were growing at a rate faster than either of us was prepared to accept or even openly discuss. It was Carmen who broached the subject the day I prepared to report back to the Saigon bureau and try to get back in the reporting business.

"Before you leave, there is something I must say to you," she said as we sat on her balcony enjoying an early breakfast. "When you come back to Saigon, I would like to see you, but you're under no obligation to do so." Her eyes locked onto mine as I listened to her.

She leaned across the table and placed her hand atop mine. "I've never had to make a speech like this before. I don't quite know what to say."

I lifted her hand and kissed the back of it. "You've said enough. I don't think either one of us needs a speech this morning."

"I know. It's just that I don't want you to think that you have to...I don't know...That you're under some type of obligation to me."

I stood and pulled her up with me. "Unless you tell the guards down there to shoot me on sight, you're going to see me every time we're in Saigon at the same time. You, my dear. No, you, my love, will have to keep me away."

"My God, Nito. There's something about you..."

Fighting the desire that threatened to take control, I released her so she could meet the driver the State Department sent over each morning. "You know I won't be here when you get back. I'll leave word if I can as to where I'm going. If not, I'm sure Wess will be back in town in a week or so. He'll know."

I heard Mai open the door for the driver downstairs. "You've got to go." I gave her a playful push toward the stairway.

As she walked down the steps, she turned once and looked back in my direction. She held my gaze so long that it was almost uncomfortable for me. Then, without speaking, she turned and left the house.

In less than an hour, I packed the few things I had with me and had Mai get me a Vietnamese taxi to take me to the bureau. Although I knew I would not be in Saigon, physically, for several weeks, I also knew my mind and a piece of my heart was staying behind in that old French villa where my lady of a hundred flames would sleep that night.

DATELINE: SAIGON, SOUTH VIET NAM

Anthony and Cleopatra.

George and Martha.

Rick and Ilsa

Great romances, both real and fiction, from the past. What draws two relative strangers together? A Roman and an Egyptian. A farmer and a young neighbor. A salon owner and an old flame that never burned out. A man old enough to be the father of the love of his life. None of it makes sense, but does emotion ever?

In a war zone it's entirely possible to find love. Men, and perhaps women, although history is very vague on that, have been finding it since the first rock was thrown or arrow shot or whatever early man did to settle disputes. I see it all the time here in Viet Nam. The men lucky enough to not be out in the field have the time to cultivate a relationship. Unfortunately, many of them do it with women who want nothing more than to escape the horrors of the war, and there is very little, if any, real love involved. Others will establish a steady relationship with a local woman with no intention of letting it go any further than the day they board a flight home, leaving the woman to start all over again.

In WWII, the female population of Europe, especially England, was almost decimated by women marrying American military personnel and leaving the ravages of their homeland behind.

Can a wartime romance last? Is it something that is started and nurtured by the hardships of the country and then once the shooting stops and the shelves are restocked, the parties take a second look at their lives together? If it ends, then what? Who gets left behind?

The allied countries involved in the war here in Viet Nam are already seeing their military men returning home with war brides. How long will it take to accept them into the local society? The bride brings with her a completely different, and for the most part, a foreign culture with her. She has different religious beliefs. Her language, diet, dress, and beliefs must be accepted or changed.

What if the war bride has the same background as the person returning from the war zone?

Bogart and Bacall

Sean and…

Chapter Ten

For me, the war ended on the 22nd day of February. I didn't get hit or rotate back home or anything like that, but that was the day I knew it was all over. Over, not only for me, but for the United States as well.

I was with a small unit in the Mekong Delta region. That was the day the unit I was with captured the old papa-san they called Rice Boat Ralph. The men were assigned to the Province Headquarters and ran operations with the local forces charged with security and protection.

The late 60s marked the beginning of the Vietnamization and pacification era in Viet Nam. It was the time when the politicians in Washington realized the war was going to last forever if they did not come up with a way to end it. No one expected, and would not say it aloud or put it in print, that the Vietnamese could not, or would not, fight the war by themselves. The political solution was to win the hearts and minds of the people. The general feeling among the troops was to grab them by the balls, and their hearts and minds would follow soon enough.

By February, I had been in-country for over two years. From necessity rather than desire, I learned to speak the language. I could hold my own in a limited Vietnamese conversation. If I was with a small unit and they captured an enemy combatant, I sometimes got to listen in on the initial interrogation of prisoners. That's how I knew the war was over. It happened during Rice Boat Ralph's interrogation.

The men at the Province Headquarters knew about the old man long before they even went looking for him. Sometimes, in the field, the Americans got intelligence they knew was good but, for various reasons, didn't act on it right away. That's how it was with him. They knew about him before Christmas, but every time someone got ready to plan an operation, something bigger came up. In mid-February, everyone said, "Screw it, let's go get Ralph," or something like that. The Province had gone through the Tet holiday with little problem, so the general feeling was that something was working and perhaps the end was in sight.

The American and Vietnamese military established a program called *Chieu Hoi*, which literally means 'open arms.' It encouraged the hardline NVA, the North Vietnamese Army, and the Viet Cong to stop fighting and become loyal citizens of South Viet Nam. It was a successful program, and as a result, many of the military members who gave up joined the fight against communist philosophy and became valued assets for the Americans. These men were called Kit Carson Scouts and were instrumental in leading patrols and operations to enemy camps and weapons caches and gathering intelligence.

One of the Kit Carson Scouts working with the Navy Seal Team in Ca Mau told the men where they could probably find the old man. "He makes the same run every Tuesday and Friday," the scout, a former Viet Cong, said.

The seals did not want to waste an operation on a target of such low value, so they turned it over to the men at Province. I arrived at the Headquarters the day prior. I wanted to do a story on how the seals and the Americans worked together. Since they weren't working together on this operation, my focus was on the Americans.

The operational order was simple. Take a helicopter out of the canal where Ralph ran his delivery service, fire a couple of shots across the bow of the boat, have him pull to the side of the canal, and bring him back for interrogation. They called it a hit-and-get operation. I requested permission to accompany the team, and it was granted with the usual caveat. Don't interfere, don't get in the way, and for God's sake, don't get killed. No one was ever concerned about my death as much as they were about the paperwork it would cause.

The choppers picked us up at the landing strip across the dirt road from the Province TOC around two in the afternoon on Monday. None of the

Viets would leave until then because of a neat little custom they practiced. It was a two-hour lunch break. The military from the North and South stopped the war from twelve until two. Nothing or nobody could get them to change. So, shortly after two, a lift of three choppers landed, and thirty-one of us loaded and headed south. We flew an almost straight line toward the mangrove swamps just outside Nam Cam.

The flight took less than an hour. The landing zone was a field of elephant grass. From the air, it was impossible to determine how tall the grass was; thus, the pilots never knew how high to hover. They had a very good method of determining the height of the grass. Once the chopper was over the grass, one of the Vietnamese military would either volunteer to jump, or if none volunteered, the shortest man would be tossed out. Once he was on the ground, he held up his hand to indicate the depth of the grass. It was crude but effective.

We landed in the elephant grass after determining it was only up the shoulders of the man. We were about seven klicks from the location intelligence said we would find the old man. I was with two of the five men from the Province team and with Lan, the interpreter. In addition, we had twenty-seven Vietnamese with us. I thought the number of men on the operation was far too many to capture one old man and a boat, but I didn't make the rules, so I figured they knew something I didn't.

By the time the last rays of sun left the flat Mekong Delta, we reached the spot where we hoped to find the old man at first light the next morning. We quickly set up the night perimeter. The Viets placed out claymores, ate a dinner of cold C-rations and rice, and prepared to do battle with the number one enemy for everyone in the Delta: mosquitoes.

It was an uneventful and routine night. We had the normal problem with people sleeping, some, especially me, snoring, and twice someone stood up to take a leak. For some reason, I always expect one of the little people to get shot one night doing that. That's going to be one hell of an explanation the commander will have to make to his next of kin. I can imagine the letter. "Nguyen was killed by a friendly. He was standing up in the middle of an ambush. Be assured your son died a hero. Nguyen died with his crank in his hand."

The first boat on the canal passed us about an hour before daylight. With dusk to dawn curfew, these guys obviously were local V.C. coming home. I'm certain the team made a mental note to come back later for them. We continued to wait.

Lan was the first to hear the boat. The old man had a small, gasoline-powered engine mounted with the long propeller shaft so common on these sampans in the area. Top speed for him was barely faster than a good dog paddle, so we had time to get set and wake everyone before he came into view.

We were in a linear ambush along one side of the river. As soon as he cleared our end position and was in the kill zone, Dai Uy Toi, the senior Vietnamese officer with us, stood up, fired one shot from his .30 cal carbine, and yelled, "Dung lai!"

To my surprise, the old man responded to the command to stop. He nosed the boat over to our side of the bank and cut the engine. As he drifted with the current, I could see at least five large bags of rice and a small yellow, red, and blue Viet Cong flag on a pole about two feet long protruding skyward on the front of the boat.

While Toi and his men got him out of the boat, Sergeant Shelly, the senior NCO on the team, called for the choppers to return for us. We weren't in a great deal of danger, but we had accomplished our mission, and it was time to un-ass the A.O. Toi had almost four hundred pounds of rice, and three of the little people, as the Americans referred to them as, had already left in the boat headed back to their village with a short stop at a used boat dealers shop in Ca Mau. To the victor go the spoils!

While we waited for the pick-up, Toi came over to me and asked if I would like to have the flag we captured. "It will be worth much money in Saigon." He spoke using Lan as the interpreter. Although I understood without using him, I responded through Lan and assured him I would repay his generosity with a bottle of good scotch as soon as I got back to a liquor store in Can Tho, or Saigon. There was a thriving market among non-combatants in some of the larger cities for captured flags, weapons, uniforms, and anything else that could be used to tell a good war story once they returned home. The only thing more valuable than a flag was a bottle of good scotch. The Americans had their standards; the Viets had theirs.

The old man was blindfolded for the trip back to the Headquarters. The plan was to hold him there until a Military Intelligence team arrived. Although they wouldn't press him, the Province team would first try to get some intelligence about operations in their area from him.

The Province Headquarters was located at the edge of a large village complex in the Delta. As a courtesy to their allies, the Americans let the Vietnamese have first crack at Ralph. The first stop once we got off the choppers was the large, thatched roof, open-sided hootch, which served as a club, guest quarters, jail, gambling den, or any number of other purposes depending on the needs of the day. Today, it was for interrogation, and it worked remarkably well.

Rice Boat Ralph was delighted to talk.

I stood beside Toi as he spoke to the prisoner. The old man, who long ago had been dubbed Rice Boat Ralph, said he was sixty-eight and had two sons. Both had been gone for more years than he could remember. Each Tuesday and Friday, he went to a designated place just off the mouth of the Mekong River. It was probably a drop-off point for a ship coming from North Viet Nam that managed to slip through the Navy patrols.

Once there, he picked up a load, usually rice, but occasionally men, and on three or four occasions weapons, and took his cargo to a spot on the Nam Can River. The cargo sometimes changed but the instructions never did. Take the cargo, fly the flag, return home, and do it again in three days. He seemed to be under some sort of protective custody by the local V.C. If he did what they said, they would not screw with him. It was basically a gentleman's agreement as he saw it, and it did not bother him to be a party to it.

I was taking notes. I knew this was a story that would get a good reception back in the world. With my notebook in hand, I stepped in to ask him how long he had been doing this. "Since before my first son left to go fight," he said. For the first time, he seemed to recognize Shelly and me standing

113

beside Dai Uy Toi and the rest of the Americans in the room.

He started first at Sergeant Shelly. Shelly was short, with red hair. Tattoos covered both arms. After a long silent moment, he directed his first question to Toi.

"Who are these men? They don't look like the other Frenchmen I've seen." Toi and I looked at each other in shock.

"French? Old man, they are not French. They are Americans! Just like the many others who are helping us throughout the Mekong Delta. French, my ass!" Toi was leaning across the table, almost nose-to-nose with Ralph.

"Americans? They fight Japanese. Why are they here fighting the Frenchman's war against the Viet Minh?" Ralph's innocent sincerity was obvious as he continued to look at me.

I think Toi realized the significance of what the old man said at about the same time I did. How could we, or they, ever hope to win a war when the enemy did not even know who he was fighting? Everyone in the room who understood not only what the old man said but the significance of it stood back and took a breath.

The old man had limited intelligence value. He told us where he picked up his load and where he dropped it off. The drop-off points were never the same, but they always crossed one of two canals in the area. Both were marked for future operations, although everyone knew as soon as the VC found out he'd been captured and his schedule and route were compromised, they would find another method of delivery. We found out during the interrogation that one of his sons had been killed fighting the French as a part of the Viet Minh and another son had left many years ago, he wasn't sure how many, to fight and had never been seen again.

There was very little compassion shown enemy combatants, but I made a plea to Vin to put in a good word for the old man when he was taken away. Like his sons, I don't think he was ever heard from again.

I still have the flag we took off the old man's boat. Later that afternoon, when Ralph was placed on a chopper bound for Ca Mau, Toi wrote the date and grid coordinates where we captured the flag in the lower right-hand corner of it.

Now, every time I see the small red-and-blue flag with the yellow star, I can read the date the war ended.

DATELINE: SAIGON, SOUTH VIET NAM

Christmas.

Anniversaries.

Weddings.

When you're stuck in the middle of a war zone, and an occasion arises that requires a gift, what do you do? Send a card with a couple of large denomination (MPC) Military Payment Certificates. Those are the multi-colored bills the military and civilians use to keep greenbacks off the black market. How about one filled with Piasters, the local currency? Both are worthless unless the recipient is in Viet Nam. A gift? Just what the newly married couple needs: a bottle of nuoc mam, the local fish sauce that is put on everything and smells to high Heaven. Maybe a six-pack of Beer 33 for the graduate? A captured Chinese or Russian SKS rifle for Uncle Fred's Christmas gift?

The choices are severely limited, but there are some things that can be sent. The first Christmas I was here, I found a man outside the PX who was drawing long scrolls on heavy paper. Each had a Christmas scene, as seen from the Vietnamese point of view, along with the names of the recipients. The one I selected had a distinctively Asian Santa Clause atop a sled pulled by what looked like dogs with antlers. I had the names of my mother and father written on it in a very fancy scroll. I sent another one to my grandmother, who lived with my parents. Hers had the same type of Santa and sled, almost crashing through the roof of a house with no chimney and a roof of straw thatch.

This year I got a different gift and it wasn't Christmas.

I recently participated in an operation in the Mekong Delta region where an old man was captured. When he was undergoing the initial interrogation, I was there. I now speak enough of the local language that I can hold myself in a conversation with children and old people who do not speak above my capabilities. The old man, everyone called Rice Boat Ralph, fell into that category. Ralph was a simple man in his late sixties. He had the weathered look of a man who had never known an easy day in his life. His skin was the color of a plug of chewing tobacco, wrinkled and scarred by the hardships of the life he had lived. He had never ventured more than ten miles from the village where he was born. I asked him to point in the direction of Saigon. He got it on the fourth try. He did not recognize the name of the president of Viet Nam. Unusual? Not as much as you would think. Outside the major population areas, you will find thousands upon thousands of locals who just want to be left alone to tend their crops, raise their animals and their families, and get on with the life their ancestors lived. Most don't have a lot to offer.

Ralph is the exception.

He gave me a flag on my mother's birthday.

It's marked with the day the war ended.

Chapter Eleven

During the early days of television, there was a series that always talked about the "million stories out there in the city." The same could be said about Viet Nam. Each person involved in the war was a part of thousands of stories, each intertwined. Each touched another to make the whole of Viet Nam.

Anytime a group of us got together, like the military, we had stories we liked to tell. And, like the military, we knew some were total fabrications. That was the beauty of war stories. It got so bad that you would often hear people, both military and civilian, sitting around, and when they had consumed enough alcohol and run out of things to talk about, someone would say, Tell war story number twenty."

"No. I'm tired of that one. Tell thirty-one," some other inebriated soul would say. The stories passed hand so much they began to joke that they were numbered.

Other incidents and stories we knew were real, but for various reasons, we did not, or could not, report them. Often, it was the lack of one key piece of the puzzle that gave it sufficient credibility to use as a dispatch. We knew it was true, but we couldn't prove it.

Such was the case with Sergeant Harry Wingate. The story got a little better each time it was told. Because of how it happened, it was impossible to verify the majority of the most pertinent details. But the fact remains. It did happen. At least the beginning. I know. I was with Harry's platoon that day.

I tried for months to verify all the facts. It was an exercise in bureaucratic futility. For Harry, I'm sorry. For the others involved, they will forever be one of the million stories out there in the city.

When I came to Viet Nam, I was given two very loose missions. My boss in the States, who was paying me, said he wanted me to ferret out the stories that the bigger news agencies did not report. These stories would be printed in the newspapers his syndicate owned or offered to other newspapers. I was fortunate in that my dispatches were getting more popular, and he was making more money from them. He raised my salary as a result. That was my first and, for him, my most important mission.

My second mission was to write a weekly column. After a few weeks in country, we both knew a weekly column was not practical or possible in many cases. He wanted me to distill the war into something readers who were not interested in the facts and figures could relate to.

I was in Saigon and had a few days to work on both when the story of Sergeant Harry Wingate came up. I decided to combine the two missions and write his story as a column.

DATELINE: SAIGON, SOUTH VIETNAM

This Is the Story of Sergeant Harry Wingate

One of the most dangerous jobs in Viet Nam is that of a tunnel rat. These are the men, mostly volunteers who, for reasons I still don't understand, volunteer to go alone into tunnels where they know the enemy is lurking. The dark tunnels are filled with the enemy. The bad guys also have a bad habit of placing booby traps, rats sometimes snake like cobras, and other things that can kill the men crawling in the dark in the blink of an eye.

Tunnel rats are normally the smallest man in the unit. He is regarded as both a hero and a fool by his fellow soldiers. When the unit encounters tunnels, he is called to the front, and after stripping down to the boxers, he is handed a flashlight and a silenced pistol and points to the tunnel opening. Due to the size of the tunnels, he is generally alone. If he runs into trouble, he must resolve the situation on the spot. Several tunnel rats have been pulled out feet first after being killed inside. Being a tunnel rat is not a career choice for most sane people.

When Sergeant Harry Wingate emerged from the tunnel complex, he was wearing only a pair of cut-off fatigue pants and jungle boots. In one hand, he held a Smith and Wesson .38 caliber revolver with a silencer screwed neatly to the end of the four-inch barrel. In his other hand, he clutched a large flashlight and a bulky canvas bag. Wingate was a tunnel rat for an infantry division in Viet Nam. "The guy down there didn't want to give up his little bag. He don't need it anymore, now," he said as he handed the bag to the officer standing by the tunnel entrance. "I checked his pocket, and all he had was thirty-eight cents and this old Zippo lighter. Let's see what's in the bag!" He said as he finally stood upright in the sunlight.

"Holy crap!" said Wingate as he and his platoon leader, a Lieutenant from Ohio, opened the bag. "I've heard about this, but I never thought it would happen to me. Look at all that money!"

Wingate watched in fascination as twenty stacks of nearly new, crisp, wrapped bundles of American one-hundred-dollar bills were placed on the ground in front of him. "There's got to be a million dollars there. That guy was probably a V C paymaster or something."

Some of the other men in the patrol gathered around and we watched as the platoon leader counted the neat stacks now on the ground. "The total comes to a little over two hundred thousand dollars." He said it as if he had been making change for hamburgers at an all-night burger stand.

I listened as each of the men speculated on how he would spend the money if it was his. Women came in first, closely followed by booze and happy smokes. One young man, a PFC from New York, had the audacity to suggest he would invest it. He was quickly labeled a commie and a pervert.

"We gotta send this back to Battalion Headquarters. I'm sure there'll be something in it for you, Harry. At least a promotion, probably a reward. Maybe they'll even give you a hero button or two." The Captain, who had been summoned by his junior officer, assured Sergeant Wingate he would take care of the find and see to it. Harry was duly rewarded.

I followed the Captain back to the Battalion Headquarters, where the Captain asked to personally see the intelligence officer. I followed him into the S-2s office. "One of my men made a hell of a find today." He said as he placed the Zippo, the thirty-eight cents, and the bag on the desk. "Look inside. There's one hundred sixty thousand in greenbacks in there!"

I protested, saying the find had been for almost two hundred thousand, but the two officers said the proof was on the desk in front of us. The count was correct and that was that. End of argument.

I watched as he counted the money and then counted the stacks a second time, with the same results. One hundred sixty. "You know what this means," he asked.

"Hell, yes. Someplace, the VC is getting greenback dollars. Somebody back in the world in supporting them."

The S-2 looked at me. "Were you there when the Sergeant found this?"

"I was, and…"

"And this not to be reported. We can't take a chance on the enemy knowing we have the intelligence ability to intercept one of their currency shipments," the S-2 looked at me. "If the word gets out, I assure you that you will not be welcome in any military Headquarters in the country. Do I make myself clear?"

It was clearly a threat, and I knew it. Being welcome, or at least tolerated by the military, was my lifeblood. He could cut it off, and both of us knew it."

Rather than agree, I turned and walked out of the room. Everything else in Sergeant Wingate's story is from reports and interviews I managed to do since that day. From this point only, I can only report what I heard, but cannot verify. I have taken some editorial license in reporting actual conversations.

"I'm not quite sure what to do with this. We've got to brief the old man on this." The S-2 or Intelligence Officer put everything back in the bag, and we went into the Battalion commander's office.

Like the Captain and the S-2, the Battalion commander felt the need to take it higher.

To obtain the most information from local intelligence, it must be examined by experts at all levels, having, as the military calls it, a "need to know."

"Sir," said the Battalion commander to his boss, the Brigade commander, "I need to brief you on something. We've got a hot item on our hands. One of the men in our Battalion came across quite a find in a tunnel yesterday. There's over a hundred and ten thousand dollars in that bag!" The two men, each experts in the area of analyzing and accounting for enemy intelligence, went over how they could best handle this situation. At the suggestion of a Major who was the Brigade intelligence officer, a courier was selected to take the find, by helicopter to his counterpart at division Headquarters.

By late the next afternoon, the discovery made by Sergeant Wingate was being quietly discussed in Division Headquarters. His talents as a tunnel rat were widely known, but to find a Viet Cong paymaster carrying a canvas bag with a Zippo, thirty-eight cents, and well over forty thousand green American dollars was almost unheard of.

The armed courier sat in the jeep next to the division officer who was entrusted with taking the find to Saigon. Just prior to leaving, an officer from the division commander's office addressed them. "Be careful, men. Remember, you're carrying almost twenty-five thousand green dollars. See that it gets to intelligence in Saigon. They'll know what to do with it. We may never know how many

American lives a find like this will touch. Think of the arms and equipment that kind of money will buy on the black market."

Men in Viet Nam's outlying areas did not often get into the big city of Saigon. The three men in the jeep enjoyed the short respite the trip provided.

After a quick stop at the post exchange at Long Binh and a trip to the money order window at the Post Office nearby, the officer handed his intelligence items to the officer outside the door guarding the entrance to the security area.

"I'll need you to sign for this. One of our men, Sergeant Wingate, risked his life to crawl into a tunnel for this bag, so I need to know someone is responsible for it."

An almost illegible signature was written on a receipt for an old canvas bag containing a Zippo lighter, thirty-eight cents, and ten thousand dollars in American cash.

The bag was taken inside and given to the intelligence team chief. It was then entrusted to the two intelligence analysts who went through the contents of the bag.

"This guy Wingate must be crazy! Imagine crawling, half-naked, down into a tunnel just so you can have a shoot-out with some guy for a Zippo, thirty-eight cents in change, and an old canvas bag with five thousand dollars in it." They checked, as best they could in the war zone, the serial numbers to see if the money had been stolen from any U.S. payrolls or finance centers in Viet Nam. "Let's finish this report after lunch," one said as he finished with the serial numbers. The two of them pressed a buzzer, and the outside door opened.

Tuesday was the day they had tennis courts reserved for their weekly match with the Red Cross girls, so the two men did not return to the intelligence center until the next morning. "Do you think we should send back some kind of report so this, uh, this, Sergeant Windlee, can get a medal or something?"

"Naw. They'll probably do it at his company or whatever back in the woods." The man was idly moving the coins around on the desktop next to the empty canvas bag.

"What should we do with this stuff? I think the bag would be nice for keeping my tennis socks and shoes in. Kind of a combat tennis bag. Just throw the thirty-eight cents into the coffee fund."

"Here, Tom, you're always looking for a light. Have a Zippo, compliments of Sergeant Winfield or Windlee or whoever."

Chapter Twelve

Few people would admit it at the time, but those of us who were there did have some fun in Viet Nam. With a few exceptions, most of the men and women, regardless of the branch of service or type of duty, had a lot of free time on their hands. A lot of it was spent in some of the most God-awful places in the world, but a portion of it was spent in places like Hue, Saigon, Cam Ran Bay, and a couple of other out-of-the-way places in Viet Nam where we could relax for a few days.

One of the most popular places was Vung Tao on the South China Sea. Wess and I planned a trip there together. We heard rumors about both the VC and the Americans sharing the same beach area as an R&R site. He went down three days before me. I planned to meet him at a place on the beach Dennis McDonald told us about.

The sun had cracked the early morning when I got to the beach and picked out my chair and umbrella for the day. With a little imagination, I could almost picture myself in Miami Beach, watching the elderly Jewish couples make their way down the beach from their two-room apartments where they planned to spend the rest of their money and their lives, in a constant memory reflection of better days in New York or Jersey City.

The only difference was a few of the couples I saw were Vietnamese. They were the lucky ones. Probably deeply involved in the government, the military, or the black market since that was the only way a couple could afford the time or the money to take a vacation. They would be lucky to make it to the age where most of the ones on the beaches of Florida began to enjoy their lives.

The other couples I saw were almost made up of a military man and a local Vietnamese woman. The woman may have been his steady girlfriend who thought she was going to be his wife and be taken to the United States, or she more than likely was a local lady of negotiable affections. She could be his by the hour or whatever they could agree upon.

I had a cooler of beer and two magazines I picked up in the post-exchange the day I left Saigon to fly to Vung Tao. They were lying on the sand next to my throne room for the day. I settled into the lounge to wait for Wess. I reached for the first magazine when I heard someone walking toward me in the sand.

The steady "flip, flip, flip" of the rubber shower shoes we all wore stopped as the visitor got beside my chair.

"Now, there's something you don't see every day. Look at the tits on that young honey down there!"

He was about twenty-six or seven, tall with dark hair. He had a slight mid-west accent. Maybe Missouri, perhaps Ohio.

"I wonder if she bought them at the PX? It's hard to tell from here what she's got in that little bikini top of hers. Not a bad-looking ass, either." For the first time, the man standing beside me seemed to acknowledge my presence. "She with you?"

"No, I'm here by myself. Right now, but I'm waiting for a friend." I shaded my eyes with my hand as I looked up.

"You won't be waiting for very long once the local girls start working the beach. If you are, it's your own fault. Your friend male or female?"

"Male. Want one?" I sat up in the chair and shaded my eyes from the sun to get a better look at the man. I reached for a beer.

"Don't mind if I do. I'm sure it's happy hour somewhere in the world." He leaned down and picked up the beer. "My name's Russell. What's yours?"

"Sean. Is Russell your first or last name?" I extended my hand.

"Happy to meet you, Sean. It's my last name, but it's been so long since anybody called me by my first name, except my Mama, I've almost forgot what it is."

As we opened the beers, another equally well-built Vietnamese joined the first one on the beach. Both were at the water line, but it was obvious neither planned to get wet. "Some of them got a lot of French blood in their background. This is the second generation of trying to catch a G.I. for some of these young ladies. Their Mamas tried it with the French when they were here. Now the daughter's doing the same thing. Same war, second verse." He downed his beer in one long gulp.

"Have a seat," I said as I turned the lounge to fit under the protection of the umbrella.

"Thanks, don't mind if I do. Who are you with down here?"

I tried to place the accent. It seemed he was working some of the words to place a bit of a country twang to them.

"I'm a civilian. A correspondent. My Headquarters is in Saigon, but I'm all over the country. How about you?"

"This is my twenty-seventh month together. I did fourteen months a couple of years ago, and I've been here thirteen months so far this time." He finished his beer and crushed the can. "Can't be too careful. Charlie'll take old beer cans and make little souvenirs out of them. Things like grenades and booby traps. Speaking of boobies," he said as he stood up, "let's see if the two ladies down there are within the remaining punches on our ration cards. I've got a couple of liquor punches left for this month. You game?"

Before I could answer, I heard Wess yell my name and wave. "Over here, Wess," I said as he made his way toward my chair. "Man, you look like shit! What'd you do last night?" He said when he first looked at me. I had a hangover, but I didn't realize it was that obvious.

"That who you're waiting for, Wess?"

"Yes. You two know each other?" I asked as Wess dropped his chair beside mine.

"Russell. It's good to see you lived through the night. Hey, this is Sean. The guy I was telling you about." Wess blinked a couple of times to dislodge some of the gremlins living in his head at that time.

"I got to sit down. Sean, don't ever start drinking with this guy. He takes no prisoners."

"I was just about to see if Sean and I could talk to those little darlins' down

126

there." Russell motioned toward two women on the beach.

"Sean's got his own private thing in Saigon. I know he's not gonna take a chance on trading her in for a local. I, on the other hand, am unburdened currently. If I can stand up, I'll go with you." Wess moved very slowly.

"You guys go ahead. I'm gonna stay right here for a long time." I settled into my chair and popped another beer.

They walked toward the women, and I didn't see either of them again until almost 6 pm that evening.

When Wess returned to the hotel, I had already spent a day at the beach, wrote a couple of letters back home, and had taken a relatively warm shower and prepared to go to dinner.

Wess didn't look much better than the last time I saw him.

"There's something about that guy that really pisses me off. He's almost like a wet paint sign. I know I'm gonna get my fingers messed up, but I gotta touch. Any beer left?"

"In the cooler. What happened today?" Wess was now stretched out on the bed. "You guys get the two girls?"

"Boy! I'll say. But that's one of the things that bother me. There's something there." He sat up again as he spoke.

He began to tell me about their day.

"When we left you, he walked in their direction, and then he slowed until I caught up with him. We were still twenty-five yards from the women when they turned in our direction.

"Looks like their radar is working today. They picked us up from way out here." Russell said as he zeroed in on them.

Unlike Miami or any other beach back in the States, Wess and Russell did not have to play the mating game. It was not done on the beach at Vung Tao.

Wess said he asked Russel if he thought they spoke English.

"He told me they probably spoke it like a graduate from Harvard, but he said we'd never know it. He said it'll be just enough to get whatever they can from us and then move on to bigger and better things." Then he wanted to know if I spoke Vietnamese."

"You've picked us a lot since you've been here. More than me " I added.

"I told him I could get by in a pinch if necessary. That's all. Sean, I swear Russell was losing his accent. He laughed and told me I'd need my Vietnamese language capabilities and my pinch before the night was through."

Wess told me that Russell gave him a little tap on the arm and motioned for him to follow as he led the way to where they were.

"When we got to them, we stood close enough to the women to tell that neither of them had to buy anything in the PX to enhance their bodies. Both stood about five feet and had raven hair hanging straight to well below their shoulders. No shit, Sean, they were beautiful. Like most of the women in Viet Nam, they had really smooth complexions with small features." Russell spoke to them in English. 'Would you like to join us under my umbrella back there? He pointed, using his hand instead of his finger.' He didn't even wait for an answer. He moved beside the one he spotted first, gently placed his hand to the small of her back and indicated I should do the same to her friend. His only concession to them was to talk slowly and plainly. 'I'm Russell, and this is my friend Wess. What is your name?'"

""I am Angel, and this is my friend Suzi,' the one with him said. I assumed that Suzi was my date or whatever they were going to be."

"She latched on to you right away?" I asked as I cracked open another beer.

"Yeah. Suzi placed her hand on my arm to steady herself in the sand as we walked." "This is your first day in Vung Tao?"

"I told her no. It was my third," he said as he motioned for me to hand him a beer. "Then she started asking questions."

"You are stationed around Vung Tao?"

"No, I live Saigon."

"Sometimes I come to Saigon. Maybe I see you there," she said as she tightened her grip on my arm. Then Russell stopped and turned to face me. 'Wess, my friend, I think these ladies are capable of handling sentences of more than three words. You'd be surprised how much you can pick up hanging around the right clubs.' Even Angel and Suzi laughed. I'm telling you, Sean, the guy was smooth."

Wess popped open his beer.

"It was while we walked back to the lounge that I noticed the small bag Russell held in his left hand. It looked almost like a ladies evening bag. It was leather. Had a zipper running around three sides. From the way he held it and the indentation of the stuff inside the bag, it was not too difficult to see one of 'em was a pistol. The outline was an automatic. Too small be the standard issue .45. My guess was a Browning 9mm."

"I told Wess I saw no reason for it on the beach, but we were in a country at war, so what the hell."

Wess held his beer and looked at it like he had never seen one before.

"We continued to where we had the lounge chairs, and when we reached them, Russell pushed the two women down on the wooden and canvas structure. 'You ladies just wait right here. We'll go get another couple of chairs and another umbrella, and then we can talk about what we want to do today. We'll be right back.'"

"You got any nuts or chips?" Wess began to rummage through a bag of pogie bait we had brought with us.

"Where did ya'll go?"

"I thought Russell had a stash of beer or something, and we were going for that, but he stopped and turned back so he could see the girls." 'Not bad for a morning's work for them, and it's not even ten hundred yet. We should look like a couple of corkscrews by this time tomorrow.'" Russell said.

"I had to stop him, Sean. I said, let's take a minute and figure this thing out, if you don't mind. You've been here to Vung TaoToo before, I haven't. I'd like to know a little more about what I, or rather you, have gotten me into."

"Did he explain what was going on? Was he just a super horny GI looking to get laid, and you were his wingman?"

"No, he tried to explain. 'He said he was sorry, and that we did move a little fast down there. He explained that we had two Vietnamese whores who work the crowd at Vung Tao. Pure and simple. They just happen to be much better looking than the average, but that wasn't going to be a problem. We just have to pay a little more for the premium stuff. It's like going to the Safeway back in the world. You pay more for a USDA prime cut of steak than you do for a choice cut. And I have to say, Sean, those ladies, my friend, were Prime."

Wess opened a can of peanuts from the P.X.

"Are you staying here? Are you stationed in the area? Just how did you happen to be on the beach by me this morning?" Wess said, asking Russell as he tossed some peanuts into his mouth.

"Is that Wess who is about to get laid speaking, or is that the reporter?" I asked.

"Does it matter? For the first time, he looked me in the eyes when he spoke to me. Weird guy, Sean. Really weird."

"What did he say to that?" I reached for some of the nuts.

"He said, 'I'm just checking. I'm an advisor. But I'm like you. My unit keeps moving around. We happen to have a couple of days to spend refitting after an operation, so I fixed myself up with a pass to the beaches of Vung Tao for two days.'"

"Sounds like a reasonable explanation to me," I said as I poured some of the peanuts in my hand. "And then?"

"We picked up the extra chair and another six-pack of beer and made our way back to the two women waiting for us. I felt almost like a teenager just coming back from the concession stand at a Saturday night drive-in movie. We were talking about who was going to do what to his date as we took the lounges next to them. After we sat down and passed beers around to them, we made what I took to be small talk. Where are you girls from? Do you work for the Americans? What do you think about the war? After a few questions and even fewer minutes, I knew we were getting the stock answers given to the men with whom they had spent other days on the beach."

Wess stopped talking for a moment to gather his thoughts.

"By noon, Russell was speaking to them like we knew everything there was to know about these two women whom we had never seen before and very likely would never see again, once we severed ties with them on this trip, and each of us settled back into the life we came to the sand to escape. 'I tell you what, Angel. Let's you and me go up to your place and get ready for the evening. You can show me where you live and how you manage to make it by just hanging around the beach.' Russell stood and gently but firmly pulled the girl to her feet."

"My friend Suzi must go with me. We live same house."

"Now ain't that just too convenient. Two ladies! And they share the same house. I guess me and my ol' buddy Wess better find out where this house of beauty is, don't you think?"

"Russell was already folding up the umbrella and lounge chair. We left the beach and followed them up to the alleyway between the largest of several villas fronting the beach. As we got to the street, Russell flagged down two pedicabs, and each of us took one of the man-powered vehicles. The girls told the drivers where to take us. While we were riding I turned and took a couple of shots of them together in the pedicab. Each time I shot one, Russell pulled her over toward him or scratched his nose or something. Almost like he was hiding."

By now I began to really pay attention to Wess' story.

"In less than ten minutes both drivers pulled up in front of a large white villa and began to quickly converse with the girls in Vietnamese."

"You pay him five hundred piasters. He drive hard to bring us here." Suzi had turned in the seat and was getting very close to me and the pocket with my money in it.

"As I pulled a single note from the small roll of bills I carried, I heard Russell begin to raise hell with the driver of his pedicab. 'Bullshit, five hundred P! You get two hundred.' He handed his driver the two one hundred P notes without waiting for Angel to translate. Somehow, I didn't think it was necessary. By then, my driver had resigned himself to the fact that he was not getting the stated amount. For whatever reason, I gave him three hundred, and he began to pedal almost before we got out of the back seat."

"The drivers accepted the money and left without an argument?"

Wess just nodded as he took a drink. "The girls had slipped into a pair of shorts and pullover shirts prior to our leaving the beach. As we walked up to the front of the villa I couldn't help but notice how attractive they were. It was evident from the first time we saw them on the beach, they spent their time with the Americans. They could pick up a couple of G.I.s once a

131

week or so and by the time they left, the girls had more money than half the women in the country. I also knew Russell and I were about to add to their coffers."

"Nice clothes and I suppose it was a nice villa?"

"The house was elegant by Vietnamese standards. Once we got inside I saw they had a small black and white television, a refrigerator, and electric fans hummed in each of the four rooms. One of the rooms served as the kitchen, another their living/dining room and Suzi and Angel had a separate bedroom. Although there were no doors to close, between any of the rooms, each opening was covered by long floor length strands of brightly colored plastic beads.

As we entered, an old woman came up to the girls and took the small bags they carried. After a quick command to the woman from Angel, she left and quickly returned and handed us bottles of cold beer. The one thing we had seemed to avoid talking about all day was rapidly brought to the surface.'

"How long you can stay here?" Angel asked me in a business-like voice."

"I think the lady wants to know how much money we got on us, Wess. What do you think? I've got the next two days. You want to take it a day at the time or stay here for the entire time?"

"Good questions. What did you say?"

"I found myself in a position that I had not anticipated when I came to Vung Tao. The thought of getting laid was high on my list of things to do, but I planned to take it a little slower and perhaps make the decision myself without having a virtual stranger act as a pimp for two Vietnamese women on the beach. As I stood there thinking about the situation, Suzi began to stroke, first my arm and then areas of much greater importance to the decision-making process. I guess this is all right with me. But let's take it a day at the time."

I reached for my money. "How much is this gonna cost me?"

I smiled as I pictured Wess. He had one great weakness. Women.

"Russell said, 'If you pull out a roll, it's gonna cost you everything you have. And if you go to sleep tonight, it's still probably gonna cost everything you brought with you.'"

Russell was painting a not too bright picture of life in the Vung Tao fast lane for 'ol Wess.

"Russell motioned for the old woman to bring us another beer while both girls went into their bedrooms to do whatever women do in bedrooms at three in the afternoon."

"While they were gone, he told me, 'Pay 'em in M.P.C., and we can get a much better rate. They can change it on the black market for much more than we can, so they get the benefit of a positive exchange rate.' As he spoke, he moved around the room. It was as if he had been there before or was looking for something. He picked up several small statutes and gently turned each over to look at the bottom. As he walked around the room, he spent a lot of time examining their radio."

"You know anything about radios? This almost looks like a short wave of some sort. I guess they want to keep up with the worldwide weather forecasts."

"When they were back in the room, I knew what women go into bedrooms at three in the afternoon for. Each of them wore the very sheerness of see-through nightgowns. Underneath, they were both completely nude. I gotta say, they were beautiful, Sean."

"Partner, you are now on your own!" Russell reached out and picked up Angel as if she were a tiny doll and carried her into the bedroom from which she had just emerged.

"I suppose you did the same with your newfound lady friend. I could see a story coming that would never made newsprint but would be one for bars in Saigon for a long time.

"Bet your ass, I did. And by the time I did the same with Suzi, I could already hear Russell and Angel in the throes of passion or what would have to pass for the intimacy that afternoon. As Suzi and I got on with the business at hand, I heard Russell as he talked to Angel. I couldn't hear all the conversation, as I had other things on my mind and various other parts of my anatomy, but it did sound like he was asking her about things that had no relevance to the situation at hand. I'm certain I once heard him ask if she had ever considered joining the Viet Cong!"

133

"Not to be personal, but how long were you with her?"

"We stayed in the separate rooms with only the girls leaving once to have the old Vietnamese woman bring a couple of beers to us. It was hot and I kinda got sweaty with Suzi so I told her I'd like to take a shower before we leave. She took me by the hand and led me to what appeared to be a closet but was a shower stall on the first floor of the house."

"Come with me. We will shower together," she said as she stepped into the small room.

"I needed no further invitation to join her. By the time Suzi and I, and then Russell and Angel, showered the four of us agreed to go to dinner at eight. While we were waiting for the girls, Russell wanted to see my camera. When I gave it to him, he fiddle-farted around for a minute, then popped open the back. I lost the roll I shot today. I'm still not sure it was an accident."

"The pictures you took of him and the girls?"

Wess just nodded his head in disgust.

"We were ready and standing on the street at eight. A beat-up green Citroen pulled up and we all got in it. 'I know a good place to go,' Russell said as we hit the outskirts of town. He leaned forward and told the driver to take us to the Club Regent.'"

"No, do not go the Regent! We go to Surprise Bar." Angel was quick to counter Russell's request.

"Whoa, darling. My partner and I've decided we want to go to the Regent, and the Regent it will be." He tapped the driver on the shoulder. "You keep this classic headed to the Regent."

"Angel was noticeably upset about the choice of clubs but I imagined it to be that she might run into a former boyfriend in the place. Suzi was quiet and she and I just listened to them."

"You go to Regent you go by yourself. I do not go to Regent." Angel now sat in the corner of the seat with her arms folded across her chest.

"What have you got against the Regent? It's just a club where Vietnamese women try to pick up Americans. Kind of like the beach at Vung Tao," Russell placed his hand on her bare leg.

"*You beaucoup sou!* We did not try to pick you up. You come to us. We did not even speak to you first." Angel looked over to Suzi for either verbal or moral support.

"As Russell and Angel bantered back and forth, we pulled up in front of a building with a large sign with the words THE REGENT in large red letters across the front."

"I think it's a moot point. We're here. I pulled three one hundred piaster notes from my pocket and without asking, handed them to the driver. I did not wait for either change or an argument for the expected price. Russell almost dragged Angel as the four of us entered the small dark club. By the time we stood inside long enough for our eyes to become accustomed to the dark, we were all holding drinks, although I'm not certain the girls had anything stronger than weak tea, nor am I certain who ordered or where they came from."

"Here's a table over in the corner. You can never be too careful in a place like this." Russell led the way to the table with Angel tightly in tow. "You sit here." He motioned for her to take a chair facing the entrance.

"By that time Russell's mood had changed from a good ol' boy from the Midwest spending the day in the arms of a beautiful prostitute, to a man with a mission. Unfortunately, I had no idea what the mission was, and Russell did not reveal any hints or details."

"As soon as we can, we leave here. Not good people come in here at night."

"Suzi leaned over and tried to whisper to me, but Russell saw her and she stopped in mid-sentence. I felt like Russell was one of the ones to whom she referred."

"You didn't leave your camera in the girl's room did you?" I asked Wess. The camera was his prized possession, and he guarded it like a child.

"Hell no. I reloaded it and had it with me. I sat in on the table in front of me."

"Tempting or challenging Russell?"

"Russell saw my camera but paid no attention to it. He caught the attention of a woman who brought us drinks. Before he paid for the round, he pulled the girls' drinks over in front of him and took a long pull from the glass. 'I just wanted to make sure I was getting what I paid for,' he said without apologizes."

"Midway through the first drink, I took Suzi's hand and pulled her to the dance floor. Let's get out and see what we can do out there."

"You come with us," Angel said to Russell as we left the table.

"I think I'll just stay here for a little while." Russell spoke without looking up.

"Why your friend act so crazy?" Suzi slid into my arms as she asked about the man as if I had known him for years instead of hours. While we made a half-hearted attempt to dance, I occasionally glanced over at the table where Russell seemed to be waiting for someone or watching for something. He constantly swept the room with his eyes, taking in everyone and everything as he did so. If asked to describe everyone in the room, I sure he could have done it without missing more than ten percent. The second song finished, and we went back to the table."

I wished I had been there to see Wess on the dance floor. I've seen him in the past, and he's worse than I am.

"I was pulling out the small wooden chair for Angel when the three men coming in the door caught my attention. Two American Army officers walked into the bar accompanied by a Vietnamese man in civilian clothing. Even in his non-military dress, it was not hard to believe he was a member of some type of military or at least para-military organization. I was not the only one to see them. Russell made a slight but obvious wave to the two Army Captains and they slowly made their way over to our table."

"Won't you join us, Captain?" Russell stood and offered his chair to the first of the two Captains to arrive at the table.

"It was a very nervous Angel who watched as the men approached. Suzi placed her hand on her friends arm and both sat silently as the men walked almost directly to our table."

"Pull up a couple more chairs," Russell said.

"Without more than a glance at the two men at the table, the Vietnamese national began to speak to Angel. His tone went from firm to hostile in the span of less than five sentences. When she did not respond to a question directed to her in Vietnamese, the man flashed his hand across the distance between the two of them and slapped her. Before the sound died from his hand across her face, I was on my feet and as I reached for him, in more of an instinct than anything else, I was greeted by the short pistol held in the hand of the taller of the two Captains."

"He slapped her?" I asked more in shock than curiosity. "What did you say or do?"

"Would you guys like to tell me just what the hell is going on?" Wess said he asked.

I knew he had his camera and I hoped he was able to get some photos of what was going on. He said Russell was the first one to speak.

"Why don't you just go around the room and see if one of the other girls want to dance. Better yet, how about if you take little Suzi here and find a pedicab that will take you home."

"How about if you tell me what the…Before he could answer me, Suzi stopped me in mid-sentence.

"Do not ask. You cannot help Angel."

"Help?" Wess said, "What does she need help for? She has four men standing in front of her, and at least three of them carry weapons. Isn't that right Russell? You got your little pistol with you, or did you leave it in your beach bag?"

Wess was getting emotional with anger.

"While I was talking and trying to sort out what was happening, the Vietnamese man was still with Angel. By now, he was speaking to her in a series of shouts, and she was crying. For the second time, I heard him slap her. That was too much for me and this time I got to him before the others got to me. I gave him one quick, short, left hook that was more of a sucker punch than even I expected it to be. The little guy went asshole over teakettle across the table behind him and I got a round of applause from the men who were watching the show. I also got another gun stuck in my face! This time from Russell, who must have had it in the waistband of his pants."

"Damn, man. You must have started a riot." Now, it was getting to me as well.

"Russell was yelling. He was telling someone to get my camera and bring it to him. I'm sure he thought I had managed to get some more photos."

I could picture utter confusion at that point.

Wess said he was in the grip of the two Captains now. One had his camera.

"You just don't understand, do you?" Russell said as the Captains held Wess.

"Hell no, I don't understand. Three guys come in here and start slapping a woman around, and you not only let them, but you're also keeping me from doing anything about it. You've got two apes holding me. What's not to understand about that? It happens every day back in the States."

"That's the point. You're not in the States. It's a whole different world over here."

"While he spoke to me, he reached into the large cargo pocket on the right side of his fatigues pants and extracted a small notebook. As he handed it to one of the Captains, Angel made a grab for it."

"I found this in the woman's room. It may be what you're looking for. Take the film out of his camera. It has a button on the bottom to open the back." He pointed to my camera.

"That is mine. You cannot have! Angel was almost screaming, making more noise now than when she was slapped."

Wess finished his beer and opened another one. He was getting wound up now.

"That was no accident today, was it Russell? You purposely exposed the film I had in my camera. He trained the gun on her now instead of me. 'Don't get the wrong idea, guys. We're not going to hurt you or Suzi. We just...' What about Angel? Can you say the same for her?" I tried to get my anger under control.

"That's not the question here. The question we have to sort out is how many of our men has this little darling already hurt and how many more are targeted in this book of hers."

I slowed my anger a little. "Just what the hell are you talking about?"

Wess took a long pull from his beer.

I just sat and listened to him relate the story and the conversation.

"Before he answered, the Vietnamese man I knocked on his ass was up, and I think he was ready to take me on next. From the look in his eyes, he did not relish the thought of an American taking him out in a Vietnamese club full of women, even though they were prostitutes for the most part, in his part of the world. 'These men are going to take Angel down to their Headquarters and ask her a couple of questions. If she has the right answers, she will be back on the beach looking for another G.I. tomorrow morning,' Russell said."

"And if not?"

"Then it may be long time before she sees the beach at Vung Tao."

"What gives you the right to do this? You're setting yourself up as judge and jury. We've got rules….I was confused and pissed."

"No! Over here, there's only one rule. Only one. Survive."

"Does that apply to her, too?" I pointed to Angel.

"Not if it cuts down on my chances," he said with no remorse.

"For the first time since the commotion started, I was conscious of Suzi standing next to me with her hand on my arm. I didn't know what she and Angel were doing or what they were even being accused of or investigated for doing or if Suzi was involved. All I knew was that I suddenly had the feeling I had been set up. And it had been done by an expert. And furthermore, his name was Russell."

I nodded in agreement with his assessment.

"I shook Suzi off my arm and advanced toward him. As I did, one of the two Army Officers made a move to get between us. Russell, you son of a bitch. I don't know why, but you set me up. You used me to get to these women. I've never threatened anyone before, but I'm going to do everything within my power at the news bureau to find out who you are and what kind of game you're playing. I was fuming! I may not have pictures, but if you want to stop me, you better take me with you, and don't ever let me out of your sights!"

"What did he say?" I asked.

"Don't even try it. It's a waste of your effort. Spend your time telling the people back home how it really is over here. Tell them about the Viet Cong going into a village and killing all the people just because some of the young men joined the GVN forces. Tell them how they are treating the "yards" up in the highlands. Wess, you send them a picture of an American with his head cut off and it sticking on a stake to warn other G.I.s not to fight in an area. Use all that energy to do that. Let that be your job in Viet Nam, and let this be mine.'"

"Then what happened?"

"The small club became a haven once again for the military men and their Vietnamese lady friends as the four of them walked out with Angel. Drinks were ordered, and the band started to play. I think I was the only one who had any lingering interest in what was to become of Angel."

Suzi was crying. "I know she talks to a man who is V.C. She ask me to go with her to a meeting one time. I tell her no. I do not think so. That is why they come for her. I am afraid for her. I think I will never see her again."

"As she spoke, she looked blankly across the room. She directed her comments not so much to me but to anyone who cared to listen. We sat with her for a few minutes, and then we left together."

Wess was clearly shaken by the time he finished telling me what had happened. He and I had seen some horrible things in Viet Nam, but most of the involved armed men from both sides of the conflict. This was the first time either of us had seen it involve women.

Wess went back to her house, and they spent the night together. The next day, I left for Saigon and spent two days trying to find out what happened to Angel and who, or what, Russell was. As he had predicted, I could not.

It took almost a year, but I finally got an official in the American government to acknowledge that Russell and the Phoenix Program did, in fact, exist.

DATELINE: SAIGON, SOUTH VIET NAM

Look!

It's a bird. A plane.

No, it's a city.

It's a secret.

My father, a WWII veteran, still maintains contact with some of the men with whom he served. Some of them started as early as 1941 at Fort Benning, Ga then deployed to England for the D-Day invasion of Normandy. Those who survived found themselves six months later in a little town in Belgium called Bastogne. Four years of unbelievable horrors of war, and they lived through it. They were like a family. They had reunions, sent Christmas cards, and, unfortunately, attended funerals.

This was not the case in Viet Nam.

Most of the men over here went through several months of training in the United States, got thirty days leave, and the next day landed in a war zone. Most came as replacements. They were the FNG in a unit filled with FNGs. They knew if they could keep their head down and not do something stupid, they would catch a plane called the Freedom Bird and fly home in twelve months. Viet Nam would be put behind them as they go on with a life disrupted by a draft notice and twelve months in a country halfway around the world. They would forget the country and the men in a short time, and it would be a memory, either good or bad, depending on what they did in the country. For them, the rules were definite. Known. Most are written down someplace.

For the residents of Viet Nam, it was a whole different story. The only rule they had to follow was: In Viet Nam, there aren't any rules, but you must follow those rules very closely.

Sound confusing?

Welcome to Viet Nam.

In WWII, the enemy wore uniforms. If you were in Europe, you knew what a German uniform looked like. The same was true for those in the Pacific. The Japanese had uniforms. The uniform in Viet Nam? North Vietnamese Army regulars wore them. The Viet Cong did not. In areas controlled by the VC, who was the enemy? How could you tell? He, and more and more frequently now, she looked and dressed just like anyone else. That attractive young woman in the Ao Dai who drove the motor scooter to work at the base barber shop every day wore the same thing at night when she planted a bomb beneath the barber chair. The old man who picked up the trash on the base and brought his two little girls to help him was, at night, a leader of a VC raiding squad that killed five Americans.

No way to tell who was who?

Not so fast.

There is a little-known program called Phoenix that is designed to ferret out the barber and the trash man and deal with them. Harshly. People can report their neighbor and be rewarded when the person is identified as the enemy.

But what about the person who says my neighbor is VC and they're wrong, or they have a personal problem with the neighbor, and this is a way to solve it?

Few people know it even exists, especially those in the United States who would be opposed to the very concept. That's why it's a secret, and I don't know if this column will make it to print or not, but someday, the truth will come out, even if it must wait till I catch my own Freedom Bird.

Chapter Thirteen

U nlike the U.S. military, even those who, like me, volunteered for Viet Nam, I could return home anytime I so desired. My decision to leave, had I elected to do so, would have had no greater impact on my career than my choosing to stay. It was my choice, and although I exercised the option mentally to leave daily, I never put it in writing. I think it had a lot to do with my dad and his attitude toward the military. He was a mechanic in WW II. He was trained to work on half-tracks used in tank destroyer units. I can still hear him describe his first day at Ft. Benning. "They put us in jeeps and had some of the other men drive a jeep out in front of us with a big wooden sign on the side that said "tank." We were supposed to shoot it with a long piece of round wood like a tank gun. We yelled 'bang! bang!' a couple of times, and when the corporal in charge left us, we all took one of the jeeps and went to Columbus and got drunk. That was the first time I went AWOL!"

It was not the last. He spent most of his time in the states AWOL in Columbus or Phenix City or on extra duty for going there. That lasted until December 1941.

He and his brother, my Uncle Jim, were at Fort Benning training and going AWOL together. When war was declared, my dad's unit went to Europe, Uncle Jim went to the Pacific. Dad said it was to keep them from coming up with a way to go AWOL and stay that way. I never believed it, but that was part of his war stories.

Uncle Jim had a different one.

Shortly after Pearl Harbor, his unit was attached to a force going to the

Pacific. Just after that, they settled in on their island, where he was reassigned and classified as a supply clerk. Three days later, they were paid their first visit by someone whom they, and I, for years to come, would hear about and known only as the "Snap Jap". He said the man flew over them every night at about eight in a rickety old plane. None of the men on the island could even identify the plane it was so old.

"That old piece of shit was held together with a big rubber band. We were all waiting for it to snap. That's how we expected him to die…when his rubber band snapped and he crashed. He took a few potshots at us, but he never hit anybody."

When he told the story, he always stopped and mentally regressed to 1942.

"Seemed like he never really tried. We never tried too hard to shoot him down, either. If we did, the Japs would replace him with a pilot who took the war a hell of a lot more seriously than the Snap Jap."

I never thought about that until Uncle Jim started telling war stories or someone mentioned a similar incident. I didn't think of it, that is until I got to a base camp in Zion and found out we had our own version of the Snap Jap at the 5th Mechanized Infantry Division's base camp.

I was at the base camp with the 5th Mech just after the big push near the Cambodian border. I spent almost three weeks with them, and by the time we got back to the division rear, all of us, whether we were military or not, were ready for a hot bath and a hot meal.

Cambodia invoked memories of sleepless nights and days running together, forming a solid dark fog bank memory of nothingness. We needed Zion.

The first two days for the military were devoted to the necessary but much-hated job of cleaning equipment, refitting units, and preparing for a possible return. Wess joined the unit the last two weeks I was with them, so he and I also had our jobs to do.

I knew it would take at least two days for Wess to come down from his high. Each time he found himself in a hairy situation, his order of priorities was to burn up as much film as he could, stay as close as possible to the action, and worry about the danger or the consequences later, if ever.

144

He had a habit of cracking his knuckles when he was nervous. Wess was on the verge of needing a full-knuckle transplant after the last two weeks.

He and I were given a small room at the end of a tin Quonset hut normally housing Australian students at the Advisor school.

We tried not to dwell on the past, either in Viet Nam, Cambodia, or back in the world, especially when we got the chance to sit in an air-conditioned bar away from Saigon and drink a cold beer with some of the men who fought the war.

We popped a beer and slid into a booth at the NCO club at Zion. For the first time in four weeks, I heard Wess take a deep breath, exhale, and slowly relax. "That was a tough one," he said. "I had my doubts back there a couple of times. How about you?"

"Yeah, me too."

"Did we do any good out there? Is it gonna matter?"

We, by virtue of our jobs were supposed to be objective. "Be open-minded." That's what the boss at the syndicate headquarters told us. It was easy for him to say. He wasn't still trying to wash a thick coating of red Cambodian dust from his body and perhaps his soul. We were.

Wess and I were sitting in the club, the Red Dog Saloon, at the bar when the First Sergeant sitting next to me first mentioned Shithouse Charlie. I had just bought a round of beer when he pointed to the slogan on the can and said, "It might be the water that makes this beer, but it's trying to get rid of it that's such a bitch around here after dark." With that profound statement, he hoisted the can and chugged it.

"What do you mean?" I asked as I read the label and then followed suit, chugging my beer.

"There's some gook that snipes at people going over the bridge to the row of latrines out by the school. He's holed up in a spider hole in the rice paddy outside the berm. He must work the afternoon shift 'cause he only comes out at night."

As he talked, he held up his hand for the Vietnamese bar girl to bring us another round. Of course, since I was asking the questions, it was at my expense. That was his way of charging me for a story he knew would interest me. "He can only get a clear shot when someone crosses over the bridge going to the shithouse. The bridge makes a little arch and puts the target just high enough for him to get a shot. He's never actually hit anyone, but he's sure scared the shit out of a lot of guys going to the can."

"Why hasn't someone sent a patrol over there and blew him away?" I asked.

"If they grease him, the bad guys will just replace him with another one who can shoot. At least this way, he can still do his part in the war effort and not hurt anyone. The guys here say they might not be so lucky next time."

I thought about Uncle Jim and his stories of the Snap Jap. Maybe our wars weren't so far apart after all.

"He's a rotten shot, but someday he's got to get lucky. While you guys are staying over at the school, remember what I said, if you need to go to the can at night. Walk low on the bridge, and if you can find one, take a weapon with you when you go. Speaking of going, it's time for me to do it. I got troops that need tucking in at night."

We decided earlier in the evening to go into the village for a non-G.I. meal. Even as repetitious as Vietnamese food sometimes got, it was a welcome change to the steady diet of C's, LRRPs' and the mermite cans containing unidentifiable rations we got while we were in the field. Normally, we could have picked up a thick, medium-rare steak at one of the clubs, but with everyone returning at the same time, the delicacy was in short supply.

"I know a place where they have prawns as big as lobsters. We can get some fresh fruit, a couple of bottles of 33, and who knows, maybe we can get through in time to stop at the steam and cream." Wess finished his beer and crushed the can.

"Of course, the trip to the steam and cream is just to get the steam and a massage. If we did anything else," he said, "you'd never respect me in the morning."

"It's not my respect you have to worry about in the morning. It's tearing out all the plumbing when you find out you got more than a cream," I said.

We left the saloon and walked across the edge of the motor pool parking area toward our hootch.

"I'm going to stop by the Brigade Headquarters and see if the phone lines are as good as Colonel Morris said."

"You're going to try to call Carmen?"

"If you get her, tell her to check out a donut dolly for me by the name of Shirley. She's supposed to be working out of the USO in Saigon. One of the guys in Cambodia called her "short-time Shirley." Tell Carmen I want to do a story on her for one of the skin books back in the world. Mention that I'll need extensive research, hands-on, and plenty of full-frontal nudity shots."

"I always thought your brain was in your pecker. Now I know it!"

"Look who's talking. Before you met Carmen, you'd be trying to charter us a chopper to the Saigon USO with the information I just gave you!"

"That, like you, is simply a part of my sordid past." We parted, with Wess going on to the hootch while I went to the Brigade Headquarters.

I saw Major Edwards, the S-3, sitting inside the building when I entered.

"Sean. Welcome to the puzzle place. What can we do for you?"

"I want to try a call through Zion switch to Saigon. You had any luck getting through today?"

"Not too bad today. Static is light. You can use the phone in the S-1's office. He's not here." He said as he pointed to the room with the door half open. "You'll have some privacy if you need it."

It took less than five minutes to get the call routed to Saigon and to the State Department.

"2183. May I help you?" The female Vietnamese answered in excellent English.

"Carmen Cienfuegos, please. Tell her it's Sean Kelly. Don't put me on hold. I'll lose the line," I added.

The light static popped and cracked as I held for her. In the background, I could hear the Vietnamese women who answered ask for Miss Cienfuegos. I wondered what she would do if I asked for Carmen by her full family name, Maria Carmen Lucia Cienfuegos!

Let her try to pronounce that, I thought as I waited.

"Sean. Where are you? Are you all right?"

I hesitated, savoring her voice. "It's so good to hear your voice again. I'm fine. I'm in back in country...up north." I didn't give my location as the communication lines in Viet Nam were not as secure or operational as you would like. Anytime the phone system in Viet Nam was used, it was a race to see if the conversation was completed or if the line went dead first. I knew we had only a few minutes at best.

"I'll be back in town in about a week. Will you be there?"

"I'm going south for two days, but I'll be back on Saturday. I'll be here, Mi Nito, she hesitated. "Waiting. *Vaya con Dios.*" she added.

The line went dead.

I replaced the phone handset and left the room.

"You get through all right?" Major Edwards asked as I walked out.

"Typical. Five minutes. Then we lost the line. But I said what I needed. Thanks."

I walked back to the hootch I shared with Wess. By the time I got there, he had already been to the long shower building and got his ration of sun-warmed water.

"The shower feels great today. Hurry up. I want to get to the village. I've worked up a big appetite today. "

"For what?" I asked.

"Vietnamese."

"Food?"

"Hell, yes! What did you think I meant?"

"Wess, with you, the possibilities are endless."

We went to a restaurant recommended by the airfield commander. It was small, with only five tables. Each table had four mismatched wooden chairs, some obviously from military dining halls. In the middle of each table sat a clear glass with several pair of wooden chopsticks for the diners.

A Vietnamese girl, no more than fifteen, brought us a menu printed in Vietnamese and English. The English was an obvious translation from a dictionary. On the menu were such delicacies as chicken with chest and hip pieces and cow.

We ate, and then Wess and I parted. I went back to the compound. Wess went to a massage parlor.

By the time the last bugle notes of taps faded, I was in my mosquito net-

148

covered bunk and almost asleep.

I drifted in the twilight between sleep and awake for a few minutes. Each time I felt my brain begin to slip into neutral, something from the last several weeks hit the right button, and I immediately felt a short shot of adrenalin, and I was awake once again.

After a while, my adrenalin pump grew tired, and it, too, slipped into neutral as I went to sleep.

My eyes flew open, and I was wide awake as soon as the first pain hit me. It was excruciating! I could not move. The knot in my stomach felt as if someone had planted a mortar roundaround there, and it had just exploded. Any minute now, I thought as I lay there, my skin was going to rip open, and everything inside was coming out.

I had two choices. I could lie there and wait to see which end opened up first, or I could try to make it to the latrine and get whatever I had eaten in the village off my stomach. As soon as I moved, I knew the choice would be made for me. I mentally tried to calm myself to keep from blowing my cookies.

Slowly, and with great concern for my life, I slid out of bed. For a minute, I sat on the edge of the bed, talking myself out of getting sick there on the spot. It worked, and I got a temporary reprieve. I stood and shuffled on shaky legs across the room to my nightstand. There I inched my feet into a pair of shower shoes and opened the drawer where I picked up my pistol. Even in my present condition, I remembered what the First Sergeant said. I did not want to go out at that time of night without a weapon.

The few times I had been forced to cross the bridge to the latrines at night, I always thought about Shithouse Charlie. So far, his stories and a shot fired one evening before we returned from Cambodia at dusk at one of the students was all I had seen or heard from the mystery man with the rifle.

As I slowly inched my way toward the bridge, I lowered my profile by bending over. That sent fiery lengths of pain shooting through my body. An additional pain was caused by the hammer of the pistol in my waistband cutting into my flesh as I crouched.

I surprised myself by breaking into a trot as I made it across the bridge without incident. "One more trip for the good guys," I said half aloud as I straightened up and resumed my brisk walk to one of the three little houses directly ahead of me in the moonlight.

The three buildings contained a sitting room for six. Each was a two-holer. The back bottom half of each opened to reveal large sections of 55-gallon drums cut and placed under the two holes. The cans were removed, filled with diesel fuel, and set on fire daily, burning the contents. This detail was usually accomplished by a Vietnamese hired for just that purpose. However, prisoners from the division stockade were occasionally utilized. It didn't take long for the word to spread through the stockade that prisoners were being used for shit-burners. That information was enough to make them model prisoners for a while.

The light gravel in the red dust crunched under my shower shoes as I approached the first of the three buildings. I convinced myself that I wouldn't blow my dinner, but if I made it inside the building, the burners would earn their pay the next day. My thoughts were filled with making myself calm enough to carry out my plan when I heard a noise coming from the direction of the building. The knot of sickness in my gut was immediately replaced by another composed entirely of fear.

Could a V.C. have made it inside the compound and been waiting in ambush beside the latrine? Had Shithouse Charlie changed his tactics? Was he here in the compound? Despite my fear of the situation, I cautiously moved forward. My hands and palms were sweaty as I heard what I thought was a low moan coming from the direction of the last noise.

I unconsciously wiped the sweat from my palms across the front of my cut-offs. As I did so, I felt the butt of the pistol that I had placed there. Cautiously, I pulled it from my waistband. I heard a sound that should have made me stop dead cold in my tracks. From inside the latrine came the unmistakable sound of a round being chambered. Someone inside the building less than twenty feet away was prepared to blow me away!

I flashed back to the pistol range the Marines constructed in Be Bop. I tried to remember everything about firing the weapon. As I quickly went over the slow squeeze technique of firing they taught me, the problem with my stomach was quickly downgraded to a role of somewhat lesser importance than the situation now confronting me.

I slowly pulled the hammer back, preparing the pistol for firing. Firing! That was the hairy part. Should I shoot through the door? If so, to the left or right? What if I yell for help? I could keep the door covered and tell the person inside to come out with his hands up and keep him here until the MPs arrived. I was learning more of the language daily; however, if I had to say it in Vietnamese I didn't think I could get the man to come out and have him give up his weapon.

It was too late when I realized that while I had been thinking of alternate plans I had been continuing my slow shuffle to the building. I was now within three feet of the front door.

My initial impulse was to kick the door down and start shooting. That, I cautioned myself, was probably bad form since I was not sure where the enemy was in the little house. I thought about pushing the door open and throwing myself up against the side of the building. That's how I had seen the good guys do in all the WW II movies. My gut feeling was that that would expose my position and still not tell me where he was. With my pistol held tightly in my right hand at almost eye level, I decided to quickly and firmly push open the door and rush inside.

The steel of the pistol in one hand was offset by the feel of the rough boards on the door against the other. I took a deep breath and prepared to push. My eyes were accustomed to the darkness and would not change dramatically when the darker interior of the building was exposed. I shook my head quickly and firmly to rid myself of the sweat forming on my forehead and threatening to run into my eyes. I wished for a drink of water to lubricate my parched tongue and throat.

No more stalling, I told myself as I began to apply pressure to the door. With one quick and flawless motion, I pushed the door open and shoved my arm with the pistol in it into the darkness.

In the back of my mind came a voice from the Gunny Sergeant at Be Bop. "Be sure of your target. And then shoot to kill. You may not get a second chance."

In the millisecond needed to take up the slack in the trigger, I did my target identification. Less than three feet away from me was a man holding a pistol in very much the same manner as I. One distinct difference was that I was standing and wearing a pair of shorts. He, on the other hand, was sitting down on one of the two holes in the seating area, and he was completely naked except for an Australian Army digger hat sitting on his head!

Both of his arms were outstretched. They held, with the end of the barrel less than six inches from the end of my pistol, his service revolver.

I waited momentarily for my life to flash in front of my eyes. Before I could complete the squeeze on the trigger and shoot to kill as I had been taught, he spoke to me.

In a voice that could have been the worst imitation of a British accent I ever heard, he said, "I say, mate, we almost 'ad a go of it, didn't we? Care to join me? There's room for two in 'ere, ya know." He spoke calmly as if nothing unusual had happened. He lowered his pistol and motioned for me to join him.

For me, it was too late!

DATELINE: SAIGON, SOUTH VIET NAM

Same song, second verse.

Some things never change.

As a correspondent, I'm considered a non-combatant here in Viet Nam. If I get myself in a situation that changes that status, it's usually my fault, and I must suffer the consequences. I suffered those consequences once already when I was wounded during a road-clearing operation with the 4th Infantry Division. I do not wish to do that again, but to do my job, I am forced to spend a great deal of time with the combat troops.

Many times, when I am with them, something will remind me of a movie, a book, or a story from past wars, especially WWII. This week, I experienced something that was straight out of a WWII after-action report.

152

I talk a lot about my dad and his service in WWII in my columns for two reasons. First, I love and respect my dad and his service, and I hope I, nor anyone else on the planet, ever has to go through that again. This time, I must mention his brother, my Uncle Jim. Dad served in Europe. Uncle Jim was in the Pacific. Both men had more war stories than I can ever relate. They didn't talk about the terrible things they saw and did, but they would tell a funny story at the drop of a hat or the cap from a bottle of beer. Uncle Jim's favorite was about a Japanese pilot who flew over their camp every night in a plane that hardly was able to stay in the air. The pilot would drop a bomb, which never did any damage, and then fly away. The next night, the same thing all over again. They called him the Snap Jap because they said the plane was powered by rubber bands that were sure to snap one day.

The 5th Mechanized Infantry Division at a base camp in Zion, South Viet Nam, had a similar situation. They called him Out House Charlie. I cleaned up the name a little for this column, but regardless of the name, he must have had Uncle Nguyen, who served with Uncle Jim and got the idea from him. He was a sniper, and every night, if you went to the row of outhouse latrines, you took a chance of being shot, or at least shot at when you crossed a small bridge that elevated you over the surrounding landscape.

I spent three weeks in the field with the division, and when I got back, one of the first things I wanted was a hot shower and a hot meal. I got the shower on the base, and my friend Wess and I went to a Vietnamese restaurant in the local village for the meal. About six hours later, in the middle of the night, I found out about the meal, and I did not agree. We were arguing violently, and the meal was winning. Against my better judgment, I had to head for the aforementioned outhouses and cross the bridge to get there. Mindful of the warning, I carried a pistol I won in a poker game with me and headed for the latrines. I made it over the bridge and to the latrines, but when I got there, even in my agonizing situation,

153

I thought I heard someone inside the little house. I'm sure I also heard him cocked a pistol. Throwing caution and common sense aside, I extended my arm, pistol at the ready, and pushed the door open. I was greeted by a naked Australian wearing nothing but a digger hat; pistol extended like mine, who, in a clipped accent, asked me to join him.

Unlike the Snap Jap or Out House Charlie, I accomplished my mission. I just didn't make it inside to do it.

Chapter Fourteen

L ieutenant Jefferson Davis Riley was fishing off the rear of the large gray swift boat, or patrol boat riverine as the Navy like to call them, when the first round hit the side of the PBR. The impact of the B40 rocket was enough to tear a hole in the port side of the boat, destroy one of the side-mounted .50 cal. machine gun positions, and blow Jeff off the back and into the canal.

Like the other men on the boat, we knew we were in an area that was hotly contested between the local Viet Cong and government troops. There had been little activity for the last few patrols, so the general feeling was that whatever the Army and Navy were doing, it was working. It was an oversight to be sure, but one that would prove to be quite costly to all concerned. I was sitting on the front of the boat, a cool can of beer in hand, working on my tan. Jeff was on the ass end of the boat with a new Zebco 33 fishing outfit.

I wanted to do a story about the Brown Water Navy, as it was called, that ran Patrol Boats, Riverine, or PBRs in the Delta. They navigated the many tributaries and canals that extended from the mighty Mekong River in some of the most hotly contested VC areas in the country. I had put in a request to go on patrol with one and waited for it to filter down to someone who could make it happen. When I was notified by the commander of the Navy base in Can Tho, the boat commander contacted me and asked me to do him a favor. He asked me to bring the rod and reel to him from the post exchange in Can Tho when he found out I was coming down to spend a few days on the boat with him and the men on his crew. He had just baited the twin hooks on the thin steel leader he used and cast them out when the rocket hit.

I first met Jeff, like so many of the men I came to know in Viet Nam, in a bar in Can Tho. It was on the Army side of the base. He was stranded there one night when his jeep and driver suddenly disappeared into the nightlife of the largest city in the Delta.

"Aren't you taking a chance? I mean, a Navy type in a bar filled with grunts and chopper pilots?" I asked as he searched the room for a place to sit. He took one look at the jacket I wore with the word "Correspondent" over the left pocket and decided I was one of the friendlies.

"No more of a chance than a noncombatant!"

Without asking, he pulled out a chair and sat at the small wooden table with me.

"Touché'. Buy you a beer, sailor?" I asked.

"Don't you people drink anything besides beer? You never heard of rum and coke?"

"The rum ration goes to the Navy. That's where all the rummies are. And besides, we never seem to have any cokes up here. You don't need a mixer with a warm beer."

"Here's to Navy rummies," he said and held his beer high. "I'm Jefferson Davis Riley. And you?" He held out his hand.

"You'd feel silly as shit if I said my name was Abe Lincoln, now wouldn't you?"

"I'd have to be a lot more drunk than I am right now to care about some whistle dick named Abe Lincoln." He began to raise his voice to be heard over the jukebox. "When you've been Jefferson Davis as long as I have, you learn to be un-amused at the misfortune of others who happened to be born with simple names like Joe and Ralph and Bill and shit like that. Now, what's yours?"

"Sean," I said. Delighted my parents had anticipated my need for more than a run-of-the-mill name at times.

We spent several hours talking and swapping war stories when Jeff suggested I join him and his crew for a couple of days of operations with the swift boats running patrols down in the Delta near the U Minh Forest. Three rounds later, I found myself promising to try to meet him in four days at the base the Vietnamese called Nam Can, or Solid Anchor, as it was known to the Riverine Force and the Seal team operating out of there.

The last thing he asked me to do prior to joining him was pick up the new Zebco. "Here's twenty dollars." He handed me a purple twenty-dollar Military Payment Certificate bill. "If there's any change, get it in rum. You know how it is with us rummies!"

The next day, I checked into Four Corps Headquarters and was briefed by the G1 and the G3. Both the personnel and operations officers had an interest in having the press give them good coverage. It was good for business back home and especially for the hard-charging light Colonel running the operations office. For a West Pointer, it was a great way to add to his wartime scrapbook. He was so obvious and obnoxious about himself and his perceived accomplishments during the war that not only did I openly question why anyone else was still in the Delta fighting, but I purposely avoided mentioning him by name in my dispatches.

The heart of the Vietnamization program was in the Mekong Delta. It was here the war could be lost to the Viet Cong if, and when, the South Vietnamese local troops lost interest in their war. If the Americans were fighting or leading the South Viets into battle, it was as close to a conventional war as we could get, but in the Delta, it was strictly a war for the advisors and the local troops. This was the gist of the briefing I received in the war room. I saw how many hamlets had been declared clear of the VC and NVA and were now solidly in the GVN column as Safe Hamlets. I saw the red lines slowly fade to blue in the elaborate three-screen slide show the Corps Commander had ready for the media. It showed how the land was being reclaimed by the good guys, and during the briefing in the main compound building in Can Tho, I saw the Americans give equal credit to the Australians and New Zealanders for their contributions to the success of the war in the Delta. When the briefing was over, the Lieutenant Colonel said I needed a chop from the Navy command since it was their boat, so he contacted his counterpart at the Navy base and made an appointment for me.

The Navy was happy to see me and gave me permission to accompany Jeff

Davis Riley on his boat as long as I wanted, but as usual, I got the caveat of "Don't get killed. The paperwork would be a bitch."

I thought about that as I flew over the green of the rice growing into the horizon of the land, which could easily feed half of Southeast Asia if given the opportunity. Here was the ideal land for growing the staple of the Asian diet. Rice. Green in the summer when it was rich and growing and golden brown at harvest time. I had even heard people compare it to the great wheat fields of our own Midwest back in the States. No amber waves of grain here, though. It was grown for food, not beauty and poetry.

I landed at Solid Anchor and went into the small hootch that marked the end of the American presence in Viet Nam. By standing behind the building, I was suddenly and dramatically the last American on Vietnamese soil. There was no one any further South than I!

"Can I help you, sir?" I was looking toward the main compound when a man in bits and pieces of a Navy uniform approached.

He had on cut-off fatigue pants, no shirt, and was wearing a pair of brown leather sandals. I had no idea who he was or what his rank was.

"Yes," I replied, "I'm looking for a Lieutenant Riley. Do you know where I might find him?"

"You the reporter from Can Tho? He's been talking about you. What the hell do you want to come all the way down here to Mosquito Junction for? You guys run out of stories about how we're winning the war in Saigon?" He stopped talking and pointed in the direction of the large wooden pier extending out into the river, entering the South China Sea in Nam Can. "You'll find Jeff over there. I'm Senior Chief Barrons."

"Good to meet you, Chief," I said as we began to walk toward the dock. The chief made no effort to assist me with my baggage. "We can find all kinds of stories in Saigon, but it's good occasionally to get out and see what the real world looks like. What am I gonna see down here?"

He reached into the back pocket of his cutoffs and extracted a foil pouch of Beech-Nut chewing tobacco, and after packing the left side of his mouth full, began to mumble, "You're gonna see some real good Navy. Both theirs and ours, and that's Senior Chief Barrons.

158

I stopped him in mid-sentence. "When you say *theirs,* do you mean the GVN or the Viet Cong?" I asked, uncertain if the VC or NVA even had a Navy presence that far south.

"Both. You'll see the little guys working on both sides of the river. They've got some Riverine patrol boats just like ours, and the bad guys got a sampan Navy that will blow you all to shit if you're not careful!"

We stepped out onto the dock just as one of the patrol boats fired up its diesel engine and prepared for a trip into the Nam Can forest. "That's Jefferson Davis Riley's boat over there," he said, pointing to the third boat in the pier area. "The one with all them little rebel flags painted on the side."

As I stood looking at the gray hulk, the three rows of neatly painted Confederate flags came into view. Like planes in the Army Air Corps of WWII, the flags were neatly lined up forward on the starboard bow. Perhaps this was his kill log. Did these represent VC sampans or operations or confirmed enemy kills? The nine flags were a definite conversation piece that I planned to discuss.

"Hey! Sean, over here!" I had been spotted. Jeff was on his way over to meet me.

"You really came. No shit. I didn't think you'd do it." He came down the steps to meet me. "I figured once you thought about the lack of air conditioning and ice for your drinks, you'd leave us river rats to be an uncovered page in the history of Viet Nam."

"Why should you guys have all the fun? I heard the Navy has great chow down here. I'm tired of paddy rats and rice with the grunts up north." I sat my bags down and pulled the long round tube protruding from the corner of my duffel bag. "I believe this belongs to you," I said as I handed him the rod portion of the Zebco 33 rod and reel combination I bought for him in Can Tho.

His obvious pleasure was almost like a child at Christmas. "I really do appreciate this. My last reel got so worn out it just quit working, and my rod got stepped on one day in a fire fight." He took the reel from its box and attached it to the rod.

"Come on aboard. I want to show you what you've got yourself into." As he reentered the confines of the boat, he quickly tossed a well-intended but half-delivered salute to the American flag flying atop the mast. Even with fishing gear in hand, Jefferson Davis Riley was, if unconsciously, a professional.

In less than ten minutes, I was introduced to the rest of the crew and guided around the vessel. I was shown where the men spent most of the time in their duty stations, what each did, where the ship had been hit on previous patrols, and where to stash my gear. The best they saved for last. "This," Jeff said with obvious pride as he ran his hand along the top of the large gray box. "This is our pride and joy. Show him Chief. You built it."

His second in command, Chief Petty Officer Rocco, quickly stepped in. "Yes, sir. This is our beer cooler and bait box!" He lifted the lid to reveal a large box with two compartments. One was filled with ice and appeared to be extremely well-insulated. Several large chunks of locally produced ice-covered at least two cases of ice-cold beer. The other half of the container held an assortment of small bait fish swimming contently as if they were on view by children in an aquarium in a doctor's office. He reached into the icy side, extracted a beer, and handed it to me. He quickly glanced at this watch and announced it was happy hour in Paris so we could legally begin drinking.

After the ride on the chopper coming from Can Tho, he didn't have to ask twice.

"You can get settled tonight. We've got nothing planned for the rest of the day, so take your time and look around. You can sleep here on the boat, or we'll put you up in a hootch in the compound. It's your call." Jeff was leading me to the stern of the boat.

"I think I'd like to stay wherever most of the others do. Where's that?" I hoped he would say on the boat. His reply did not disappoint me.

We spent the remainder of the daylight hours getting acquainted with the commanding officer of the small base and with the local Viet officials. True to tradition, we were invited to a party in my honor that evening at the district chief's house. To decline was to lose face; to accept was to awaken the next morning with an industrial strength hangover!

We choose the latter.

I'm certain there are those in the world who find the gentle rocking motion of a boat to be soothing. I have never had a problem with the rocking of a boat, however, the rocking of that particular boat in direct conflict with the rocking of my stomach and the pounding in my head was more than I could stand the next morning when I awoke. I quickly found my way to the side of the boat, and, holding onto the cool round metal post upon which one of the fifty caliber machine guns was mounted, I proceeded to blow my cookies in the river. On the dock, two Vietnamese sailors assigned to American boats laughed openly at my predicament.

As I lay upon the deck, awaiting either death or whatever my second choice happened to be at the time, Jeff slowly made his way around the corner of the deck. "I see you've made your contribution to the river this morning."

There was no need to ask what his comment meant. His ashen face spoke for itself.

"We've got a patrol scheduled for 1400. We're gonna support a small operation up around the Song On Doc River. It's about an hour's ride from here but the little people are going in by chopper. We're just going up there in case they need some heavy stuff like the fifty or mortars. Should be a piece of cake."

We went up to the river junction and fired support for the small operation the Vietnamese Regional Force Company successfully completed that afternoon. We pulled back into Nam Can just after dark. "Let's help the guys clean up, and then you and I can finish the operation report in the logbook in the hootch tonight. I've been on the boat too long. Let's sleep in the compound tonight." The entire boat crew worked as one, including all the resupply and clean-up missions.

We finished the last two beers in a pair of six packs and prepared to turn in for the night when the compound commander came over to the table where we sat. "Jeff, it looks like we've got some heavy shit on schedule for tomorrow. Your boat will be in support, so why don't you take your guest with you." He nodded toward me as he spoke.

"I don't mind a little real action. As a matter of fact, you might be interested in knowing that I've probably spent more time under fire than any man in the compound. Perhaps, even you." I tried to sound as pleasingly sarcastic as possible.

"I know you've been around," he said, "but in all your past combat operations, somebody else, not me, has been responsible for the paperwork if you get your ass blown away!"

"Boys! Boys! No one's gonna get his ass blown away tomorrow or any other day if he keeps it low enough." Jeff saw the tension begin to rise.

"Be ready for an ops brief tomorrow at 0800."

"Right, Commander. See you in the morning." Jeff finished his beer. "Don't get upset with him. He means well. Let's go over to the hootch. There should be a poker game going by now."

We played a little poker and then the men around the table began to stretch and yawn as their money or beer or both began to disappear." I think I've enjoyed about all of this I can stand for one night," I said about midnight and crawled into the mosquito-net covered bunk I was to occupy.

"See you about seven. That'll give us enough time to get a cup of coffee prior to the brief." Jeff was bumping heads with a master chief from one of the other crews. Both claimed to be just about even, but they were the only two with any money left in front of them.

By 1000 hours the next morning, we had been briefed on the day's mission. We were to take some local troops up to the edge of the U Minh and go into what almost became an amphibious operation. Like many of the operations the Americans supported, this one turned out to be a bust. Some speculated the Viet Cong had prior knowledge of our planning and simply took the afternoon off. At any rate, we met no resistance when we inserted the troops. After thirty minutes on at the station, we split. The men on the ground were now too far away to be supported by the weapons we had on board.

"Take it easy going back, Chief. I want to try out the new Zebco." Jeff gave the order for the boat to take a circuitous route back to the compound. As he did so, he settled in to take up an easy afternoon's fishing on the stern of the boat.

The first thing I remember after feeling the earthquake of the rocket when it hit the boat was thinking quickly about Carmen. I wrote her a letter the day before but I had not taken it over to the mail drop at the compound headquarters. I knew I still had it but I couldn't remember where I put it.

Chief Patterson was at the helm when the rocket hit. "Get on that starboard gun! Get that son-of-bitch going. I want some fire out there! Whitney!" He yelled at the man now working frantically to raise someone on the radio. "Get the base and tell them we're hit and taking small arms fire. See if they can get the Sea Wolves on station."

Petty Officer Whitney was already asking the base for support from the Navy Sea Wolves. They flew the Huey helicopters armed with fifty caliber machine guns and provided support to any unit in contact in the Delta.

Whitney had just made the call when the second rocket caught the far side of the canal, barely missing the boat now rapidly maneuvering along the canal. "Where the hell is the skipper? Go and see if he's been hit." The chief yelled across to me. "He was on the stern."

I had to hold on to the side of the wheelhouse as I made my way to the rear of the boat. By now, the boat had cleared the kill zone and plowed through the muddy water at a respectable speed. We left a readily identifiable oil and smoke trail behind as we ran bow-deep in the water.

Petty Officer Whitney secured the fifty calibers and made it to the stern at about the same time I did. Without speaking, we both sensed the fate of Lieutenant Jefferson Davis Riley. He was no place to be found! He was missing on a large unnamed canal leading out of the U Minh Forest. The blast from the rocket had either killed him or blown him into the water where, if wounded, he would probably drown, and if not wounded, he was almost surely a prize of the Viet Cong by now.

When we determined he had not been wounded and was lying behind his beer cooler and bait box, Whitney began to yell, "Chief! Chief! Stop the fuckin' boat. The skipper's gone. We gotta go back and look for him!"

I went forward and tried to explain to the Chief what we surmised. Regardless of our speculation, the man was missing.

Reddish brown water rapidly washed over the bow of the boat, as the chief cut the engines and prepared for a bootleg turn in the middle of the canal. His precision turn would have been the envy of any southern whiskey runner in a road race with the local sheriff.

In the distance we could hear the steady beat of chopper blades as the Sea Wolves cleared the distance to us. "Get them on the horn and tell them the skipper's still down there, and we're going back." Without waiting for radio confirmation of his message, he finished the run and gunned the now heavily smoking boat back into the direction of the ambush.

We expected the area to be quiet when we returned. We weren't disappointed.

It took less than ten minutes for us to determine Jeff was really missing and get the Sea Wolves on station to return to the area. By the time we finally got back, only a small fire started by the rocket, which missed the boat and hit the riverbank, still burned. It was a single clue to the ambush we survived.

"There's a wood line about three hundred meters to your North. We're gonna check it out. If Chuck has your man, maybe we can convince them to let him go." The pilot of the lead chopper gave us his intentions. The low-flying chopper sped quickly across the distance and fired for several minutes into the grove of mangrove and banana trees.

Nobody wanted to speculate what would happen if, for some reason, Jeff was still alive and was either hiding or captured and being held in the area now being raked with fire from both the choppers and the V.C. had a different philosophy from that of the pilot.

Chief Patterson contacted the base and told them what happened and what we were doing. Two more boats were on their way. Since it would be getting dark soon, time was the critical factor. As he spoke to the base, our boat began to cough and sputter as the wounds from the ambush took their toll. Like a man losing blood, a machine like we now used to look for Jeff could manage only so long without oil. Our time was rapidly growing short.

As we made our way back to Nam Can, I returned to the stern and picked up the thin fiberglass rod with which Jeff had been fishing when the rocket hit. The black rod had been hit or stepped on during the firefight. It, too, was wounded. Midway up the five-foot pole, the white splintered fibers protruded like a compound fracture. The seven-pound mono line was trailing in the wind from the reel. I wondered as I held it if Jeff's passion for fishing had cost him his life.

It was dark when we pulled back into the pier to tie up for the evening and report on the day's activities. Before we stepped from the boat, Chief Patterson placed his hand on my shoulder. "I don't think we better mention the skipper was fishing when we got hit. We had all the proper security, but the commander here has a dim view of things like that. He might not understand we had already finished our mission for the day and were just cruising back home."

He correctly took my silence for consent.

The chief completed his log, and Jeff was reported as Missing, Presumed Dead. A plan was readied for the next day when patrols would be sent out from the local outposts. The Sea Wolves had already cleared a mission to fly through the area to look for him or his body. Two boats were going to cruise the canal the next day and see if his body turned up in one of the many small streams running in all directions from the ambush site. Other than that, it was a routine schedule ahead. Although he would be missed, it was a fact of war that men died. Jefferson Davis Riley was one of those men. The necessary paperwork was prepared, and a telegram was prepared to be sent to his mother and father in North Carolina.

Jefferson Davis Riley was a statistic for the week of 26 July.

I went out with another boat crew the next day. We went to an area about seven kilometers from where we lost Jeff. While out, we managed to cruise the canals before the day was over. We, like the other boats, had no luck.

On the 29th I packed my gear and told the commander I would take the next chopper out going toward Saigon. I wanted to check in with the bureau and then go up with the infantry units near the Laotian border. I knew I didn't really need to go through Saigon, but I wanted to see Carmen once again prior to going back into the brush. Yesterday's mail held a letter from her that I read with the usual delight. I scanned each line and each word to see if I could pick up double meanings or innuendos, which might give away her feelings for me. My hope was that hers' were growing, as were mine.

Chief Patterson and I stood on the dock talking about the last couple of days. I made a promise, which I planned to keep, about writing something nice and mentioning the names of all the guys on the boat. I was writing down the hometown of Patterson and Whitney when we heard the first shots being fired.

Small arms fire was not an unusual occurrence in the Delta. Most of the time, it meant the beginning of a small unit ambush or some drunken Viet letting off steam if it happened in a hamlet. To hear it so close to so much American firepower was another area entirely. Neither of us had an immediate explanation.

When the next burst, which was a full magazine being spat out at one pull of the trigger, echoed down the canal, the men on the boats quickly jacked rounds into all the boat-mounted machine guns. As the last round was secured in its place in the machine guns, another burst was fired, this time accompanied by much shouting in Vietnamese, which we did not understand.

All eyes and most weapons watched the canal from where we heard the shooting. A small group of four sampans rounded a corner on the waterway. A man in uniform stood up in the lead boat and waved a white cloth tied to the end of a rifle. Before he or the others could get too close, one of the Vietnamese on the boat with us had a megaphone and ordered the sampans to cut power and wait for a swift boat to approach them. They immediately responded and pulled to the far shore.

"Be careful, them little bastards may have a full regiment of NVA regulars out there in the grass," Patterson cautioned the crew of the boat as we prepared to pull out to meet the visitors.

As the small boat coasted to the far side to wait for our swift boat to approach it, both the chief and I saw another man stand up in the second boat. He was dressed in cut-offs and had an old bush hat pulled low over the eyes. "That's what the skipper was wearing," said Patterson as he yelled at the boat next to us and ordered them to fire up their engines. "Holy shit! That's him. It's Lieutenant Riley."

There was no doubt about it. The man waving at the approaching boat crew was, in fact, Jefferson Davis Riley. He was alive, and he was standing up in a Vietnamese sampan less than one hundred yards from where we were by the pier.

By this time, most of the men on the pier had recognized the Lieutenant. While two of them went to get the compound commander, the rest waited for the swift boat to bring its cargo up to the dock.

When Jeff stepped quickly but cautiously from the boat, he was a mass of small cuts and scratches. Dried blood covered him from head to toe. He had large red splotches where innumerable mosquitoes and leeches had bitten him. Just as he arrived at the dock, Commander Starkey came in from the Headquarters. "Where the hell have you been, Riley? We thought you were dead. Or at least captured." He added as an afterthought.

"So, did I. On both counts." He stopped at the end of the pier and turned to step aboard his boat. As he stepped aboard the side of the boat, he took a long look at the ensign flying above the terribly wounded ship he had been on only three days before and, pulling himself to his full height, popped a graceful salute toward the colors. It would have made a midshipman on parade proud.

I followed the line of men who joined him. Each man in turn, saluted the colors and requested permission from Lieutenant Riley to come aboard his boat. Each man's salute was acknowledged until the deck was full, and Jeff had the opportunity to tell his story.

"When the first round hit, I guess it just blew my ass overboard. I don't remember hitting the water, but I do remember how thick and dirty it tasted when I came up to the side of the canal." He stopped and asked one of the sailors to stand up. When the man did, Jeff opened the lid to the beer cooler upon which the man had been sitting and extracted a cold can. "I haven't lost my touch," he said as the beer spewed from the opening, and he placed his mouth over it, not allowing any of the liquid to escape. "Now I feel like I'm home."

"Take it easy, Jeff. I've got a corpsman on the way over here. He'll clean up those cuts. You don't have to tell us anything if you don't want to. Just take it easy." For the first time since I arrived, I heard unmistakable concern in the base commander's voice.

"It's okay. I needed this more than I needed a corpsman." He said as he held up the beer. "When I hit the water, I guess I was lucky. I went to the other side of the canal. I came up and stayed close to the bank. I could hear them on the opposite side, so I stayed as low in the water as possible."

"Why didn't you get one of those reeds like the cowboys use in the movies and breathe through it?" One of the men asked.

"I'm sure I didn't think of it. I was just trying to keep my head and my ass down. I saw my hat float by so I grabbed it and pulled it down and put it between my legs to keep it out of sight." As he spoke, several of the men were taking pictures. It was their first visit with someone who had come back from the dead.

"After I knew the firefight was over, I took a chance and peered through the grass on the side of the bank. I didn't see anyone, so I crawled out and began to un-ass the area as quickly as possible. I knew they were on the other side, too. I kept low, but after making about a hundred yards, I began to run though the grass. Thank God I didn't lose my shoes. That elephant grass cut the shit out of the rest of me. I don't think I could have made it without these old boondockers."

"Didn't you hear us when we came back to look for you?" Chief Patterson wanted to know.

"Damn right, I did! And I want to talk to you about that, too. I was in the wood line behind a fallen coconut log when the Sea Wolves started blowing everything to shit. I couldn't even stand up to try to get their attention. With those bastards in there blowing everything away, how was I supposed to make it back to the canal? By the time they left, so had you guys."

Although there was excitement in his voice, I didn't detect anger.

"When I saw I couldn't get picked up that night, I started to move to the southeast. I knew we were running patrols in the area, so I thought if I could just make it through the night, I'd get picked up in the morning." He stopped talking, drank the rest of his beer, and tossed the can aside. "Somebody hand me another beer." He added.

The corpsman arrived and wanted to treat his injured. "Sir, you better let me clean you up. There's no telling what kind of bugs and shit have been biting you for the last two days."

While the corpsman cleaned the multitude of small wounds, Jeff sat back and closed his eyes. As he relaxed, obviously for the first time in several days, it became evident what a lucky man he was.

Jeff suddenly sat bolt upright, eyes wide open. He turned to the commander. "Did you send a telegram to my folks?" He didn't wait for an answer. "What did it say, and when did it go out? If it's gone already I want to take a chopper up to Can Tho and make a call from the Red Cross. I don't want Mom and Dad worrying about me." He brushed the corpsman aside as he stood up.

The look on Commander Starkey's face was enough to tell all of us that he had sent a telegram.

"What did you tell them? Did you say I was dead?" Jeff was almost shouting.

"Based on what information we had, we had to list you as missing, presumed dead," Starkey said quietly.

Not a man on the boat spoke. We all thought of the scenario that Jeff's parents were about to undergo. Like on the boat when it first happened, my first thoughts were of Carmen. How would she react to a report of my death or capture?

"I want a chopper right-fucking-now," he said as he moved about the boat.

"You've got to sit still if you want me to clean all those cuts." The corpsman was trying to keep up with him as he paced.

"The hell with these cuts. Do you know what a telegram like that will do to my parents? It'll kill them. They'll be the ones who need a funeral, not me. Commander, you've got to get me out of here."

"We've got one of the Sea Wolves en route now. They should be here in ten more minutes. Chief, how about packing him a bag to take with him up to Can Tho and to the hospital? Between the doctors and Naval Intelligence, we may not see him for a week." His final words were accented by the sound of incoming choppers. "Sounds like them now. Turn to Chief. At least get him some clean shorts."

"I'm already packed. I think I'll go on the same chopper with him if there's enough room for me." I said as I prepared to depart the base for the second time.

As we jumped on board the chopper, the corpsman handed Jeff a large tube of white salve. "Put this on the bites. It'll keep them from itching too much until you get to the hospital."

"Thanks, guys. I'll see you again as soon as I can." Jeff leaned back in the webbed seats of the helicopter and let the realization of what he had been through sink in. As he sat there, I watched him begin to shiver.

I yelled for him to put on the shirt I pulled from my rucksack and handed him. With a smile, he accepted, and I left him to his thoughts.

In less than an hour, we could see the large Red Cross painted on the flat green roof of the wing of the hospital going out to the chopper pad. I felt the ship begin its banking turn as we made our approach. With a touchdown as gentle as a kiss, we landed. Jeff was escorted to a waiting gurney, where the staff wanted him to lie while they rolled him into the hospital.

"Get me to the Red Cross so I can make a phone call, then you can do whatever you want to with me." Jeff refused to stop until one of the doctors promised to take him to the Red Cross.

I sat in the room with him for over two hours while we waited for a telephone line to the United States. Each time he got an operator, he was cut off somewhere in the process of linking the phones in Viet Nam to the local system, reaching North Carolina.

It was a red-eyed Jeff Riley who emerged from the small wooden room serving as a phone booth in the Red Cross office in Can Tho, Viet Nam. Without asking, I knew his parents had already received the telegram sent by the military.

"Our minister was with them. They got the news about three hours ago. I don't think it had time to really sink in yet." He stopped to look out the window. For a minute, he was silent, and then he turned to me. "You know what my dad said to me after I got on the phone? He said he wanted to make sure it was me and not some nut trying to hurt them even more. He asked me the name of my dog when I was a kid in Wilson, North Carolina. When I told him Teddy, he began to cry. That's the first time I ever heard my father cry. He's fifty-four, and that's the first time I ever heard him cry."

Jeff was processed into the hospital without incident, and the doctors took care of his multitude of cuts and scrapes. He called his parents again the next day and I placed a call to the State Department in Saigon and spoke to Carmen.

Jeff got a Purple Heart and four days in Can Tho. His parents got their son back, and I left for Saigon and Carmen.

DATELINE: SAIGON, SOUTH VIET NAM

Three strikes, and you're out.

Four balls, and you walk.

Four attempts to gain ten yards.

In sports, we get second chances to accomplish a goal. In life, we hardly ever do. Navy Lieutenant Jefferson Davis Riley got a second chance. It wasn't to play baseball or football. It was a second chance at life.

Jeff was the officer in charge of one of the many PBRs that patrol the Mekong River and the canals and rivers that run from it in the U Minh Forest in the southernmost regions of South Viet Nam, and the Mekong Delta.

He and his crew were on a routine operation, if anything in the country can be referred to as routine. It was a mission where he and another boat were supporting a group of Vietnamese local military units. They completed the mission without incident and were on the way back to the Navy base at the southern tip of the country when they ran into a well-placed and well-executed ambush. The local VC fired several rockets at Jeff's boat. One hit the part of the boat where Jeff was standing. The mark of a good ambush is to catch the people you are trying to ambush by surprise and in the kill zone. This was what happened to Jeff. It was a surprise, and his boat was in the kill zone. The first rocket round hit and knocked Jeff off the boat and into the canal. No one saw it and no one saw Jeff disappear beneath the brown water.

171

Long story…short version.

An extensive search was made for Jeff for two days. Boats cruised the waterways. Helicopters flew overhead to no avail. The military has certain requirements when something like this happens. One is to report the person in a situation like this as Missing. Presumed dead. The report goes to the next higher headquarters and then to the next of kin. The wife. The mother. In his case, since he was not married, his parents were notified that they had probably lost a son.

Second chance.

Jeff was found. Alive. Three days of bug and mosquito bites, cuts and sores from leaches, and innumerable contacts with thorns, etc., covered his body. He was alive. But his parents thought he was dead.

He was able to contact them while a minister was with them. His father, thinking the call was a cruel joke, asked Jeff for the name of his dog when he was a little boy. The correct answer caused Jeff to hear his father cry for the first time in his life.

Jeff got a second chance.

His parents got their son back.

Chapter Fifteen

The war in Viet Nam has produced some of the finest and best-trained elite forces the United States or the Free World's military services have ever seen. We have the Army Special Forces (call one a Green Beret and see what happens), SEALS, Rangers, Air Force Special Operations, LRRPS, SOG, some of whose missions and, identities, and names may never be known or acknowledged. The one thing they all share is their dedication to their units and their mission. Most of the people who know of their existence treat them with great respect. They also go out of their way to stay clear of them. All are slightly eccentric, and most were crazy to boot!

I encountered them quite often as I moved about the country. I often saw them in basecamps, in the brush, or on operations as we passed through the same heliport. I once promised myself I would spend some time with one of the units and see if I could find out what made them tick. I got my chance after meeting a recon team Sergeant in a bar. Where else?

After three days in Saigon, I was ready to hit the woods again. I spent the first day in the city getting dispatches ready to send out and catching up on mail to my boss in the States. My evenings were spent at the Continental with Carmen. We watched the moon rise over the city, and one night, we sat on the rooftop lounge until the sun began to break the darkness to the east. We just sat and talked. All night. Sometimes, we talked without making audible sounds. She knew what I was saying, and I could look into her dark eyes and hear the same thing. Carmen was occupying more of my time when I was in town, and all thoughts when were in the brush. I knew that could be dangerous. I had been lucky this far, and like some of the grunts, I sometimes thought I was bulletproof.

I went over to MACV Headquarters and asked the J3 Operations section to assist me in my quest to find a RECON or SOG team with which I could spend a few days after talking to the Sergeant. My credentials and security clearance were picked apart by the Intelligence Officer, and when he found no holes in my qualifications, he turned me over to a short, stocky Lieutenant Colonel who tried to impress me with his knowledge of the field of journalism. "I've got a master's from the University of Mississippi," was the first words he spoke to me when we were introduced. After that, he took great delight in spicing his conversation with terms like "deadline", "proofs," "blueline," and an assortment of terminology unique to the teaching of journalism, but not always used in the real world.

"With such an interesting background, how did you wind up in the Army in Viet Nam?" I had to ask.

"I was in the National Guard in Jackson, Mississippi, and working on the city newspaper when I had a little, uh, let's call it a problem with the daughter of one of the largest advertisers in the city. I found out she was pregnant the same day she found out I was married. My city editor found out about us and gave me a deadline to get out of town and the newspaper business. I found out I could volunteer for duty in Viet Nam. So here I am. I'm a Mississippi weekend warrior doing his thing in Viet Nam."

"You going back to Mississippi?" I asked as he lit a cigarette.

"Fuck no!" He said, pronouncing the word in a strong Southern accent, making it sound as if it had two syllables. "At least not for the next eighteen years. I have what you would call an extended family in the state. My wife won't give me a divorce, and my…uh…" He took a long pull at one of the unfiltered cigarettes as he searched for a word. "My friend had a little boy and called him Truman L. Hopper Jr." It was not too difficult to see who Truman Sr. was. The nametag on his jacket said Hopper.

We walked down the corridor to the small snack bar and bought a cup of coffee and two of the greasy donuts the Vietnamese cooks made daily. "Can you get me hooked up with a team," I said as we sat.

"On one condition."

I waited for him to ask for a two-page spread in the local Jackson, Mississippi, suburban disturber. He surprised me with his request.

"Don't mention my name in anything you write. I don't care if it's in the country or for dispatch to the States. I don't want anyone at home to know where I am. And I damn sure don't want any of those crazy bastards you're going to see to know who gave you permission to be with them." He spoke with deliberate slowness to emphasize each word.

"You got it," I didn't want to alienate anyone if possible. This was something I had waited on for almost a year. "I'd like to go as soon as possible."

All I can give you are some RECON or SOG teams up in the Highlands. If you want SEALS or Air Force, you've got to go to their office."

"How long can I stay?" I tried to see why he was being so agreeable. "What kind of restrictions are you, or they, going to put on me?"

"One operation. If they stay for two days, you stay for two days. If they go out for six weeks, you go for six. Unless you get killed or wounded, there's no extraction." He blew a thick cloud of smoke skyward. "And damn little chance if you do," he added.

For the first time, I was having second thoughts about this mission. I had been out for as long as three weeks with the First Cavalry division once, but we had regular resupply, and I could have taken a chopper out almost any time I wanted. This was a tough call. But I knew I was going.

"I've been in the brush, off and on, for the last two years. I think I can handle myself."

"Let me tell you something right now. If I hadn't checked you out and believed you could make it and would do them a good job, your ass wouldn't be sitting across from me." He finished his first cup of coffee and stood up to get another.

We continued to banter back and forth for the next thirty minutes until he finally said, "Let's go back to the operations section, and I'll see what I can do for you."

Unlike past wars when the forces occupied whatever houses or buildings that were available, the United States in Viet Nam had custom-built headquarters. The MACV building was a large, sprawling structure with hallways running in all directions. Like any military building, it had bulletin boards filled with permanent, temporary, and daily notices. The walls were covered with posters cautioning the occupants to lock up their documents and keep their mouths shut about sensitive material. I found the posters about the phone system to be the most amusing. One of the big jokes in Viet Nam was the poor telephone service. It was not uncommon to walk down the hallway and hear someone shouting into the handset. "BEARCAT! THIS IS MACV. GET ME REDLINE SWITCH! ...DAMN THESE TELEPHONES!"

I once was on a telephone in Da Nang talking to Saigon. Midway through the conversation, we were interrupted by a loud cracking and popping noise on the line. In a second, I heard two unfamiliar voices talking. "Hey, can you guys hear me?" I asked.

"Who the hell is that?" One of the two men asked. I identified myself and gave a general description of my location, telling them I was north of Saigon.

My announcement was followed by a hearty laugh by one of the men. "I don't think I'd be giving away any secrets if I told you that you have Air America operations in Saigon talking to Guam!"

We talked for a few minutes, and then, just as quickly as they came on, the line went dead.

Truman and I went into a room, and he quickly and quietly closed the door behind us. "How about if I put you with a team working with some yards?" He asked, as he once again lit a cigarette. "I can do that or you can go in with a team sitting up on the trail near Laos. They're due for rotation in about a week. We can have you up there for that."

"I'll take the team in Laos."

"Dammit! I said, *near* Laos. I didn't say they were in-country. If you don't know the difference, perhaps you better stay down here with some of the REMFs." His friendly mood quickly changed.

"Loud and clear, Colonel."

"You can take a Caribou north in the morning. I'll give you the name of a contact when you get on the plane." He leaned back in his chair, and for the first time, I saw him relax. "Now tell me how you came to be in Viet Nam."

Although my story was by no means as interesting as his, he did soften a little as we began to find a mutual background in the newspaper industry. "I've even thought about trying to get on with Stars and Strips. Either here or Japan," he said.

We spent about two hours together, and towards the end of the conversation. I invited him to accompany me on a trip sometime.

"I think I'll pass. I spent a year on the police desk in Vicksburg. I've seen my share of crazies. I don't need to go looking for them again."

I spent the evening drinking with two Australians from one of their network affiliates. We hit several local bars, and they spent about twenty dollars in one on Saigon tea with some of the best-looking hookers in the city. The money bought one round, and when they found out we were not military, and further, we were not interested in what they were renting by the hour, we were quickly left to ourselves, and they found a group of more likely prospects.

We left for the Continental at about eleven to beat the curfew. When we got back, I looked in vain for Carmen. I knew she was not in Saigon, but I slowly scanned the terrace, hoping she might have made it back. When I finally decided she was not there, I left and went to my room.

I met the Caribou the next morning at daylight thirty. At least, that's what time my head felt like. My only hope was that the flight would be smooth and uneventful and that I could recuperate during the trip.

By the time the plane touched down at a small strip far to the western edge of Viet Nam, I was batting five hundred. The flight was as smooth as any I had taken, but my head was ringing, and my stomach felt as if the green cans containing the Australian bitters I consumed the night before were slowly being digested in it. I knew if I blew my cookies, I would rip my throat to shreds with the metal from the cans coming up.

We landed, and I made my way over to the operations officer who was running the strip. This, like so many duties in Viet Nam, was in addition to whatever he had been sent to the war to do. It was not a full-time job since we were the first fixed-wing aircraft to land in four days.

I'm supposed to meet a Captain Brown. Do you know him?"

"Brown's over at the Headquarters. Let me make sure this bird takes off and don't crash on my strip, and you can ride over there with me." He looked at me and my duffel bag sitting beside the small wooden shack he used as an airfield headquarters and asked me what I did in the war.

"I'm a correspondent. I work for a syndicate in the States. I'm doing a story on some of the troops up here."

"Aviation?"

"No," I hesitated to tell him whom I planned to see. "I'll probably work with some of the recon or LRRP teams. If there are any in the area," I added, not wanting to appear too knowledgeable about the troops and their operations.

"You must have a death wish, my friend. Those guys are about as squirrelly as any group of people you'll ever find in captivity." He finished his paperwork and watched the plane as it broke ground on its way to the next stop. "We can go now. Once the wheels leave my Province, I couldn't give a shit less if it falls from the sky or not. It's somebody else's problem then. You ready?"

We went to a Quonset hut painted in alternating light and dark green splotches in a sort of homemade camouflage pattern. "This is what we call the Pentagon West out here. Somebody figured out our coordinates one day and said we were the westernmost Headquarters in Viet Nam. Since then, everybody's called this piece of shit the Pentagon West." He opened the screened door, and we entered the tiny building.

It was divided into two areas. One large portion contained the desks and chairs for what appeared to be a Province or Headquarters staff. The back of the room was divided off with its own door. A sign on the front said PROVINCE SENIOR ADVISOR. The door was closed.

"Come on in, I'll introduce you around. That's Captain Brown at the end of the table over there." He pointed to a long green table with a hand-cranked mimeograph machine on the end. Beside the machine was a box containing the masters typed to produce the light blue pages. I momentarily wondered if fresh mimeograph sheets in Viet Nam smelled like they did so long ago in grade school.

"You must be Sean Kelly. I heard from the Colonel in Saigon you were coming. You just get in?" The man came over to meet me. He seemed unusually old for the rank of Captain. Perhaps he had been an enlisted man for a long time prior to getting a commission. I made a mental note to find out.

"He told me to talk to you, and you could possibly help me get a story on some of the men in the area." Once again I tried to be a vague as possible, not knowing how the sensitivity of the teams was treated.

"Let's go into the PSA's office. We can look at his maps, and I can answer most of your questions."

The sparsely furnished office was dominated by a wall-sized map. On it, the Province was outlined in red. Throughout the Province area on the map, pins of different colors dotted the terrain. A legend at the bottom identified them as depicting safe and secure hamlets, suspected Viet Cong infiltration routes, and locations of enemy activities.

"You can tell from the map we're a pretty secure area."

I almost laughed aloud as he said it. We were less than three klicks from the Laotian Border and the Ho Chi Minh trail, and he said they were secure. I started to ask for the operations officer's map, but hesitated. No need to make enemies on the first day.

"That's fine. I think. Although I must admit, I was hoping to find a little activity to write about." Mentioning they might get into print usually started most people talking.

"I think you'll find enough to write about. Let's take you over to the team hut and let you meet the men you'll be working with." We walked through the building, and he stopped at the senior NCO's desk. "I'll be over at the Zoo if you need me."

I could see the black door on the team house as soon as we went around the corner from the operations building. It was painted black and had a skull and cross bones placed about head high so anyone approaching was face-to-face with it. This was not a painting of a skull and cross bones. It was the real thing! Sitting on a small shelf on the door was a human skull. Underneath it was a pair of crossed bones that, at one time, probably were the legs of its previous owner. Painted in red letters over the skull were the words *SAT CONG*! Kill the Viet Cong.

As we approached, I could hear the mixture of country and western, soul, and other music being played simultaneously. They couldn't agree on their music as easily as front door decorations.

"Lieutenant Snow! It's Captain Brown! We're coming in." He stood outside the door and announced our presence and intentions prior to carefully and slowly opening the door.

"The Lieutenant ain't here. You wanna talk to someone else?" A voice spoke to us from behind the bar in the far corner of the large open room as soon as we entered. It took several seconds for my eyes to adjust to the darkness of the room. Once inside, I was greeted with a feeling uncommon this far out in the brush. They had an air conditioner! Their hootch was probably the coolest room north of Da Nang.

"I guess you'll have to do, Sergeant Harley. This is Sean Kelly. He's a reporter. Wants to do a story on you animals. Can you help him out? He's got permission to talk to you guys and go with you on your next trip to the woods. I'm going to leave him here with you." He turned to me just as he was about to leave. "It's still not too late."

Sergeant Harley motioned for me to place my bag against the bar, and he handed me a can of beer. "The first one's free. After that, they cost a quarter apiece. It's on the honor system till we catch someone trying to screw us around, then we hurt him."

"I'll remember that," I said as I drank my beer.

"What kind of story you want to write? Who's it going to back in the States?" By now, several of the other men had gathered around and introduced themselves.

"I'm just doing a story on the war in this area. I thought the best way to find out about the local activity was to ask the experts. So here I am."

My comments were greeted by several positive comments about them being the experts, and the rest of the men in the entire country were a bunch of REMFs. Sergeant Harley and I were on our second beer when the Lieutenant came into the room. He assumed the role of one of the boys, and they accepted him as such.

He brought a large acetate covered map into the room and spread it on one of two round poker tables in the main area of the room. "Come on over here, guys, this is as close as you're gonna get to a briefing."

The map contained several areas circled in red. Each circle had a numerical designation of the known NVA or Viet Cong units working in that area. "This is where we're going tomorrow and," he hesitated as he looked at me, "this is where our guest is going with us."

"Lieutenant, I don't think we should take a civilian if this is a real area. What happens if we make contact?" One of the men, a Specialist Fourth class from Ohio, wanted to know.

"Good question, Moose. Maybe we better let our guest answer."

All eyes turned to me. I remembered having a new Lieutenant tell me one time the most frightening thing he ever faced in combat was the first time all his men's eyes were on him, and he had to tell them what to do, knowing his actions meant life or death for many of them. I knew how he felt.

"It appears to me if I know, and understand, the mission of a RECON team, that it's your job to snoop and poop and not be seen or heard. It's my job to write about what I've seen. If either one of us screws up, the other is likely gonna get his ass blown away." I paused and moved over to the refrigerator,put a dollar's worth of MPC in the open-top coffee can sitting on the first shelf, and pulled out another beer. "I know you guys can do your job. I'll do mine."

My answer seemed to calm their fears of having me with them ,and we proceeded to plan for the upcoming operation.

Lieutenant Snow gave out the operation order in an abbreviated form. It was a method they were used to working with, one in which all the information he knew and could reveal to the men was shared. "This is gonna be fairly easy. We'll be over the border and just west of the trail." As he spoke, he pointed on the map to an area inside Laos by about five klicks. So much for Lieutenant Colonel Truman L. Edwards Sr.'s denial of cross-border operations! "We'll be there for five days. Our mission is just like the last trip. Watch the trail. Don't make contact and un-ass the AO if we get compromised. The only extraction we can expect is on our side of the border. That's where we go in and where we come out. We've got a pick-up at 0600 tomorrow morning. We have twelve hours to get our shit together. Sergeant Harley will have a weapons and equipment check in three hours. Final check at 0430. Any questions?" He waited for a few seconds for anyone to ask questions about the operation and then turned to me. "I'd like to see you alone in fifteen minutes." He made one last comment to him men. "The roster will be posted in ten minutes. If you're on this one get ready, if not get the hell out of the way so the rest of us can get ready."

The Lieutenant was from Arizona and had gone through ROTC. He seemed to have a great relationship with his men. This is what I expected to see in this type of unit. There was no room for the dissension we so many times heard about and sometimes actually saw. If a casting director for a Hollywood movie came by and asked for a typical Lieutenant, Snow would not get the part. He looked more like an insurance salesman than a man who sat quietly beside a trail for days at a time, counting enemy convoys.

As we talked in the cool darkness of their hootch, I could smell the acrid smoke of a charcoal fire outside the door. "What the hell is that smoke?"

"We've got a grill out there. We always try to scrounge up some steaks prior to going out. You know what they say about the condemned men getting a last hearty meal."

We dined on some of the finest New York cut steaks to be found in Viet Nam that evening. After dinner, there was a movie at the combined club, which some of the men watched. I, like several of the others going out the next morning, wrote a letter. Theirs were to wives and families. Mine was to Carmen.

The choppers sat us down in a small clearing the next morning. To say we walked through the jungle is to give us the benefit of the doubt. We hardly moved. For two years, I had been trudging up and down hills and mountains in the Northern sectors and trying to stay afloat in the Delta, but these jungles were the thickest I had ever tried to traverse. Overhead, the sun shined on the tops of trees so tall and heavily laden with vines and undergrowth that often we did not even know if it was shining. At times, it was so dark in the brush that we could have used flashlights to illuminate our way.

Sergeant Harley was the third man in the group of seven. I was fourth. Lieutenant Snow was behind me. Moose Roberts was the point man. It was his job to give the warning if and when we approached any type of danger area. That could be a clearing, a trail junction, or that hardest one of all to describe, the place where gut feelings and instinct takes over and tells the senses something is amiss. Hear it and live. Ignore it and suffer the consequences.

SP4 Moose Roberts held up his hand, and we immediately stopped. Each man turned either to his right or left in a prearranged move. This gave us protection on both sides. As soon as his hand went up and we began to turn, Sergeant Harley moved silently to a position beside him. If the Lieutenant was needed, a hand signal would ripple down the seven-man column, and he would move into position beside the two men kneeling and looking at a small acetate-covered map. After a few silent seconds, we moved on.

My legs told me we had moved for days. My watch spoke the truth. When I finally let myself look at the stainless-steel wristpiece, I was shocked to learn we had been traveling for over three hours. With no sun and few shadows to go by, I could not tell how far we had gone or even which direction we were traveling. I was mentally running over a trip to Bangkok to keep my mind from the heat and humidity of the jungle when we stopped for the second time.

This time, Snow came up and motioned for me to follow. As the four of us huddled together, he spoke in a near whisper. "That trail we passed about four hundred meters back," he pointed a sweaty finger on the map, "is where we will set up. We'll stop here to see if we've been followed. If we don't hear anything in an hour, we'll go back and set up."

He turned to his Sergeant. "Harley put everyone on fifty percent, and let's eat. Sean, you stay with me."

We used an old practice of moving through an operational site and then doubling back. This afforded us the opportunity to see if we were now being pursued. After thirty minutes, it became obvious we were not.

The men ate silently. It was like watching a group of ghosts as they prepared for an outing. Each moved carefully and cautiously. No motion was wasted. No effort went unused. I could feel the men watching me as they checked their weapons and gear for loose fittings and pieces that might rattle or snag in the growth, which would be home for the next five days. My deliberate moves made enough noise to roust an entire NVA Division I was sure, and I tried harder than ever to keep quiet. The p38 I used to cut the top out of a can of fruit sounded to me like I had cranked up a chainsaw and was revving it with each twist of my wrist.

After an hour, I felt the tap on the shoulder. I turned, and Snow was motioning for me to stand and to pass the signal up the line to the man ahead of me. We finished eating, cleaned up our empty cans, and walked back to the site Snow had indicated. We moved in, settled down, and became still. We were quickly greeted by the first enemy of the jungle. A multitude of ants, bugs, and mosquitoes began to inspect our little group of invaders. Liberal splashes of Army issue bug juice brought little relief against the insects but were used extensively, especially once the first leach was discovered. I watched George Peters mouth a silent oath as he squirted the juice on a leach stuck to his right calf and waited for the bloodsucker to lose its grip so it could be pulled away without losing its head.

George Peters was the new point man. Roberts was now the rear security.

Since I was expected to be a fully functioning member of the small team, I carried a rucksack filled with extra radio batteries, a first aid kit, and several smoke grenades. I had no weapon other than the small .38 hidden under my jacket. I had put several small notebooks in my ruck. Each was in a plastic bag that had once covered a radio battery. When we were in position, I, like every other member of the team, found a small place to call home for the next five days and slid the aluminum-framed canvas bag off my shoulders.

Back at the base camp, it was determined that we would function as two teams. I would be with Snow and Moose Roberts. Sergeant Harley would have the other three men. By a toss of the coin, it was determined his team would take the first watch. The three of us pulled back approximately five meters and gently cleared a place on the ground to spread our poncho liners.

As the moist ground under the camouflage-pattered quilt shifted to fit my body, I allowed myself to think only one of the question I felt certain I would ask a thousand times in the next one hundred hours. "What the hell am I doing here?"

A recon team's mission is to do just that: recon. It is not a combat patrol. It is to avoid contact at all costs. With only a limited number of men and very little firepower, it would be suicide to engage the enemy, except as a last resort. The men knew this. They also knew they were outside the artillery fan of any friendly fire they might have under normal circumstances. Medevac was out of the question. We could not see the top of the jungle. We could not expect a chopper pilot to be able to see us. No reactionary force was standing by to pull our nuts out of the sand. Recon teams lived life on the edge, and they loved it! All were volunteers, and most had extended stays on the teams. It was a strange and potentially deadly force of men with which I spent my first night in Laos, a country where we were not supposed to be and where, if we were killed or captured, the US military would deny our very existence.

When the men were not on duty, and it was during daylight hours, they either tried to sleep, pulled maintenance on their weapons, ate, or read the small paperbacks which they brought with them wrapped in plastic radio battery bags. The nights were spent sleeping in shifts or deep in one's own thoughts.

Even I had gotten used to the sounds of most of the animals by the second day. We saw an assortment of small rodents dart by our position. On occasion, some even stopped to stare at us. We heard what we thought was a deer and some type of wild cat in a death struggle about sundown, but it was well out of our line of sight, so we could only speculate. Everyone kept a special watch for the small snake the guys in Viet Nam call the "three steppers." Three steps and you're dead if it bites you was what we were told. I don't know anyone who was bitten or even saw one, but it made us all cautious.

It was about three in the morning. Moose, Snow, and I were keeping watch. It was as dark as a whore's heart, and we could not see three feet in front of us. To our rear, Harley and his men were sleeping. I tried to avoid hearing what I knew was coming in loud and clear in my brain. SOMEONE WAS ON THE TRAIL! Not just a someone, but a lot of someone's. Moose touched my foot and gently shook it to be certain I was awake. I slowly waved my hand to indicate not only was I awake, but I touched my ear, indicating I had heard the noise on the trail.

Moose tugged gently at a small cord tied to Harley's boot. Instantly, the man was awake and fully alert. With a single touch, each of his men was awakened to a similar state of readiness. Peters depressed the handset on the radio in a prearranged sequence of long and short squeezes to tell the radio watch back at the headquarters we had possible contact. There was nothing to do now but wait to see who and how many they were.

We could hear the movement. It was slow and cautious in front, to the rear, and to our left side. From the sound, I expected their flank security to stumble over any one of us at any moment.

For the second time in my life, I placed the small pistol I carried in my hand and prepared to shoot at another human being. I tried not to think of all the times I heard the guys in Viet Nam describe how it felt to take a life. I never expected to find myself in a situation where that was necessary. The sounds in the jungle around us were enough to make me think the time was rapidly approaching when I would have to place my convictions on the line.

The movement was becoming more defined as we heard the undergrowth pulled slowly apart to allow passage through the green landscape now shrouded in darkness. In front of my position, I heard what I thought was a grunt or cough as the jungle gave way. Behind me I could hear the radio being keyed in a rapid series of signals giving our location, situation and I hoped, requesting an immediate pick up or air strike or nuclear attack or something to get us out alive.

As the noise level picked up, Moose moved between each of us and said, "We've got a pick-up scheduled at dawn. We've got to stay quiet or fight our way back to the pick-up point if necessary. Snow will give the order to fire or get the fuck out. It's his call." My sweaty palm around the pistol said I was ready for either, but the heart pounding in my throat voted for a move-out.

I heard Sergeant Harley try to yell just as the breath was knocked out of

186

him. As he rolled away from his attacker, he managed to fire the claymore in front of his position. As the deadly steel balls cut through the jungle, Moose was grabbed from behind as he lay at the rear of the ambush site, trying to provide security. By this time, I knew we were surrounded!

Noise and light discipline went down the tubes when the first claymore was fired. I tried to find a target in front of me and could not. I saw Snow move to a crouch and fire the combination M-16 and grenade launcher he carried. Moose got off one load of buckshot by the time Snow finished the thirty-round magazine.

"Pull back to our last rally point! Kelly! Get over here with me." He stopped to reload and turned to the right flank of the position where he covered Peters. "Let's go. Get the fuck out of here! Is anybody hit?"

Snow moved down the line of the positions when he stopped next to where Moose lay on the ground, bleeding from several large wounds. "Peters! Get that aide bag over here. Harley! Get a head count."

As he leaned down to assist Moose, he saw the other body lying next to the man. "Harley, get over here! What the fuck is this?"

Harley and I pulled up next to the Lieutenant at the same time. We came from different ends of the ambush.

"What you got, *Trung Uy*?" Harley was crouched as he continued to cover his end of the ambush. He used the Vietnamese term for Snow's rank.

"Beats the hell out of me. What do you think?" He asked as the two of them bent down to examine the casualty next to Moose.

Lying on the ground was a dark, hairy figure. Its large, shaggy appearance, at first, gave the impression it was wearing a coat of some sort. As the three of us got closer in the limited light available, we heard Peters begin to swear as he, too, discovered the cause of our having to fight our way out of the recon site.

"It's a fucking monkey? I just shot a monkey!"

"Get over here, Peters, and bring the radio. We've made enough noise to have every black hat in the valley down on us." Snow took the headset and spoke into the mouthpiece. "Beer base, this is Lone Star. We need an immediate extraction. We have been compromised. I say again. We need immediate extraction. We are proceeding with the wounded to our pick-up point. Do you copy?"

"Roger, Lone Star. What is the nature of the wounds, and how many are there?"

"One on a poncho." He indicated Moose would have to be carried.

"How long before you reach the pick-up location? Are you still taking fire?"

"Negative fire. Bad guys are neutralized or gone. Three zero to pick up."

"I don't believe it. We were attacked by a bunch of fucking monkeys!" Sergeant Harley stood with his hands on his hips as he surveyed the damage done by and to the recon team. We could now make out at least four hairy bodies lying in and around the position. The claymore had taken out many more outside our location. The dead one next to Moose had slashed and bit him all over his body prior to Moose dispatching him to that great tree swing in the sky.

"Let me help carry Moose," I said as Peters made a hasty stretcher out of a poncho.

"We'll all be carrying him through this shit." Harley bent down and assisted Peters as they bandaged the still bleeding and unconscious Moose.

"Give me a head count, and let's get out of here. I've got his weapon. Harley, you get his ruck." Snow was ready to move his team out.

Just as we lifted Moose and began the arduous trek back to the pick-up point, Lieutenant Snow turned and, in his best command whisper, said, "The first one who says anything about his is dead meat! That goes for you too, Kelly!"

As we made our way through the underbrush to the landing zone for pickup, I kept speculating on the possibilities of what we would give as the reason for busting the recon. What was our body count? How did Moose get wounded and not shot? I thought of an endless stream of questions. First, they were to speculate on the answers and second, to take my mind off the load Peters and I were carrying.

As we approached the edge of the prearranged clearing, I heard the chopper pop through the air in the distance. Harley eased out into the middle of the

188

area, prepared to flash the strobe each team carried for just such emergencies to bring the chopper into our position. If we had not been in a place where the United States denied our operations, a smoke grenade would have been used to mark our pick-up location. The strobe light was just enough in the early morning dawn for the pilots to see and land.

"No shit, guys. Our body count was four, and we think we wounded several more. They stumbled into our site just before daylight. We had no choice but to open fire in self-defense. That's the story. Is everybody clear?"

He was talking to everybody, but he was looking directly at me. "I don't think you have anything to worry about, Lieutenant. I'm sure none of us want to be guilty of killing Cheetah." I said as the ship landed.

On the chopper back to base camp, we pledged our loyalty to the team and its reputation. As far as the official record was concerned, a small force of North Viets attacked the recon team. Four were killed, several were wounded, and the team suffered one friendly wounded, for which SP/4 Moose Roberts received the Purple Heart.

Until now, only a small group of seven men knew the team was attacked by a herd of macaque monkeys during their nightly feeding!

Sorry about that, Guys!

DATELINE: SAIGON, SOUTH VIET NAM

It's no place to be monkeying around.

War is serious business. It's just as serious, even if they call it something besides war. The men who gave their lives in the Korean Conflict are just as dead as those who lost their lives in WWI or WWII. The jury is still out on what the action in Viet Nam is or will be called. Some say it's a conflict; others call it a police action. Neither term does it justice. It is, in my opinion, a war anytime somebody in a uniform different from the one you are wearing is shooting at you and trying to take your life.

Such is the case in Viet Nam. Men in different uniforms with opposing political, social, religious, economic, and many other views are charged with killing each other. As far as I can determine, they are doing a pretty good job of it. Not everyone in Viet Nam is a combatant, although there is always the possibility one of the bad guys will not recognize the difference and a good guy who is a cook, a clerk, a mechanic, or a driver for a senior office will be killed.

And not every day is spent in combat. And not everything here is as serious as you would think befitting a war zone. People do laugh and have a good time on occasion. They laugh at the comedians the USO brings to the country. They laugh at the jokes and cartoons published in each issue of the magazines, especially Playboy, which gets passed around, usually with the centerfold missing.

They also laugh at themselves. Some things are inherently funny, but you must be a part of it to appreciate it. My dad used to say there is a fine line between humor and horror, and it depends on the situation and who it happens to for it to be judged.

Such is the case with an operation in which I recently participated. Like the television show back in the world, only the names will be changed. This time, it's to protect the guilty.

I accompanied a small unit on a mission in a location I cannot reveal. We were supposed to spend a couple of quiet days monitoring enemy activity. Ours was not a combat patrol but just the opposite. Making contact with the enemy meant the mission was compromised, and the unit had to quickly be rescued, as they did not have the firepower to do more than fight their way to an extraction point.

The second night, we were attacked. We heard them coming, and there was nothing we could do about it. We were surrounded. Suddenly, they were inside our little protective perimeter. Claymore mines were fired in the dark, and the deadly steel balls tore through the attackers. Small arms were fired. Magazines emptied. One man was bleeding and needed medical attention. It was just at dawn and in the limited light, the patrol leader had to check on his wounded and do a body count of the enemy.

What he found was not what he expected.

The enemy lay bleeding and dead all around our position.

The enemy did not wear uniforms. They did not wear anything.

We were attacked by a vicious, and hungry group of large monkeys on their nightly feeding frenzy.

The names were left out to protect the men who got Purple Hearts for monkey bites.

Chapter Sixteen

Even now, when people talk about WWII, they often call it a two-front war. They could be talking about Europe and the Pacific or, in the case of Germany, the eastern and western fronts. In Viet Nam, the two fronts were the one here in country and the one back home. The home front. There was no denying the effect the anti-war movement had on the men and women on the ground in Viet Nam. They either agreed with it, saw no reason for their being here, and did what they could to make their feelings known, or they opposed those demonstrators and made those feelings known as well. Since they were wearing a uniform, there was little they could do either way.

Almost every time I met someone new in Viet Nam, they had two things in common with everyone else with whom I had spoken. They all had a war story they wanted me to write, and each wanted to be mentioned by name if that story was going back to the world.

The one exception was Doug Lambert, a Marine lance corporal assigned to a Naval gunfire team I ran across along the coast near Chu Lai. He had a name he wanted to be mentioned and a war story he wanted to be told, but both were about his cousin Jimmy. I was on the last night of four days I spent with the gunfire unit when we met while he was sitting on the top of the berm surrounding the artillery piece they used to fire support for Marines in combat.

After sharing a lukewarm can of Coke, he pulled out of a chest that normally contained ice, but was empty, he sat back and we talked about nothing for a few minutes. He knew I was a correspondent, and I felt that, at some point, he would open up to me with whatever was on his mind.

"You write stories about the men you meet over here, right?" I nodded in agreement since he had already asked the question at least twice.

"Would you write about somebody who's not here?" He hesitated. "I mean, he was here, but not now. He's…he was…he was killed. Here about a year ago. But that's not the story. It's what happened later."

There was no way I was not going to pull out a notepad and ask him to continue.

Jimmy's story began during the siege of another Marine firebase and ended near Richmond, VA.

I had been in country less than six months when I realized things happening at home sometimes had a greater impact on the men and women in Viet Nam than the armed enemy. We quickly saw how the evening news at home was exploited by the VC and NVA to their advantage. Fortunately, the men fighting the war in the brush did not have access to televisions, but it was no secret that we tried to keep abreast of stateside news.

Jimmy's story made headlines only in his local hometown newspaper and the Pacific Stars and Stripes, where he was listed in the column marked "killed as a result off hostile activity."

Jimmy's story was one Doug asked me to tell someday. That was a request, like many others, made to me over a bottle of 33 beer, a shared C-ration, or a night watching a far-away firefight. Some I knew I would never fulfill the promise, but several hours later, I realized I was listening to a story that should be told for Jimmy and Doug, the others whose families went through similar ordeals back home.

I made notes while I listened without interrupting him.

"There were three of us. We were cousins, but since we were all within about a month of two in age, we were more like brothers. We did everything together. It was me, Jimmy, who we nicknamed Doc, and Don. Me and Jimmy joined the Marines, but Don got caught up in the anti-war movement and stayed home. All of us still lived at home. Jimmy lived with his mom, our Aunt Millie. His dad died before he finished high school.

Me and Jimmy went through boot about a month apart. He graduated first, so he got here before I did. He was only in country three months when.."

Doug choked with emotion, and stopped talking. He was holding back tears, and I knew if he didn't get his emotions under control, as a Marine, he would stop talking. He could not let himself be seen as emotional. After a long silence, he began again.

"After three months, Aunt Millie quit answering the phone when it rang in her small house just east of Richmond. She had the number changed and when the new one was found out, she came up with a simple system for her friends and family to contact her.

She told everyone to let the phone ring twice, hang up, and call back. Then she'd answer. She couldn't get to it in two rings anyway. It worked for a while. Her friends called her, and she made calls as usual. One evening the phone rang twice, quit, then started ringing again.

She told my mother it was almost eleven. She'd fixed a cup of coffee and was sitting down to eat the last piece of pound cake from the Sunday dinner she had cooked three days earlier. It was for the usual Sunday dinner she always came to at our house."

Doug stopped, and I could tell he went back to those happier times when the family was all together, and there was no war to talk about.

"When she heard the phone start ringing the second time, Mama said she slowly moved the chair back from the oval kitchen table. I can see it now. The table was covered with the oilcloth she bought from K-Mart."

He looked at me and smiled. "Funny, but I can smell that old tablecloth now just thinking about it."

"I've heard smell is our strongest sense."

"As soon as she answered the phone, she knew her system had failed once again.

Mama said Aunt Millie said *Hello* several times, but nobody said anything. Mama told me that all she heard was heavy breathing. Said she's heard it before."

"Did the person ever say anything to your Aunt Millie?"

"Oh, yeah. This is where it starts getting interesting. He told her she was getting smart, but not smart enough. Like Jimmy, he said. He wasn't smart enough to stay out of Viet Nam. Now he's dead. Just like all the people he killed in Viet Nam. Now that's not too smart. Is it? Maybe now you know how all the wives and mothers in Viet Nam feel. They've lost a lot of sons, too. Just like you."

"You're kidding?" I said, knowing he was relating just what his mother told him. I was getting it third-hand, but I believed every word was imprinted for eternity on the brain of Millie, Doug, and his mother. I did not question the accuracy.

"Each time he called, she wanted to hang up, but she couldn't. Maybe Aunt Millie felt by taking the abuse on the phone, she was sparing Jimmy further pain.

Jimmy was killed during a rocket attack one night. The Marine Captain who came to see her said Jimmy was being awarded a Silver Star posthumously for his actions during the siege of the Marine base.

Mama said Aunt Millie had not pressed him for details and did not fully comprehend what was on the award citation they gave her. She accepted it just before the honor guard fired their rifles, and two buglers played Taps.

She put the flag, the box of empty shells, and the large plastic folder and case containing his medals on a shelf in the hall closet. I can picture that place because that's where she always made me and Don and Doc hang our coats and kick off our sneakers when we came home. I know she thinks a part of him is still there.

Mama kept me updated on what was going on in her letters. Aunt Millie was her younger sister, so they were really close. She was worried about her because she'd just sit for an hour or so at a time thinking about Jimmy. She told Mama she even tried to speak to Uncle Frank, who'd been dead for a long time. She'd ask him how to handle the situation."

Jimmy's father, Frank, was killed in a car accident. A drunk driver hit him head-on one night. Millie was still up with three-year-old Jimmy when the state patrol officer came to her door to tell her of the accident on the highway. From that day on, Jimmy knew only Uncle Frank from photos and what Aunt Millie told him.

Doug finished the warm coke, crushed the can, and tossed it aside.

"On Saturdays, Aunt Millie usually came to our house in Mechanicsburg. It was an easy drive, so she didn't mind the trip or the visit. Lots of times, our other cousin Don was there. His open opposition to the war and anyone who participated in it was no secret. The two of them argued about it a lot. Aunt Millie had no real opinion, but since Jimmy had volunteered to go to Viet Nam, it was legitimized in her mind. Mama said she started listening more intently to Don, but she didn't know why. She said sometimes Don got in her face.

"Aunt Millie, how can you sit here and know you lost your only child in a war he should have never gone to? All he had to do was go to school and not try to be Mr. Hero. There was no reason for his joining the Marine Corps. If you asked me, Doc watched too many John Wayne movies."

"What did your aunt do?" I asked.

"She fired back, so I heard. Said maybe he needed to watch a few more of his movies and see how he felt about his country. Mama told her and Don to settle down. It got to the point where she had to play a combination role of referee and peacemaker. Aunt Millie would spend the night, and then every Sunday after church, she visited the cemetery where Jimmy and Uncle Frank were. If she had them, she'd put some fresh jonquils from the front yard on their graves.

One Sunday, Mama went with her, and she told her she didn't know how much longer she could take the phone calls. She said she'd tried everything to get them to quit calling. She couldn't take her phone out because she might need it in an emergency or something."

Doug stopped talking for a minute and then turned to face me. "I know everything I have told you so far is gospel truth. It came from my mother, and she'd rather swallow a bug than tell a lie."

I wrote that analogy down and underlined it.

"What I'm about to tell you now could get some people in trouble, and I can't prove it one way or another. It's based on what Mama said and what she found out." He looked at the tracers lighting the sky from a firefight on a distant hill. "You still want to know?"

I assured him I'd treat anything he told me as a confidential source, so he was protected. This is how he ended the story of his cousin Jimmy and his Aunt Millie.

"The phone rang while she was turning the television to channel 7 for the news. Since she was standing so close to the small table, she picked it up between the first and second rings, throwing the caller off guard.

"A, uh, Millie?" There wasn't a pause that time. "Have you got a new system, or have you decided to speak to everyone now? By the way, I went by the cemetery today. The flowers were a really nice thought, but they look so dead, lying scattered all over the grave. They're all crushed and broken. Someone even sprayed some black paint on Doc's stone. They…'"

"What did you say?" She demanded.

"'Black paint.' He said someone sprayed black paint."

"No, where did they spray it? On who's stone?"

The line went dead.

Millie had no calls about Jimmy in the next two weeks. Each time the phone rang, she still got a bitter taste in her mouth as she picked it up and waited for a response to her greeting.

"Millie, are you coming this weekend? We missed you last week. Even at church…." Her sister spoke more rapidly than Millie at times.

"Yes, I'll be there." As she spoke, she slid her fingers over a carved wooden picture Jimmy sent her from the Philippines, where his plane stopped en route to Vietnam. "I'll be there."

It was the first time she saw her nephew Don in over a month.

"My mother said Don was at the Sunday dinner, and Aunt Millie sat next to him at the table."

"Don, would you do me a favor next Sunday night? I've got some big boxes of stuff I canned this summer sitting in the kitchen. I'd like them moved out to the garage, but I can't lift them. Would you mind? I'll fix dinner for you. I'll even make one of those chocolate cakes you used to like when you and Doug and Jimmy were little."

Before Don could respond, Betty answered for him. "That would be nice. You two could use the time to get better acquainted again."

She walked over and stood beside her son as she talked.

"I don't know. I've got to get back up to school. Early class Monday." He stood, turning his back to the two women.

"I really need you to do this, Don. It will take such a load off my mind. Getting those things moved, I mean. I've been worrying about them for so long now. It won't take long."

"Oh, all right. I'll be there around five."

It cost thirty dollars for the groundskeeper at the cemetery to clean the paint from Jimmy's tombstone. "A couple of months of spring rain and summer sun and all the black will be gone," he said as she gave him the money. "I'll mail you a receipt."

The receipt came on Saturday. She took it from the mailbox as she was returning from the A&P, where she bought several items for the dinner she planned to cook for her and Don the next day.

As she held the paper, her mind drifted back to the night the voice told her about the flowers being crushed and the stone painted. She thought of the flowers, the stone, and the voice. It was the voice she tried so hard to recall. She had heard the voice only once since. It was deeper sounding, muffled as if coming through a cloth placed on the phone. Even muffled, it was still the voice.

Don arrived at precisely five.

"Look, I don't really have time to eat with you. I'll just move the boxes and leave." He spoke rapidly as he entered.

"Nonsense. I've already got the table set. Everything's ready. You move those boxes out to the garage and I'll fix us a plate. I can't afford to fix a meal like this and not eat it."

Even in his haste and obvious displeasure with having no choice, Don enjoyed his meal of fried chicken, fresh corn, beans, and hot biscuits.

"I've saved the best for last." Millie stood, turned, and walked to the long hutch where a chocolate cake sat covered by an aluminum cake pan.

"I don't bake as much as I used to. Only for special occasions like church, or when someone dies and everyone sends food." She placed the cake on the table between them. "Why don't you pour us a cup of coffee, and I'll cut a piece of cake."

Don filled two brown mugs he took from a small tree-like rack sitting next to the coffee maker. "You don't take anything in it, do you?"

"I know you're in a hurry, but let's have our cake and coffee in here." She casually waved her arm toward the living room. Frank and I, and after he was gone, Jimmy and I would sit here on Sunday night and work out all our problems." She eased into a large, overstuffed, old green chair now faded with age.

Don started to protest but instead sat across from her on the equally faded yellow couch.

"I'm sure your mother has told you about all the trouble I've been having lately. With the phone calls and all. Millie leaned forward, looking closely at her nephew. "She told you, hasn't she?"

"Yeah, she's mentioned it. Look, I appreciate the dinner, but I've got to go." Don stood and looked nervously at his watch.

"Please, Don, just a few minutes. Sit back down. This won't take long. I need your advice on how to handle my problem. It seems to me that a person who has no respect for the dead can't have much for the living, either. Even himself. Don't you agree?"

She did not take her eyes off him as she spoke. "I don't want you to get bored with this conversation, so I'll get right to the point."

The old woman placed her half-finished cake and coffee on the end table next to her chair. She then opened the table's single drawer and took out a small cardboard box.

Don watched as she opened the box, placed her hand across the dark object lying in it, and produced a snub-nosed pistol that she pointed at his midsection.

"Now, don't worry, Don. Frank taught me how to use this pistol. So just sit still and tell me what made you want to call me and say all those terrible things about Jimmy."

"Do you think it's been me calling you? Why would I do that?"

"That's what I want you to tell me." She added emphasis to this by pulling back the hammer and rotating the cylinder. The pistol was now cocked and ready to fire. "Did you hate Jimmy that much?"

"How could I hate him? He was my cousin." Don was sitting, wide-eyed, on the edge of the couch.

Millie held the pistol as easily as if it was nothing more than a flashlight. "Don't try to deny it was you, Don. We both know it was."

"What if it was? Would you shoot me?" Fear danced in his eyes.

"I haven't decided yet. Right now, I want to know why you hate him like you do." Millie's voice didn't waiver as she spoke to her sister's son.

"I don't hate Jimmy. I hate the war. I hate what he and all the others are doing. They've got no right being there. It's not our war. Don't you see, if everyone who gets killed like Jimmy did is made a local hero, it could go on forever? It's got to be stopped. Do you know the high school retired his football jersey number? No player will ever wear the same number as he did. Is that any way to treat a…a…"

"A what? Go ahead, say it. You've called him a murderer before on the telephone. Tell me to my face that Jimmy was a murderer."

"What would you call someone who goes out and kills people he doesn't know or has no interest in? This is not a war. It's a series of random killings directed at a nation we couldn't even find on a map ten years ago." His voice was taking on the rapid fire of the telephone conversations. "It's just like you right now. If you pull that trigger, you will be just like Jimmy."

"You don't think what you're doing, out marching and protesting burning flags, is not hurting boys like Jimmy? He wrote me one time about how the enemy would take pictures of people like you and show it to our boys over there." She was now moving her hand somewhat as she spoke. The pistol in it strayed up and down over her nephew.

"You know, I really feel sorry for your mother. I know the pain of losing a son. At least she won't have to put up with all the phone calls and the desecration of the grave."

With total fear now enveloping him, Don realized this woman, his mother's sister, planned to kill him. His fear was so intense, he could not move. He sat frozen, sweat beading on his forehead. It was several seconds before he realized he was crying like he had not done in years.

"Please, Aunt Millie, don't do it. I'm sorry. I see how much I hurt you.

Don't do it. Please."

The pleas of this object sitting across from her fell silently on the mind of an old lady whose world and reason for living had been killed slowly by the death of a young Marine in a country so far away and by the constant ringing of a telephone which signaled the beginning of another personal torture session.

Just as the sobs and pleas went unheard, so did the sound of the single shot that exploded forth, then echoed through the house where Jimmy, Frank, and Millie once lived.

DATELINE: SAIGON, SOUTH VIET NAM

Two sides to everything.

North Viet Nam

South Viet Nam

The Battlefield

The Homefront

Shortly after America pledged its support for the government and, by extension, the people of South Viet Nam, a second front was opened for the war. It wasn't in North Viet Nam. It was in North Carolina and North Dakota and New York and Florida and almost every other state where men were drafted or joined for the fighting in South Viet Nam. Most of the protesters had personal, more than political, objectives for the war. They didn't want to be drafted and possibly killed, and that was a reasonable objection. Taking to the streets and burning their draft cards made the news, and that gave a certain amount of comfort to the enemy. If the American people didn't support the war, how long could it last?

It was also a factor that affected the morale of the men in uniform. Who was right? The man with the rifle or the one with the cigarette lighter and the draft card? Much like the American Civil War, it divided families, and sometimes it was brother against brother as they took opposing sides of the argument.

A young Marine I met one night didn't have a brother, but he had two cousins. Jimmy, or Doc as he was called, had also been a Marine, and Don. Don took the opposite view and opposed the war and shared his views with everyone, including his family.

Doc was killed in Viet Nam. He received a Silver Star for his actions, making him the recipient of the third highest award for valor in the military. He was buried next to his father, who was killed when Jimmy was three, and whom he never really knew.

Jimmy's mother began getting harassing phone calls telling her Jimmy was a murderer for what he did in Viet Nam. The calls continued, and one mentioned that her son's grave had been desecrated. That was too much, and after determining who the caller was, she confronted him.

Millie was sixty-eight years old when she sat across from the caller. She held a small pistol and asked why. When she didn't get the answer she wanted, she pulled the hammer back on the pistol, watched the cylinder rotate, then she pulled the trigger ending the agony she had been subjected to because of a choice her son freely made.

Chapter Seventeen

By the time we had been together for over a year, Carmen and I sometimes talked about what we wanted when the end of the war came. It was obvious to both of us that the United States was rapidly having enough fun in the sun in Sunny Southeast Asia. The political situation back in the world was such that if the military didn't bring the war to an end, the people in the streets would.

That was the atmosphere when I returned to the city in November. The Vietnamese National Elections were the hot topic of conversation. I came in from the area around the Plain of Jars, where I had been with a Special Forces A-Team for a week.

Carmen met me, as usual, at the Mass BOQ for dinner. Wess was in town, so he told her I was coming back, and she was there the first night.

Even though we had been lovers for over a year, she still insisted on our keeping a "semblance of modesty," as she called it, in public. I watched her step into the bar at the Mass, and it took all my strength and composure not to run to her, grab her, and pull her to me.

I walked over to her and, as usual, gave her a friendly and formal little kiss on the cheek. As I did so, I whispered into her ear what I planned to be doing with her within the next ninety minutes. The quick dance of the gleam in her dark eyes told me more than any audible answer she could have given me.

"Sean, it's so good to see you again." She held my hand and smiled for those around her who might have been as struck by her presence as I was that first night so many lifetimes ago.

"I've missed you."

"Me too."

We went to the table I had been occupying, where two gin and tonics were waiting for us. "To... to... what? I think we've toasted to everything under the sun and the moon. Got any ideas for tonight?" I asked.

"How about a week of D and D in Bangkok?" She said.

"You're kidding? Did you get the time off?"

We had been planning a week to Bangkok for over six months. Each time one of us got the time off, the other could not. I had scheduled a week just before Christmas, and she had been trying to get the State Department Officials to let her have the same time. We called it our D and D rather than R and R since I planned for it to be a week of sheer decadence and debauchery rather than rest and relaxation.

"They said I could go if we get one more mission completed up country prior to my leaving. We're looking into the USAID people up in Quan Tim Province. It looks like some of the aide money may be going into the wrong hands. It's through the Americans this time."

I looked at the date indicator on the watch I bought my second day in Viet Nam so long ago. It said we had exactly five weeks until Christmas. If we left on the nineteenth of December, we would have been looking at only twenty-nine days until we landed in Bangkok.

I singled for another round and took her hand in mine. As I kissed the back of it, I looked into her deep, dark eyes. I saw the message she had been giving me silently for the last six months. She didn't have to say it, nor did I. It was there.

We left the Mass and caught a taxi to her place. By the time we arrived, both Mai and her daughter had already left for the day. Only the guard was out front. Shotgun in hand, he waived us into the enclosed courtyard of her villa.

On the inside we wasted little time getting to the second-floor bedroom that had become a second home for me.

Each time we made love was better than the last. She never tired of trying and learning. As we became more familiar with each other, each session opened new doors unknown during the last meeting.

Some things were almost ritualistic. She wanted me to slowly undress her as she stood by the windows overlooking the city. If the night was blessed with the glow of the moon, she took special care to have me ease the clothes from her. Her body was offered almost as a living shrine to the light from the heavens above.

She never hurried. Each meeting was as if there would be no other. Many times, I awoke the next morning to find her lying cradled in my arms. She usually was still awake and probably had been so since I drifted off.

The next morning, we went to the American Express office at the MACV Annex, picked up travel checks, and reconfirmed our reservations for the nineteenth.

All the men and women returning to the United States who completed their tours of duty between the twentieth of December and the ninth of January got a Christmas drop. They got to leave on the same day we planned to go to Bangkok.

I wanted to file one last story prior to the holidays, so I made arrangements to get a ride out to the Newport Docks and see an old friend of mine. He was an Army chief warrant officer who was in charge of unloading ships. I picked up a tip about some of the defoliants we were using down in the Delta from one of the men who worked at the dock.

"Every time we start unloading that stuff, it leaks from the barrels, and if you stand in it for a couple of hours, your lips and hands and fingers begin to go dead or tingle. I mean, man, that's some potent shit. Whatever the hell it is."

He gave me the information one night in a bar next door to a steam and cream parlor outside the gate at TSN.

"Just as long as it affects only my lips and hands. If anything else starts to tingle and goes numb, I'm gettin' the hell out," he said, and I knew he meant it.

I came back to Saigon and worked on the story. Wess and Clayton were both in the city and had plans for the holidays. Wess was going to spend it with the daughter of a Vietnamese Colonel and his half-French wife. Their daughter was the second most beautiful woman I had seen since coming to Viet Nam. Everyone who knew them wondered what Wess had done or what he had that qualified him for such a beauty.

The USO in Saigon put up their usual holiday lights and had a fake tree. That was one concession I made to myself. Never again, after leaving Viet Nam, would an artificial Christmas tree enter my home. If it was Christmas, I would have a real tree.

I went to the main exchange in the Cho Lon district and bought Carmen a new camera. She had been using an old Yashika since she arrived. I bought her a new Pentax Spotmatic with a case and light meter. I also picked up a couple of new cassette tapes for her and hoped the gift I ordered from the PACEX Catalog would arrive in time. She wanted a fine China demitasse set she saw in the catalog, so I ordered it. If it didn't come in time, I would give it to her when we returned from Bangkok.

While I was in the exchange, I bought her a single pink rose. It was the last one the vendor had, but it was a perfect bloom. I picked up a card for her and attached it to the green paper around the stem. On the card, I put one word: "Because."

We met that evening for dinner. She was in town for only one night and had to be back in the field the next day, so we made it an early evening and went to her villa.

I awoke early the next morning so I could leave as soon as the curfew was lifted at five-thirty. She had a vehicle coming to pick her up at six.

As she stood in the doorway in the early morning sunrise of Saigon she held the rose in her hand. "Why do I always feel like a teenager leaving my date after a night at the movies?" I asked as we stood there, neither of us wanting to leave.

"I guess, Mi Nito, it's because…" She spoke with her head down. As she looked up, I saw she was gently taking each petal from the rose in her hands.

"Is there any significance to your taking the petals off one at a time?" I interrupted.

"Maybe I feel like a teenager too, sometimes."

The petals continued to be detached from the stem. When the last one was removed, a smile broke over her face. "Is there something I should know? Are you telling fortunes with rose petals now?"

"I'll be back tomorrow at noon or a little after. Then, we can talk about fortunes and rose petals. Till then, *Mi Nito, besa me como si fuera la ultima vez.*"

I kissed her again and went into the courtyard. As I left, I heard the door behind me as she closed it and went back inside her home.

I went back to my office and did busy work until it was time to leave. We had no set office hours when we were in Saigon, but since our time in the field could run for days and not hours, we came and went as we saw fit. Unless I was chasing a story that I needed local contacts or information to confirm, I usually came in late, stayed until happy hour, and then left. On the days I needed to attend the Five O'clock Follies, I'd leave in time for them.

That had been my routine for the last two days when Wess suddenly appeared by my desk at about three in the afternoon. We were four days away from Thanksgiving. It wasn't a recognized holiday in Viet Nam, but Army tradition was for there to be a big feast where the officers served the enlisted men. I knew one was planned at the large mess hall at the MACV Annex. Wess wanted to take his lady friend, and I planned to take Carmen.

I could tell something was wrong when he stood without speaking. Wess was never at a loss for words, so I stopped and gave him my full attention. "Okay, what is it? You're gonna be a daddy?" I joked.

His facial expression said it was something more important or maybe even worse than being told one's girlfriend was pregnant. I stood up. "What is it? What's wrong?"

"It's...it's..." he struggled. "It's Carmen. The chopper she was on was shot down."

My vision went black for a second. I felt my heart beating in my chest and in my ears. I closed my eyes, hoping that when I re-opened them, Wess would be gone, and I would be in my bed, awakening from a horrible nightmare. I was in a dark tunnel. Darker than any place I had ever been.

I felt his hand on my arm. "Sean...Sean. You okay?"

I mumbled something to him and slowly took a seat in the chair behind my desk. "Tell me what happened," I managed to say.

He sat on the corner of my desk. "All I know now is that she was on a Huey. They had two other choppers on the flight. One was a gunship. They started taking ground fire, and hers was hit. They were close to the Laotian border, so it was a tricky flight to begin with. When hers was hit, they lost the tail rotor, and it spiraled to the ground and caught fire."

"Oh, shit," was all I could say. I had seen the results of other choppers that caught fire. Only the very lucky and the very quick got out alive. "Survivors?"

"The gunship worked the area because they could see the NVA coming out of the wood line heading for the chopper."

NVA meant hard-core North Vietnamese Army personnel. They were not big on taking prisoners.

"Couldn't they get one of the other Huey's on the ground for a rescue?"

"They finally did, but it took a long time. They had to call in another gunship before it was safe to land."

"What did they find?" I was holding my breath when I asked.

"Three dead and one wounded inside the chopper."

"Was...was Carmen...?"

"She wasn't there. They knew there were seven people on the ship. They accounted for the pilot, co-pilot, and crew chief. The one wounded was a civilian from State."

"The other three?"

"No trace," he hesitated to say what we both knew.

"Carmen is a prisoner of the NVA," I finally put into words what neither of us wanted to believe or say.

For the next three days, I almost camped out at the operations center at the Annex. Anytime an American was presumed to be taken prisoner, the first few days are the most critical for getting them back. Find them before they are moved deeper into the jungle, moved up or down the Ho Chi Min Trail, and worse, decided they were too much of a burden to their captors and killed.

I did not let my mind dwell on what they would do to an American woman. I knew, or at least I hoped, she would be of sufficient value that she would

208

be kept alive, but I had no way of knowing if she had been injured in the crash. What if she was injured, and the injuries slowed her captors down? I pushed that thought from my mind.

Thanksgiving Day

Carmen had been missing for four days. I had nothing to be thankful for. Wess convinced me to come and have dinner with his girlfriend. It was not going to be turkey and dressing, but maybe a meal with them would give me a few minutes when I was not thinking about Carmen. We went to a French restaurant I had never heard about. The food and wine were excellent, and I kept thinking that Carmen would love it here. So much for a night out without thinking of her. I knew it was not possible, and I didn't want to consider the possibility of not seeing her again.

I knew the State Department had notified her parents of her situation. I didn't know if they used the same: missing, presumed dead, designation the military used, but she was still alive as far as I was concerned.

It was the Monday after Thanksgiving. I knew if I didn't get back to work, I never would so I was looking for an excuse and a unit to visit when Wess came crashing into the office. For him to move that fast, it had to be really good news or incredibly bad, and I knew instinctively it had to do with Carmen.

"What is it?" I jumped from my desk. My heart was pumping, and if my blood pressure was taken at that moment, I knew I would blow the numbers off the chart.

"I can't verify it, but I heard from a friend at Navy intelligence that a SEAL team picked up an NVA officer in the vicinity of Carmen's chopper crash, and he may have some intel on what happened and maybe where she is."

I remember looking around like I needed something from my desk. When I realized I didn't, I grabbed him by the arm. "Let's go. I want to talk to your contact."

He held back. "Slow down. You now know all I know and probably all he knows, too. Give the SEALS and their assets time to work on the issue. If there is any intel to be gotten, they know how to get it and what to do with it." He pointed to my desk. "Have a seat. I gave my contact our office number. He's going to call the minute he hears something."

"What if the office is closed and we're not…"

"I gave him the number for the desk at the BOQ and told him to have them wake both of us." I watched him take an easy breath for the first time. I think he was as keyed up as I was.

Ten Days

I had a job to do, and I did it the best way I could. My mind was occupied with thoughts of Carmen. I had the pleasant ones of times we spent together and the horrible ones of what she may have been, or is going through, now. I managed to do a few interviews and wrote my weekly column, but as I read over what I had written, I knew my heart was not in it. I was drinking more and sleeping less. I even snapped at Wess once when we were talking about a corrupt Air Force officer who was being court-martialed.

I heard the sound in my dreams. It was the rapid fire of an artillery piece. Somewhere in my subconscious, I realized that there was no such thing as a rapid-fire artillery piece. It had to be something else. Finally, it registered. There was a pounding on my door. Once I knew what it was, I jumped from my bed, and in addition to the pounding, I heard Wess yelling my name.

"Sean…Sean…wake your ass up," was accompanied by more pounding.

Finally, I got to the door and opened it. Wess rushed inside, grabbed me by my shoulders, and said three words that I will never forget.

They found her!

I know my knees went weak for a second. "How is she? Is she…?"

"She's alive. I know she has some injuries. A broken arm and some cuts and bruises, but otherwise, they say she's okay."

I rushed to the chair where I had hung my pants and shirt from the night before. "Let's go. Take me to wherever she is."

"Not so fast. My guy said they pulled her out of a camp across the border in Laos. You know how sensitive that is. We're not supposed to be there, so they've got some CYA to do before she can talk to anyone. She's going to an aide station in I Corps, and I asked if she could be transferred to the hospital here in Saigon."

I had one leg in my pants and was hopping around trying to get the other in. "What did they say? When will she be here?"

"Nothing more, and I don't know, but if you'll stop hopping around and get dressed, we'll go and see what we can find out."

Three days later.

I sat beside Carmen's bed, holding her hand, promising I'd never let go. She was in the hospital in Saigon, and except for the cast on her left arm and a few lingering bruises from the crash, she looked as beautiful as ever.

She spent the first day in Saigon being debriefed by the State Department and then it was the Army and Navy who took over. What did she see? How many NVA were there in the camp? How were they armed? Her captors did not know she worked for the State Department. She managed to hide her credentials and her identification card in the wreckage when it became obvious that she was about to be taken prisoner.

They also did not know she spoke very good Vietnamese and was able to give all her de-briefers more intelligence information than they ever expected. She knew where the unit came from, where they were going,what their objective was, and what they planned to do once they got to it. She was a walking intelligence briefing. Like all intelligence, if it's not acted on immediately, its value diminishes by the hour. When everyone got all they could from her, she was free to rest and recuperate, and I was free to be by her side.

I never asked her what happened to her in the camp, and she never said. I tried not to let my imagination and some of the stories I had heard of Vietnamese women who had been taken captive by the VC take over.

On the fourth day, she got one of her co-workers at the State Department to bring a car to take her home. I helped her out of the hospital. She wore a gown that she asked me to go by her house and pick up. It was a long purple gown trimmed in white. The car took us to her villa, and after getting her inside and into her bed, the driver left us alone.

Even Mai and Kim left us alone after bringing a tray with a single rose I had brought over when I came for the gown, as well as two gin and tonics.

By morning, it was like she had never been gone at all.

DATELINE: SAIGON, SOUTH VIET NAM

Three little words.

Not: It's a boy.

Not: It's a girl.

Not even: I love you.

The best I ever heard.

They found her.

I have written many times about the relationships we make in a war zone. I made one. Her name is Carmen, and she works for the US State Department. I'm not sure even now where the relationship is going. We enjoy each other's company and have even spoken about plans after we leave here, when and for whatever reason that may be. Several months ago, we began planning our own R&R trip and decided it would be to Bangkok. We didn't make it to Bangkok. She was in a helicopter crash and, for a lot of reasons, had to spend some time in the hospital here in Saigon. Instead of Bangkok, we flew to the States. After not being here for several years, her parents deserved to see her. It was the best Christmas gift they ever had. We spent four days with them and then went to my parents for New Year's. I had written to them about Carmen, so they knew all about her and what had happened. They also knew how serious I was about her.

We spent a lot of time talking about all the things that are important to us. She has a great future ahead of her at the State Department and I have just been asked to go to work for one of the big three news networks. Both will take us back to Viet Nam if we accept.

I think I can speak for her when I say our future is in a little country many people cannot find on a map.

Acknowledgements

Writing a book, whether it is fiction or non-fiction, is not an isolated act conducted in front of a computer screen, an old-fashioned typewriter, or on a stack of yellow legal pads while sitting in a coffee shop. It is a collaboration of any number of people who help bring the words to life. Many of the people may never know of their contributions by way of a small snippet of dialog, a favorite phrase, or some other act or omission they may not even realize they contributed. In my own case, my fascination with "story" began when my grandmother, whom we called Mama Waller told me stories of what she referred to as the "old days." If she was not the one telling the stories, it was my Daddy, a member of America's Greatest Generation, who rode the rails on freight trains looking for work, survived the great depression and WWII, and loved to talk about it. To them, I owe my ability, if there is one, to tell a story.

To bring this book to life, I have had the pleasure to serve with many veterans who were more than willing to tell a "war story," some of which were true, some made up on the spot, and some the result of far too many adult beverages. To my very special reader, typist, and light in the darkness, my wife, Jewell. For their continued advice, encouragement, and suggestions, some of which I actually take, my daughters Colleen and Victoria.

Mistakes, errors, omissions, and other things you don't like or agree with that you may find in this work are mine and mine alone.

About the Author

Paul Sinor is a retired US Army Lieutenant Colonel.He had two combat command tours during the Viet Nam War. His other positions in his diverse career ranged from company commander to being on the staff of the Secretary of Defense. His final military assignment was the Army Liaison to the Television and Film Industry in Los Angeles.

He is an award-winning screenwriter with eight feature films made from scripts he wrote. In addition, he has been the Technical Advisor for numerous feature films, including *Transformers* 1-3, *GI Joe*, *The Messenger*, *I Am Legend*, *The Objective*, and *The Invasion*.

AUTHOR WEBSITE:
Paulsinorbooks.net
Paulsinorbooksandmovies.com

Also by Paul Sinor

JOHNNY MOROCCO SERIES:
Wrath of the Dixie Mafia
Fair Game
Picture This
Blackmail and White Ligntnin'
Double Trouble

MAX MAXWELL SERIES:
Dancing in the Dark
Sentimental Journey
We'll Meet Again
That Old Black Magic
Long Ago and Far Away
Blues in the Night

STANDALONE NOVELS:
Where There's Smoke
Operation Thunder Strike
Demon Riders

www.ingramcontent.com/pod-product-compliance
Lightning Source LLC
Chambersburg PA
CBHW020141120726

47903CB00007B/2352